PENGUIN B

TALES OF TWO PLANETS

John Freeman is the founder of *Freeman's*, a literary
biannual of new writing, and executive editor of
The Literary Hub. His books include *How to Read a
Novelist*, *The Tyranny of E-mail*, and *Dictionary of the
Undoing*, as well as two collections of poems, *Maps*
and *The Park*. He has also edited two previous vol-
umes about inequality: *Tales of Two Cities*, an anthol-
ogy of new writing about New York City today, and
Tales of Two Americas, a book about inequality in
America at large. His work has been translated into
more than twenty languages and has appeared in
The New Yorker, *The Paris Review*, and *The New York
Times*. The former editor of *Granta*, he is Artist in
Residence at New York University.

TALES OF
TWO PLANETS

Stories of
Climate Change
and Inequality in
a Divided World

Edited by

JOHN FREEMAN

PENGUIN BOOKS

PENGUIN BOOKS
An imprint of Penguin Random House LLC
penguinrandomhouse.com

Published by arrangement with OR Books, LLC, New York, 2020.

Photographs on pages 159, 161, and 163: © Lu Gang/
Contact Press Images

Pages 289–290 constitute an extension of this copyright page.

LIBRARY OF CONGRESS CATALOGING-IN-PUBLICATION DATA
Names: Freeman, John, 1974– editor.
Title: Tales of two planets : stories of climate change and inequality
in a divided world / edited by John Freeman.
Description: New York : Penguin Books, 2020. | Published by
arrangement with OR Books, LLC, New York, 2020.
Identifiers: LCCN 2019039029 (print) | LCCN 2019039030 (ebook) |
ISBN 9780143133926 (trade paperback) |
ISBN 9780525505716 (ebook)
Subjects: LCSH: Global environmental change—Literary collections.
Classification: LCC PN6071.G54 T35 2020 (print) |
LCC PN6071.G54 (ebook) | DDC 808.83/9355—dc23
LC record available at https://lccn.loc.gov/2019039029
LC ebook record available at https://lccn.loc.gov/2019039030

Printed in the United States of America
1 3 5 7 9 10 8 6 4 2

Set in Adobe Caslon Pro

This book is dedicated to Barry Lopez,
for showing me that storytelling is stewardship,
and the world is more vast and beautiful than
any of us can appreciate on our own.

CONTENTS

INTRODUCTION

John Freeman

IT'S 109 DEGREES in Paris as I type this. Outside, on place Saint-Sulpice, a half-naked man washes himself in the great marble fountain. The sun has baked the limestone buildings around him a blinding shade of white. He takes his time, soaping his body: soaking his neck, his shins, his damp head. Not far away, a group of men sprawl on the ground. They look like they've been dropped from the sky. One wears only his underwear. No one else is around. The roaring splash of water is the only noise. It's 3:00 P.M. and it will remain this temperature well into evening, by which point five people across the city will have died.

■ ■ ■

The complete name of the fountain at Saint-Sulpice is actually la Fontaine des Quatre Points Cardinaux, which means the Fountain of the Four Cardinal Directions, since the structure faces north, south, east, and west. It was designed by the Italian architect Louis Visconti at the behest of Claude Philibert Barthelot, comte de Rambuteau, prefect of the department of the Seine. Rambuteau's mission as prefect was "Water, air, shade," and his plans for delivering them to Paris residents were as ambitious as his name was elaborate.

During Rambuteau's tenure, which began in the 1830s following a devastating cholera epidemic, an explosion of public works began. Destruction came with creation in equal measure. Boulevards were widened, slashing through ancient and never-to-be-recovered city lanes. But sewers were modernized, and over one hundred miles of water mains laid down. Rambuteau planted trees along avenues, installed pissoirs so men weren't urinating in the street. And, most startlingly, in a city where drinking and bathing water was taken from public fountains, he built more than 1,700 small fountains, so that the large decorative ones didn't have to serve as water sources.

La Fontaine des Quatre Points Cardinaux was completed in 1848. It stands today, nearly two hundred years later, in part because Rambuteau imagined that an apparently impossible problem could be solved. How could a city that had become a terrible breeding ground for disease, a city that occasionally burned and seethed with fire, a city ruled arbitrarily by a king, no less, be transformed into a place of water, air, and shade? Paris provides all three things to many (though not all) of its visitors today.

■ ■ ■

Rambuteau's success was enabled by another architect, though, a far less famous urban planner—Charles Axel Guillaumot. A few decades before Rambuteau began the city's building spree, Paris was sinking. All of the mines and quarries that had been dug in the city for centuries—going all the way back to the Roman era, when the city was called Lutetia—had honeycombed its underground structure. In the 1770s, sinkholes began to develop across the city. Whole buildings and street corners would suddenly, violently collapse into the dark, cavernous space beneath the city streets, killing pedestrians and raising a public alarm that perhaps

Paris was built on borrowed time. In 1774, a quarter-mile trench opened up one day on what is now part of boulevard Saint-Michel, swallowing horses, houses, people—to a depth of eighty-five feet. Perhaps all the rock and stone that had gone into creating Paris would be the source of its demise.

Guillaumot, who was born in Sweden to French parents, was not a notable architect until he began what would become his life's work—rebuilding the city under the city of Paris. As Graham Robb beautifully describes in his book *Parisians*, Guillaumot possessed the imagination to see what had actually happened. "As the city spread from the island to both banks, the quarries deepened and Paris began to devour its foundations." For three decades, Guillaumot set about quietly, in the dark, completing the largest architectural project in Europe: shoring up the city's entire foundation, and mapping it upon the city streets to a scale so grand that when Paris's cemeteries ruptured, his vast halls and reconstructed galleries were capacious enough to also absorb the million-plus bodies of the city's dead. Today, they are simply called the *Catacombes*.

Attempting to solve the problems created by what had been extracted from the earth: it sounds like a very modern problem.

■ ■ ■

We face a similar calamity in the making, all across the world today. For two centuries, by taking and taking from the earth, we have rendered our ability to live here an open question. Burning fossil fuels has heated the planet. How much and how fast the temperature rises is a matter of debate. That it's happening, and why, is not. Ninety-nine percent of scientists believe that this warming has been caused by human activity. We call this development climate change, a term that doesn't describe the violence of what has been happening. Earthquakes, fires, floods, die-offs

of species. Sinkholes, tornadoes, tsunamis, and volcanic eruptions.

Instead of acting on this enormous problem, as Rambuteau did
many years ago, with drastic action, we—*especially* those of us in
the global north—have dithered, argued, denied. And waited.
We've waited for record heat waves to break, for the forest fires to
burn out. For the floods to abate. For migrants to stop leaving
parched countries and turning up at borders throughout the
world. We have been waiting for ice shelves to cease their melting,
for the droughts to end, as if all the signs of catastrophic climate
change might be magically waited into submission.

While governments and our own individual wills have fal-
tered, these events have only grown in size, frequency, and destructive power. The future so often predicted by climatologists
is here, and yet large numbers of the world's most powerful residents cannot grasp what it means.

To turn away from the greatest threat humankind has ever
faced has required a staggering dedication to distraction and lack
of empathy for the suffering of others. Evidence of what's happening to the planet is everywhere one looks; the facts have been
checked and rechecked and benchmarks of acceleration routinely
surpassed. Rather than deal with what these forces are telling us,
much of the world—especially the global north—has retreated.
Many of the richest countries have elected nationalist leaders
who campaigned on us versus them platforms, and who are at
war with the power of facts. They are often in the pocket of fossil-
fuel companies. Many of them are triumphantly xenophobic, fla-
grantly demonizing anyone who travels from elsewhere in search
of a better life.

These leaders know something so blatantly true that it's about
the only aspect of climate change that is not debated: this crisis
has been affecting the world at different rates. Right now is a

great time to live in Brittany; it's not such a good time to be in Bangladesh. Or Chad. Or Burundi. Or Thailand. Or the Sahel. Climate change is affecting us all, but it's going to hit the poorest parts of the globe first, and hardest. It's also going to transform Asia a lot faster than it will the rest of the world. The Paris Agreement attempted to limit global warming to 2°C above pre-industrial temperature levels. That now looks impossible, and with a 3.2°C temperature increase predicted by 2100, nearly 300 million people will be displaced—large portions of cities like Osaka, Hong Kong, and Shanghai, with its 24.4 million residents, will be underwater.

■ ■ ■

There we go, though, see? That's *over there*. Unless, of course, you're reading this in Shanghai, let alone Dhaka. Or Miami for that matter, a city predicted to be underwater in a few decades.

One of the greatest casualties of this spasm of self-interest we're witnessing in rich countries of the north is that these delays—and in some cases, returns to increased fossil-fuel consumption— compound catastrophic circumstances in parts of the globe that cannot afford incremental change. Paris is experiencing repeated heat waves that kill three, four, or five people; meantime, Phuket suffers a tsunami that leaves nearly five thousand dead and as many missing. Regions that are paying first are facing outsize climate bills run up by the carbon emissions of the rich northern countries.

It's foolhardy to think this first round of catastrophe, even if it avoids the richest countries, will not blow back on them. The 300 million people who will be displaced by the end of this century will have to go somewhere. To put this in perspective, that's more than five times the number of displaced persons in the world at the present moment: and look how destructive that crisis has been to liberal governance.

This test of the values of liberalism has failed magnificently in all but a very few places. That's because a gremlin lurks within the founding documents of many nations—and the attitudes of their societies: the fractionalization of the value of human life. That somehow, some lives are just worth more. Of all the nations, America must be one of the guiltiest on that score: a global disaster is not one until, so often, an American has perished. Nationalism is the incarnation of this value. To believe in a nation has increasingly meant to believe in a certain kind of person. Increasingly, it means *my nation's citizens are worth more than yours.*

This is an outrageous proposition. Do we really believe that the lottery of birth should be so definitive? No one gets to make a choice to be born in Conakry versus Cleveland, but from the moment of birth very different prospects unfold. What if we believed, stupidly or hopefully, that every living life mattered equally? That it was possible to act as if this belief were a value worth defending, to tell stories as if it could be observed? Climate change will not be "solved," but we might survive some of its worst effects if we work collectively.

■ ■ ■

By assembling tales from all over our world about what it feels like to be alive today in this time of crisis, this book is an attempt to resurrect that collective spirit. This is not a book about policy or about statistics. We are swimming in facts, but a fact does not fully obtain the depth of a fact, the power of a fact, until it becomes part of a story. Too many of our stories about climate change are about fear—fear felt in the north about what is coming. Not enough of them are about how the climate crisis is being experienced across the globe now.

We need to create a new language to deal with the scale of the crisis we face. A new lexicon of life in a time of natural disaster, or a different species of grief. How do we truly imagine our own possible demise? How do we face someone else's? Is there a complex context for what is coming? On a narrative level, this is not a problem for one royally empowered prefect, or an architect happy to work in the bowels of just one city: we need many writers in many parts of the globe thinking on it all at once.

This book contains the work of thirty-six such writers, from points as far and wide as Hawai'i, Port Harcourt, and Freetown, from Bangkok to Maori territory in New Zealand, and from the banks of a river called Slaughter near Buenos Aires to a very wet village in the Himalayas, where fresh water is precious. Two writers come from Iceland, whose landscape has never afforded its residents a feeling of stability or calm, with its near dozen active volcanoes, its melting glaciers, its deep and mysterious crevasses. An ideal book might have featured writers from one hundred more destinations. Yet I wanted one that might fit in a person's hands.

■ ■ ■

What a story these writers tell—here is the thrust and heave and beauty of life on a planet that seems hostile to our presence. In Andri Snær Magnason's essay, he describes walking up onto a glacier in Iceland that his grandmother mapped seven decades earlier; looking down into a crevasse, he gets the sense that the earth has always been a precarious place. "We are standing on a thin crust on a ball of boiling magma floating around a burning sun," he reminds us. But something has changed—we used to live in a world in which the earth aged in geologic time, while we arrowed through it in human scale; now we've forced the earth onto our own brief time frame. Thinking of glaciers melting, he notes that 2 billion people rely on the frozen ice that lives at the top of the Himalayas. Writing from that region, Anuradha Roy shows what that daily trek for water looks like for people in her village, and what happens when floods and drought make it that much harder to do.

There's a biblical feel to the weather events we're experiencing. In her poem "Tracking the Rain," Margaret Atwood captures the polarities of emotion that arise in a time of wild temperature fluctuation. "We stand on the non-lawn, / arms outstretched, mouths open. / Will it be burn or drown?" But we don't have to go back to ancient texts to recall why these images feel so familiar. After the 2010 floods in Pakistan displaced 20 million people, Mohammed Hanif saw a sudden replay of that nation's partition from India, the pictures of mass displacement, "grandmothers separated from their families, walking in a daze, toward a destination they have no clue about."

Migration is a recurring theme in this book. When crops dry up, when city streets are flooded with water, what else is there to do? "The state of our earth is inscribed on refugee bodies," writes Sulaiman Addonia, who left Eritrea during its war, spent time in a Sudanese refugee camp, wound up in England, and now teaches writing to men like him—in Belgium. Burhan Sönmez learns this journey the same way, leaving Turkey for political exile, only to rediscover upon returning home a new group of emigrants living his experience in far harsher terms. Sitting up one night drinking tea, he notices who the new outsiders are—it is the Syrians who come to work the fields like he once did. They sleep in the barn, with the animals.

Leaving, in some cases, is for the lucky. Some don't have the opportunity, even when it's advisable, like the people Juan Miguel Álvarez meets in a Colombian town beset by catastrophic landslides. Many of them have lost everything. It's not folly that keeps them there, as Mariana Enriquez points out in her essay on Riachuelo, the heavily polluted river that runs through Buenos Aires. "People use cesspits, and they don't throw their garbage in the nearby streams that flow into the Riachuelo because they're evil or dirty or uneducated or apathetic. They have no other option. . . . It's not a matter of changing habits: it's a problem of development."

Too often, that development is co-opted into escapism for the rich. Or the enshrinement of new classifications that make movement harder for the not-rich. In his futuristic piece about present-tense Bangkok, Pitchaya Sudbanthad chronicles how a city that is sinking and flooding is in response building upward, catapulting its wealthiest residences above the smoggy air. "Champagne-worthy sunsets are yours every evening," co-op ads beckon to buyers. In a story set in an alternate Tokyo, Sayaka Murata depicts a world in which residents are classified by their potential survival rate. In her tale, a pair of star-crossed lovers struggle to figure out what to do with their divided fates.

You needn't read into the future, though, to imagine such a tale. Just read Eka Kurniawan's love story set in contemporary Indonesia, where a boy and a girl are split apart by a simple change: after droughts and floods destroy crops, one leaves, one stays, and from that division flows a world of pain. Left behind in Port Harcourt, Nigeria, at a time of power cuts and international bluster, the narrator of Chinelo Okparanta's story thinks on similar things. How the precariousness of the world has sharpened fate's blade. "One never knew whence happiness would come, like the song went, just as one never knew whence happiness would slip away."

■ ■ ■

Anger is not surprisingly a big part of the response to what's happening across the globe. As complex as the sources of climate change can be, the obstacles—at least on a governmental level, sometimes on a global level—are infuriating. Lawrence Joseph's ferocious poem takes aim at a preening U.S. president who jubilates in the pain of others—in denying what is patently obvious about the climate. Khaled Mattawa rages in a poem at the absurd bargain many of the world's citizens are meant to swallow—their resources stolen, but told to stay put when they can no longer survive in landscapes that have been hollowed out. A second, awful debt is coming due. Many nations have seen it coming. "In the terrible country," Tahmima Anam writes in her short, powerful fable of being from Bangladesh, "climate catastrophe had already happened."

This crushing debt is being passed on, though, sometimes merely from the rich to the poor within nations. Lina Mounzer writes with black comedy of the hubris and greed of Beirut developers, who can game the political structure. They get their comeuppance from the overtaxed sewer system—which explodes in a biblical storm of filth when one building too many goes up. Rot is not a metaphor when it is so obvious. Growing up in Guatemala, Eduardo Halfon used to go swimming in a crisp, blue lake, close to where his grandfather had a home. Then the dead body of a guerrilla soldier washes up, and so begins the long dying of the lake. Gaël Faye writes of the holocaust of the fireflies in Burundi, which had given his youth, before that country's brutal civil war, such a luminescent beauty.

What many governments have done in recent years has made the sudden shortages and downfalls much worse—especially for their poor. In "Machandiz," Edwidge Danticat recounts a trip to Haiti during the buildup to a series of gas riots; the Haitian government had been part of a Venezuelan gas-purchasing scheme. But although the money was supposed to be invested, it was pocketed. In 2018, when suppliers began withholding new deliveries, gasoline surged to nine dollars a gallon in a country where the average person earns three dollars a day. These moments are even more bitterly felt when a government in power has not been elected by the people who live there. Walking across a diminished wadi near their home in Ramallah, Raja Shehadeh and Penny Johnson describe how for every example of hope and resilience in the destroyed landscape, many other possibilities—for preservation, study, and care—are shut down by the Israeli occupation.

Nowhere has this total shutdown of popular efforts to grapple with the cost of development—the price of a lack of stewardship—been more brutal and consequential than in China, where the photographer Lu Guang traveled and worked, recording, in essence, the stories of what had been hidden from the public eye by censorship: AIDS villages. The smog- and smoke-filled regions that literally fuel China's enormous economic growth. Writing on Lu's work, the photographer Ian Teh pays tribute to the power of Lu's art and what it records. "His images do not question the value of market reforms that lifted 800 million Chinese from poverty since the late 1970s; they are instead a heartrendingly persistent reminder of the suffering it took to get there."

■ ■ ■

The vigorous effort by many public figures, governments, and everyday citizens of the world to ignore climate change has forced storytellers to confront some dark forces in human nature. Namely, our greed, our stubbornness, our willingness to get ahead personally no matter the steep collective cost. We are so deep into this crisis and the stakes are so high, it feels as if a certain powerful segment of the population has simply decided to take what it can in the time we have left. In her chilling fable "Everything," Daisy Johnson conjures a woman who is given one awful, sweeping power to get what she wants—but often at great cost to others. Does she ever renounce it? In a harrowing brief poem, Lars Skinnebach sings an ode to grabbing and smashing in the voice of a greedy antienvironmentalist. It sounds like Patrick Bateman—the Wall Street broker turned serial killer of Bret Easton Ellis's *American Psycho* come to life in a new way.

The word "psychotic" comes up more than once, especially in Joy Williams's essay on the moral bankruptcy of big-game hunting. If there's anything that effectively epitomizes the inequality of this planet, it's our treatment of animals, whom we've bred and dominated and hunted into extinction everywhere—sometimes merely to mount their heads on the wall in a deranged sense of what a trophy is. Aminatta Forna describes what happens when, in the aftermath of Sierra Leone's civil war, one such persecuted animal—a chimp named Bruno—fights back and escapes his cage, going on the run. Reeling from years of being under the thumb of unelected brutes, Sierra Leoneans cheer on the escapee. "Bruno had become a simian Spartacus," she writes; "the country rooted for him." When the animals eventually do leave, we often feel bereft—as if abandoned. "At last, a week past their migration season, it dawned on me that they wouldn't be coming this year," reflects the narrator of Lauren Groff's hilarious and very sad short story "Dusk," in which a flock of cranes that used to land in the neighborhood stops turning up. "Maybe they wouldn't be coming ever again."

Cultures are struggling to come up with a language for these departures. Should we be elegizing? How do we honestly remember what was so clearly never valued? Simply watching it happen, Ishion Hutchinson makes clear in his poem on coral reefs dying, isn't enough. Some indigenous and native groups have this theft written into their bodies, into their stories. Tayi Tibble writes extraordinary poems out of this space. "I developed an early kind of kinship / with all the ways the earth hurt," she says in "That House." In Mexico, the reporter Diego Enrique Osorno hikes into the sierras of Chihuahua where the Rarámuri people, twice displaced from their land, never felt impoverished; but now that the climate has begun to make it impossible to grow maize, they have begun to feel as if they're losing everything.

Many pieces here channel a powerful sense of anticipatory loss—especially of the home. Even the Portuguese word "*saudade*," with all its permutations, from nostalgia to the nostalgia for what never was, cannot quite describe a longing for a home about to be lost by being made uninhabitable. Ligaya Mishan feels this returning to visit her mother in Hawai'i—each year the rains get harder, the soil looser, her mother's house more vulnerable to being swept away. But where is she to go? Returning to Nairobi, Billy Kahora sees a city remade by these destructions—his own neighborhood so far gone, and so transformed, as to not exist. Yasmine El Rashidi has already suffered this loss in Cairo. In her essay, she describes setting out to find a place to rebuild the home her grandmother lost—but where? Everywhere she looks, the forecast is for drought.

■ ■ ■

How do we live within dire forecasts, how do we breathe? How do we create a space to imagine both the coming destruction and the life that remains? How to go about one's daily life while knowledge of something awful hovers right there? These questions come up over and again in these essays, poems, and stories. In her short story, portraying a Korea beset by smog and dusty winds, Krys Lee puts this dilemma so aptly it could be a song. "Eat more, drink more," her character urges her husband and child, "trying to act like a mother and wife. Outside was the apocalypse."

Pop culture is saturated with spectacles of the apocalypse: cresting waves, super tornadoes. Yet these actual events are not such a voluptuous entertainment in many parts of the globe. They are realities. To put the fear of such catastrophes into literature goes only so far. What about the small, unseeable thing in a blizzard of detail? Such as the plight of a Blue Mormon butterfly in India, which Tishani Doshi renders with immense delicacy in her poem. We need to take on board what our planet is telling us, which means listening to what we are telling each other—humans and animals. "Only by putting literature into an ecological template," writes the Icelandic novelist Sjón, "can we understand what role writers might have in saving the earth and humankind."

■ ■ ■

Part of writing, the best part of it, is to wake a reader up into the present, by transporting them into a dream—one vivid enough to reorient how they see things upon waking. Sometimes I wonder if parks operate similarly within public spaces. Were they always simply meant to give us water, air, and shade? Or were they meant to remind us of a two-way relationship that has been happening for thousands if not tens of thousands of years between us and nature, one we would leave behind at our peril? What would happen if we could see the ruins our current ecosystem is built upon?

The heat wave in Paris broke, and I was walking across the city. I'd met a friend for coffee in the morning at Gare de Lyon and passed through the Jardin des Plantes on my stroll back to the apartment. It was raining now, the temperature an unbelievable 46 degrees cooler than it was one day before, when it hit 109, so chilling I'd had to wear a sweater. The abrupt swerve of weather unnerved me, so I didn't enjoy the gardens and hustled through them, on and up the hills behind, until I found myself at the entrance to the Paris Catacombs—the ossuary that was built by Guillaumot during those three decades he spent underground, shoring up Paris's crumbling underland. Functional for many years, now it is simply a sideshow. It's possible his own bones are down there; it's not entirely known. To go down into them, you make an appointment, and then, for a few hours, you're allowed to peer under the skirt of the city. Giggling travelers were queuing up, ready for a glimpse of the underworld, happy to be spooked, as if none of this would ever happen to them.

I continued on. Ten minutes later, I was back by Saint-Sulpice. The afternoon light had begun giving its towers and spires a Roman glow. A yellowish, golden umber. The church, like many of Paris's famous monuments, had been inspired by Roman architecture—in this case, the Colosseum. But as often happens with churches, its builders ran out of money while building it. Even when it opened, it was somehow a ruins. Yet how much joy it provided, what a lesson on learning to live within limits, and on the sense that all of this we call life is lived on borrowed time—moments often taken from something that came before us—and would need to be continued after. There's a sadness in that, but also a possibility, and wonder. I couldn't help but think of something Graham Robb wrote of Guillaumot, standing eighty, ninety, one hundred feet beneath the city, surveying his work as it neared its completion: when he would give the city another several centuries or more of life where it stood. "There was no doubt in his mind that where he walked there had once been an ocean."

TALES OF
TWO PLANETS

N64 35.378, W16 44.691

Andri Snær Magnason

ICELAND

I

I grew up in the United States until I was nine, and when we moved home there were many things that struck me visually. There were elements in the landscape that had a deep impact but I could not put it all into words. There were just these feelings stuck in my mind, and pictures, and things that I only understood much later.

In the north, we had an abandoned farm by the ocean, just below the Arctic Circle. It is one of the harshest homesteads in Europe, and you can see the next house only with binoculars. In the old days, driftwood from Siberia, eiderdown, seals, and trout made it a place where twenty people could live. We stayed in the old house where my grandfather was born. Nobody had lived there since the 1960s, but now my grandfather was back with his children and grandchildren to renovate and use it as a summer house.

For many years I was not sure what defined the nature there so strongly, because the most obvious thing was all the life. It is a place where you can listen to fourteen species of birds singing or quacking at the same time. Walking around on the beach or in the meadows in late June, you have to tread gently: everywhere you will find nests with eggs or small chicks. This is nature, but it is neither calm nor tranquil. It is as busy and stressful as a metropolis, the cliffs full of screaming gannets, the meadows full of birds trying to divert you from their eggs or arctic terns coming in swarms to attack you. All these elements resemble life in an obvious way, but a few years ago I found out that it was not life that defined this nature. It was death. The abundance and overwhelming presence of death. In a short walk you would find a dead bird, a dead chick, a half-eaten duck, a dead lamb wriggling with worms, dead fish, an old skeleton of a whale, and a seal's head. And looking closer, skeletons everywhere, parts of wings, and the smell in the air was actually rotting seaweed.

In the sky you would see gliding gulls threatening the newly hatched birds, swooping down and flying away with the little innocent creatures. This was a culture shock for a child; you would remember that in a park, or the zoo, in a city or on a common farm, you would never encounter death or anything dead. So up north, in this harsh nature, you had this overabundance of life, and what comes with it—all this obvious death. The children would collect the bones and the wings and play with them. Sometimes we would find a weak little bird and try to save it, but it would die in our hands. We would cry a bit and dig a small grave in the animal cemetery behind the farm.

To get up north we went over the highlands in my father's Volvo Laplander. We would travel over lava fields covered with green moss. Areas that look as if God had only two materials left after she created the earth: black rock and green moss. This alien landscape would show you that from the scantiest material you could create quite dramatic scenes. And then the moss disappeared, and we would travel through black sands for many hours. The sands looked like some kind of postapocalyptic landscape and we would listen to the car radio until we lost touch with any communication.

On one of these journeys north, we were just this one car in the black landscape, and we came across a geothermal area. We stepped out and walked into the steam and the vivid colors. The ground was full of bubbling holes with yellow sulphur around them. My mother was tense, as just a few weeks earlier a traveler had been walking at the same site and had stepped onto a thin crust covering a mud pit. He fell through the crust and his body had been boiled to the bone up to his waist when he was finally pulled up.

In the geothermal areas, our earth reveals what it is actually made of. We are standing on a thin crust on a ball of boiling magma floating around a burning sun. The geothermal area stands where the tectonic plates meet: it is like a window or a wound on the surface, you can feel the power that moves continents and you can feel the hostility, that you don't really belong to these areas, the crust can be weak, the ground is too hot to sit on, the muddy, boiling pools like something from Dante's *Inferno*. Everything seems very lifeless and dead, hostile and grim. But when you look closer, in all the Jupiter-like colors, in all this dead wasteland, you start to see all these traces of life. In a pool of bubbling 100°C water, there are some slimelike formations and you wonder what kind of life is this that can live there. You wonder if this is how life was perhaps originally formed. Between rocks and in the gravel you find small blades of grass, formations of lichen on hot rocks. Between rocks you find moss and maybe a flower, and when you look even closer, there are flowers everywhere. You wonder where these flowers come from. How can a seed find its way here in the short summer, sprout, and make a flower? In all this apparently dead landscape you suddenly understand the strength of life. In a forest, life is so obvious, so overabundant. But not in this landscape, full of sulphur, mud, and harmful gases. This life arises in areas where air and land and water seem not to be fully separated. The steam fills the air and becomes dense as a wall. The ground can be so weak and temporary. The next day it might be a boiling pit of mud. You take careful steps on the ground, trying not to make tracks, understanding the miracle of each blade of grass.

Some of the areas we traveled had been mapped and named by my grandparents and their friends. For hundreds of years, people saw no point in traveling into these deserted landscapes in the center of Iceland. It had been green many years before, but volcanic eruptions and erosion had created one of the greatest deserts in Europe. What we saw as nature was actually the ruins of something we had never seen. And what our ancestors saw as destruction became land that we loved and cherished.

II

In May 1956 my grandparents went on an unusual honeymoon. They got married on a Friday, packed their bags the same evening, and went on a four-week glacial trip to measure and map the uncharted territories of Vatnajökull, Europe's biggest glacier. They were team leaders on this trip of a group of volunteers: geologists, mountain lovers, and truck-driving mechanical wizards who could keep the snowmobile engines running in the most extreme conditions. They encountered all sorts of weather. They went into no-man's-land, had no idea where the greatest cracks would be found in the ice or what kind of weather they could expect, as forecasts were unreliable at the time.

Once they were caught in a snowstorm and they were stuck inside their tent for three days, until only the tip of the tent could be seen from the glacier's surface and they had to be dug out. I asked my grandfather, "Weren't you cold?"

"Cold?" he responded. "We were just married!"

I was about eleven when I asked and found it hard to find a rational connection between marriage and being warm.

The glacier was unmapped and most of the peaks and places were still unnamed. The place where they were stuck in a blizzard has a name now. A low-rising hill from the glacial plateau in the northern part of the glacier is now called the Bride's Belly. You can find it here on a map:

Brúðarbunga, Kverkfjöll,
1781 meters
N64 35.378, W16 44.691

Brúðarbunga is now registered as the fifteenth-highest peak in Iceland. I asked my grandmother about the trip a few days ago. She is ninety-four now and in really good shape. She is actually the same person she has always been. It is regarded as insulting in my family to refer to her as an old person. She is just "Hulda," and we don't use the word *ern* for her either. *Ern* is the word we use for an old person with an unusually clear mind.

I sat down with her with some maps and old pictures that my grandfather took. My grandmother had a nice scarf around her neck.

"Nice scarf," I said to her.

"Thank you," she said. "An old lady made it for me."

"Old lady?" I asked.

Grandmother laughed. "Well, she is actually ten years younger than myself."

We went through the maps and old logbooks. We went through the diaries of that trip and the trips after that. They built mountain huts at the edge of the glacier and on the top. The idea was that the huts should become shelters for scientists, outposts to gather information about these last uncharted frontiers of Iceland.

After a thousand years of human settlement in Iceland the country was covered by an invisible layer of stories. Every single farm, every hill, every mountain had a second meaning in history, folklore, or literature. A rock was not just a rock, it had been used in a battle in the 1200s; a cliff was not just a cliff, it was the place where *huldafolk* ("hidden people") lived, invisible people, descendants of Eve's unclean children. A farm was on the same place as the first farm had been built, layers of history surrounding everything, everywhere. But the endless glaciers were still a tabula rasa. A real blank sheet of paper, without stories or history, hardly mentioned in folklore or the Icelandic sagas. My grandparents and their expedition crew were the first to apply names and stories to this white, infinite blanket of ice and snow.

These trips became annual and are still today a vital part of the Icelandic Glaciological Society. I asked my grandmother if she was ever afraid in this hostile environment, but she just laughed and said, "It was so strange. I was never afraid. And we never got lost. If a storm hit us and we had no idea where we were we would just wait. Maybe a day or two, then we would find our way when visibility returned. Every spring I would find this smell. A scent of a glacier. I can't describe it but I would feel it. And I can still feel it during the springtime. The smell of a glacier. I miss not going on these trips."

When my grandparents were mapping the glacier, the glacier existed in the context of eternity. It had always been there, as long as any man or documents could remember, and according to their best knowledge, it would always be there. My grandfather took a 16mm camera with him on the trip. Once I said that I wished he had filmed more of my grandmother. You could always film the glacier, but my grandmother at a young age would be something more worthwhile to catch. But now if we take the glacial data from 1956 and onward, and apply that to current global temperatures and future predictions, we will see that this great body of ice will vanish within the lifetime of someone born today who became as old as my grandmother. Nature has left geological time and has started to change during a single human life span. We can calculate that the glacier is collapsing and will be only a fragment of its old self by the year 2120.

The Icelandic Glaciological Society has mapped the glacier floor. It has found invisible valleys and mountains that nobody had ever seen. You can look at these pictures and imagine these valleys in two hundred years, now frozen but at that time in the future possibly nice rugged valleys with small scrubby bushes or green moss formations. If my descendants want to wonder about my grandmother's travels and look at the old maps, they will have to imagine over thirteen hundred feet of ice above them and all around them. And they will have to imagine a snowmobile traveling more than thirteen hundred feet above them and say: "If you draw a line between these peaks, that is the path your great-great-grandmother traveled." We can take the documents of the Icelandic Glaciological Society and start naming hills and valleys. We will grieve the glacier but they will see it as I saw the landscape traveling in our Volvo Laplander. They will see blades of grass that will prove the miracle of life. They will see geothermal areas that had no name for people of my generation.

I have traveled parts of Vatnajökull with my friends, but I am far from being as adventurous as my grandmother. Traveling over Skeiðarárjökull, one of the large outlet glaciers flowing south of Vatnajökull, it is hard to believe that this vast, seemingly endless body of ice is vanishing. We travel through landscape unlike anything I have seen before, over terrain that looks like miles of turtles' backs, through a forest of black pyramids, past cracks that moan and gurgle, past streams that fall into bottomless holes that remind me of the lair of some alien, snakelike creature, an ice version of the sarlacc sand monster. The thought of slipping, falling in, vanishing, and getting stuck hundreds of feet below is harrowing. We encounter something like a road, a long, smooth highway, and after a day you feel as if you are on the planet Solaris in the novel of Stanislaw Lem. You try to interpret the forms you encounter, try to understand all these forms that almost look man-made. A pothole here, a pyramid there. A highway here. It feels as if the glacier is showing us what is killing it, from the pyramids to highways. The glacier does not leave with dramatic noises or calving ice such as we see in documentaries from the Arctic. The glacier vanishes softly, like a silent spring. It just melts, retreats slowly, calmly, but its appearance is strangely dead, almost like a slain fish. It loses its glow, lies flat and lifeless and far up in the middle of the mountain. You see chunks of ice and a line showing where the glacier was just a few years ago. And you try to grasp this great mass that is gone, to understand it has just changed form. It has become ocean and it will rise slowly, steady and calm, until a storm hits and knocks down doors and porches of beachfront properties.

III

I was writing about my grandparents' trips when I got a strange phone call. I was invited to interview the Dalai Lama on his visit to Iceland. I was wondering what I could ask a person who has been reincarnated fourteen times. It would have to be a very intelligent question. I was browsing through world history, religion, mythology—just anything, looking for something, when I started to think about the strangest figure in Nordic mythology. According to Nordic mythology the world started with a cow. It was a frozen cow and from its udders came the four rivers that nourished the world. This myth sounds like some great misunderstanding: a frozen cow in the beginning of time makes no sense. Sounds like a whispering game that went wrong as the myth was passed down generation after generation. And the name of the cow is *Auð-Humla*. *Auð* means wealth in Icelandic. *Humla*, I was not sure. *Humla* of Prosperity.

In Hindu mythology there is a Mother Earth cow, Kamadhenu, and the foundations of that cow—her feet—are symbolized by the Himalayan Mountains. You could say that the foundations of Kamadhenu are those mountains. And if you go to the Himalayas, you will find a district in Nepal called Humla. And if you follow the Great Himalaya Trail through Humla you will come to Mount Kailash—the center of the world, according to Buddhists; the throne of Shiva, according to Hindus. From this mountain come the four major rivers of Asia: the Indus, the Ganga, the Brahmaputra, and the Sutlej. A bit farther away you will find Gomuk, another source of the Ganga, one of the most holy places in India. Gomuk is a valley glacier, and the name means the Mouth of the Cow.

I am not sure if there is a real connection that can be proven. But suddenly it was as if it all came together: a glacier is a frozen cow. It keeps the water during the cold and rainy season. It releases milky white water full of silt and minerals when you need it the most. It can be all the water people have, the water that defines life and death for your crop, or the real keeper of the groundwater level.

Hima in Sanskrit means frost. *Auð-Hima*. The Prosperity of Ice. And today we still have 2 billion people who rely on this melting water, this source of life running from the Himalayas. During my interview, the Dalai Lama expressed his worries about the future of these glaciers. They were also retreating, and what would happen if up to 500 million people are met with water scarcity? Mythologically speaking, you could say that the Great Frozen Cow of Life and Prosperity is dying.

I started to feel that these issues were somehow beyond my

comprehension. Like hearing a new word before it has been loaded with meaning. Like what the words "nuclear bomb" might have meant to a person in the 1920s, before any images or contemporary victims had been attached to them. I started to think how I was worried about a dam that was being built in Iceland and the damage it would do. I was thinking how I could grasp that dam but still not understand it while I was walking on land that would soon be drowned under six hundred feet of water. That in a few years I would follow an old map with my children and I would point at an island and say: "Imagine that this was a hill, surrounded by goose nests. Imagine a roaring river under the hill, a waterfall and a rainbow. A nice place on the other side to camp, full of crowberries."

I remember how I could feel agitated and angry about this dam, but how I find it difficult to grasp or feel the great damage of the rising sea levels, warming temperatures, and melting glaciers.

IV

The old skaldic poets used a language in poetry that was saturated with Nordic mythology. To say "sky" in a poem you did not say "sky," you said "the dwarf's helmet." To say "earth" you did not say "earth," you said "bride of Odin." When the poets became Christian they were confronted with a problem. How do you talk about the Creator of heaven and earth when the language forces you to talk about God, the creator of the dwarf's helmet and Odin's bride? It took decades to find new metaphors and a language with which they could speak about God, without being drenched in the old metaphors. Imagining 500 million people affected, imagining the melted glaciers covering 200,000 square miles of land, I feel that these issues are so large that I don't really have a language to talk about them, and it seems that there are no maps to navigate properly into this future. What I see as nature is becoming something we have never seen. But of course, I hope that what I see as destruction will eventually become something our descendants can love and cherish.

DROWNING IN REVERSE

Anuradha Roy

INDIA

WILD ANIMALS DON'T BELIEVE in long good-byes, they disappear without a rustle of leaves. A few years ago we lost the foxes. In the part of the forest that went downhill to a stream, there were particular knots of trees where foxes flitted through the undergrowth as we passed at roughly the same time every day, walking our dog. Some mornings they would stand motionless, their eyes upon us, as if tied to a ritual, awaiting our arrival. Our dog raced off after them, yet though the foxes took flight in response, they went only a token distance, probably having come to the conclusion that the chase meant nothing—or there was a shared awareness of their mutual curiosity, an acknowledgment of kinship, the instinct that perhaps they were closer to each other than they could know.

At dusk, or deep in the night, the foxes often called, and in response our dog sat up very straight, raised her head to the skies, and joined them. A heartbreaking sound that was not a howl or a whine but a song of longing, the call of one wild being to another. Their echoing cries traveled across the darkness, one creature in the jungle, the other inside a house.

Then came the laying of a massive concrete water line that was to snake up from the stream to the highest ridge of our town—the pipes were to traverse great swaths of the forest to reach army units stationed in barracks on the next ridge. Reservoirs were to be built along the way. A labor force of half-starved men in threadbare shirts was off-loaded from trucks, and they camped in the woods in shanties that kept them neither fully warm nor altogether dry. Nevertheless, they made a life there and could be heard chatting, cooking, brawling, singing. They washed with water they stored in a metal drum at the forest's edge, cut dead branches from the trees to make pitifully small fires for warmth, and at the end of each day they cooked a big pot of mishmash for their meal. Trucks thundered down with construction goods. Drills went for stone and rock with machine-gun bursts of sound. It took two years for the work to finish.

Months after the men and trucks had gone and it had rained a few times, blades of grass began to spear their way up from the heaps of rubble and earth that were left behind. When another year or more had passed, the forest began to feel less ravaged, though we noticed that the ethereal banks of autumnal *immortelle* were gone and the golden *coreopsis* that lit up the ground had been driven out by a brash weed that was colonizing every slope. Something fundamental had been altered.

Nevertheless we did expect the foxes to return: cautiously perhaps, testing the ground, taking their time—but we were sure they would be back. Those small, brown, doglike creatures who had watched us, impassive and bright-eyed. We looked for them every day, going down the old routes we had abandoned in our attempt to stay clear of the pipe work. For many months we waited for a glimpse of fox eyes curtained by foliage.

Now we have given up hope.

Sometime over those years, who knows why or when, the flying squirrels that glided from oak tree to cedar and then scampered busily up tree trunks in the half dark, minding their own business as we spied on them—they too vanished. Was it because of the trucks and the water pipes and the camp of the workforce? Or was it because we had lopped a few of the overhanging cedar branches that threatened our house? Could an animal's sense of home be so fragile that the slightest change in its environment sent it scurrying elsewhere?

■ ■ ■

Once I met a man on a train that goes daily from Delhi to the Himalayan foothills. I'll call him Mr. Negi. He was from a village near the town of Tehri Garhwal, which had a population of about one hundred thousand until it was washed off the map by the waters of a giant dam built there to supply electricity to cities in the plains, such as Delhi. As they were watching their town go under, Mr. Negi said, his uncle realized he had left his typewriter in the house, locked away in a battered metal box, during the town's evacuation. His uncle was an old man, half blind from peering at that typewriter over a lifetime of work as a lawyer's clerk. Black, bulky, outdated, with keys that stuck. Their whole lives were going under, his aunt's eyes red, yet Mr. Negi's uncle kept crying out, My typewriter, my typewriter.

The last building to drown was the clock tower, Mr. Negi said. An ugly structure he had never liked, but at that moment it began to feel urgent and necessary that it stay visible, because as soon as its pointed tip slid from view it would feel as if a town where every street and building held meaning for them had never existed.

Mr. Negi moved to his wife's village, which was on a nearby hill above the old town. The water from the newly formed lake now surrounded it. From being hill people, they had been turned into islanders. They had to take boats if they wanted to leave the village, but ferrying trips happened only three times a day. It was a steep climb down from his house to the jetty, followed by half an hour on the boat, and you had a long walk ahead on the other side to reach the market or hospital in the new Tehri that the government had built to replace the old one. The village had nothing now, he said—no land to grow vegetables, no forest to graze cattle, no streams to fish.

Mr. Negi had heard that to capitalize on the novelty of a giant high-altitude lake the government planned to develop a new kind of tourism around it. Midget submarines would take tourists past the underwater wreck of the old town—the palace, the market— all crumbling away, but the state had no doubt that visitors would flock there and pay good money to enjoy this mini Atlantis so far inland, a thrill very different from the region's standard menu of mountaineering and bird-watching.

He broke into a bitter laugh. Nowadays everyone says things are ruined because of climate change. Isn't it convenient for governments like ours to have climate change to blame? It is so big, it's international, it's everyone's fault—yours, mine, America's, China's. And that's worked like a dream, hasn't it, for our ministers? Drought? It's because of climate change. Floods? Climate change. Scorching summers? Climate change. What about the things our governments have done? Doesn't it change the climate to wipe out miles of trees and mountains and replace them with water?

The clock tower is undamaged, said Mr. Negi. A hydraulic probe had been sent down to photograph it. The pictures showed it green and mossy but still upright. People knew this was so years before the probe went in, he said. They had heard the clock's muffled gong down there, from below the water. In the daytime the sound was too soft to be audible over street noise, but if you sat on the bank of the lake at midnight with only a quietly hooting owl for company, you could hear it ring twelve times. Telling the time for ghosts.

■ ■ ■

The other day I met a neighbor, Sundar, who was born in the Himalayan town where I've lived for the past twenty years. My partner and I are among the very few who moved here for work—mostly, people do the opposite. They have to leave, there are no jobs here. Sundar left our town to become a police constable in Delhi and was back for a vacation after some years. It was never this hot here before, he said. It used to snow long and hard and deep in winter. And these forests—he pointed to the bushfire-charred slopes around our houses—they were thick with undergrowth and the trees were tall and dense. He'd been scared of the dark shadows when walking that route to school. It's all changed because of global warming, he said, with an air of knowledgeable gloom. Climate change, his wife nodded. We were speaking in Hindi, but these two things were said in English, as if they were new, volatile elements from the greater universe, a foreign world that could be expressed only in a language alien to them.

Sundar is lucky to have found a job, even as a badly paid constable. His brother Hira, a lanky, loose-limbed, easygoing man with a gentle smile and an amiable manner, has not been so fortunate. He lives here and works when he finds work. For a low daily wage he will cut stones, carry heavy loads, repair fences, and dig foundations. When idle, he ambles around looking for a friend in the same predicament, so that together, the two of them can feel fraternal about unemployment.

Because his earnings are so infrequent and uncertain, Hira's wife and children live from day to day, relying on a combination of charity and luck. They have no bathroom nor is there piped water at home—in common with many village families, the forest is their toilet. The new pipes carry water only for military homes and barracks, and the municipal pipes that go to middle-class homes are too expensive for Hira to install. Water in taps at home is a fantasy for many.

As it is for most women in the hills, the day begins at dawn for Hira's wife because the early bird at the community tap gets the most water—sometimes the supply lasts no more than fifteen minutes. On the far horizon as she waits in the water queue are snow peaks and glaciers that melt into great rivers; the irony is even more acute when the water supply sputters or fails during the cataclysmic hill monsoons, and everyone is soaked while waiting at the tap. Each drop of clean water she can manage is precious, and once her bucket is full she bends a knee and carefully lifts the five gallons onto it. From there she hoists the bucket to her head and, straightening up, walks upslope or down, over rocks and a carpet of slippery pine needles; a smaller bucket or jerry can in the other hand helps her balance. Later in the day, she repeats the trip.

Our water supply is erratic and brief in summer, and when the community taps dry up before everyone's had a turn you can hear violent squabbles among the women, which end with screams of rage and metal pots and pans thrown around. This is more a manifestation of desperation and helplessness than of hostility—the next day, when there is hope again, they are smiling and gossipy at the tap, and neighborhood reputations are analyzed, shredded, and consigned to garbage bins as they wait for water. They are all in the same boat, as their parents have been before them. They see no prospect of change.

It is more than seventy years since the British left India, but the number of those who are grindingly poor runs into the hundreds of millions. They do not accept poverty as preordained in the way their grandparents did: modern communication technologies have ensured a change. They are perfectly aware that countries have risen from civil wars, natural calamities, epidemics, even nuclear bombs, and that states elsewhere provide most citizens with basic health care, food, water, education. The world on mobile phone screens pulsates with color and music and food—in other places, ordinary people seem to have a better quality of life. But for most such millions in India nothing has changed. Among those over forty, there is a profound sense of resignation that nothing ever will. The young peer at phone screens as if willing the plastic to do something magical. In a country run by politicians who are almost all thugs of different shades, the poor know that governments are of the rich, for the rich, by the rich.

Where the rulers are oblivious to the needs of citizens, wildlife and landscapes exist only to be commercially exploited. An invisible web of plutocrats and corporations controls the ruling regime as well as its rivals. There is resignation, cynicism, and fury as government after government ravages the country's forests and waters in a tight embrace with giant companies. Nobody can reverse this or stop it: it has been and will be *coitus uninterruptus continuous* until there is nothing left to destroy.

■ ■ ■

A few weeks after my conversation with Mr. Negi on the train, I read *The Photographer at Sixteen*, in which the poet George Szirtes reconstructs his mother's life. He is going to write her life from end to beginning, Szirtes says at the start of the book: "Moving backwards may be like healing a wound, returning to a perfect unwounded beginning where all is innocence and potential." He quotes from a poem by Anthony Hecht in which a diver's action is imagined in reverse: "Emerging from a sudden crater of water / That closes itself like a healed wound / To plate-glass polish as the diver slides / Upwards . . ."

I wondered how often the man on the train must wish that his town, moving backward, would surge out from the water: first the tallest treetops, then the ugly clock tower, the roofs of buildings, streets and shops, all intact. A resurrection. As if no time had passed and no typewriters and tin boxes or foxes and flying squirrels had ever been lost.

TRACKING THE RAIN

Margaret Atwood

CANADA

A mist of thin fat yellows the air.
We breathe hot pudding.
The leaves in the garden are crisp,
like antique taffeta. The former garden.
A touch and they shatter.
Forget the lawn—
the former lawn—
though the dandelions prosper:
they've outlasted our flimsy hybrids.
Their roots grip baked clay.

All day it's been pending, the rain.
It gathers, it withholds.
We thumb our touchscreens,
consulting the odds
on the radar maps: green puddles flow
from west to east,
vanishing before they hit
the dot that's us.
A stretched red dot, like a comic-book voice

devoid of words,
like an upside-down teardrop.

That's where we're living now,
inside this dot
the color of a heated toaster;
inside this dry red bubble.

We stand on the non-lawn,
arms outstretched, mouths open.
Will it be burn or drown?
Though we've forgotten the incantation,
the chant, the dance,
we invoke a vertical ocean,
pure blue, pure water.
Let it come down.

RIACHUELO

Mariana Enriquez

Translated by Megan McDowell

ARGENTINA

1.

My first memory of the river: the still, black, expectant surface, its false appearance. It didn't look like water: it looked like oily plastic, and it was waiting for me. I was in my uncle's arms. The man was barely present throughout the rest of my life, but he left me with this gift: as a joke, he threatened to hurl me into the stagnant water. "I'll throw you in on the count of three—one, two, and . . ." The "three" never came, but my screams did, because I was convinced that, if he threw me in—and I had no reason to think that this man, who worked in the port, wasn't capable of it—I would be eaten by the Riachuelo, the rotten beast that lies in the south, where the city of Buenos Aires ends. The river mouth where the Riachuelo flows into the ocean is called, precisely, La Boca. It's a tourist area. It no longer reeks because, for years now, the river has been undergoing a rescue and cleaning process. Still, it will never again support life or, probably, lose its color, black and opaque like an Elizabethan sorcerer's mirror.

I wish I remembered my parents or some other adult telling my uncle to stop that morbid prank right now, not to use my body and my fear for his enjoyment. However, in my memory I hear laughter and some incredulous consolation, someone's voice saying, "Your own uncle isn't going to throw you in the water."

2.

Immigrants came to settle in the port of La Boca in the first half of the twentieth century, many of them Italian and Spanish people fleeing poverty and the European wars. Today, the neighborhood is touristy and dangerous; it has tango dancing in the street for the foreigners, and it's where the Boca Juniors stadium was erected for the country's most popular soccer team. The Boca Juniors' colors make the neighborhood's origins quite clear: the founders decided they would use the colors of the first ship that came into port, and the first vessel they saw was from Sweden, with its blue and yellow flag. The river is called the Riachuelo because, except in the port where it's wide, its course is narrow and meager: *riachuelo* is a derogatory adaptation of the word *río*, river, and it's an apt name for that insignificant waterway. It edges the city of Buenos Aires and is the geographical and political border between Argentina's capital and its largest, poorest, and most intense province: Buenos Aires, same as the city. The superimposition of names confuses something that is not confusing. The city and the province have the same name, just as Washington, D.C., is not in Washington State—it's the same kind of imprecision. It's simple: the city of Buenos Aires is a rich district. As soon as you cross the Riachuelo, though, you find the first poor cities of the province, with their sprawling slums, abandoned factories, and the ugliness that comes from zero urban planning—millions of people living the best they can and building any which way, a world of cement, speeding cars, and working-class neighborhoods. The Riachuelo extends for forty miles, and it loses its name after about nine. Technically, it's only called the Riachuelo in the stretch that borders the southern municipalities: Avellaneda, Lanús, and Lomas de Zamora. For the other thirty-one miles, the river bears the terrible name of Matanza, or "Slaughter." The area around that stretch, however, is pleasant; there are small farms, people raise horses, it's (almost) the countryside. The river is the center of a large territory of a thousand square miles that encompasses streams and aquifers. Industrial runoff, rains, sewage: it all ends up in the river. About 5 million people live in the area.

■ ■ ■

The Matanza-Riachuelo River, its complete and correct name, is the most polluted in the country and in Latin America. It is always among the top ten most contaminated rivers in the world, alongside celebrated siblings like the Ganges, the Yellow River, or the Mississippi.

3.

I was born and raised in Lanús, one of the fourteen municipalities along the Matanza-Riachuelo. On some mornings when I was a child, the smell of the river used to wake me up. Like any smell, it's hard to describe in words, but maybe I can identify its components. The strongest tone is red: the smell of dead meat, of blood; the steak that rots in the fridge inside its plastic bag. A biting smell, organic and terrible. It was worst in summer, when it seemed to stick to clothes, dishes, walls. Another tone is gray and orange: the smell of garbage, leftover food, the stench of dumpsters where fruit and plastic mix, where fires blaze and stink as well—the smell of burnt garbage is unforgettable and sad, the madeleine of poverty that augurs the end of the city where a nameless place begins among the highways, factories, and automobile graveyards. The final tone is blue: the smell of fuel, the refinery flames against the sunset, the wake of the boats and ships that somehow manage to navigate that black water—these days, it's illegal to have boats on the river. That was the smell that wafted, before a rain or on a breeze, to my school playground, to our sidewalk games, to the breakfast table. There's something that is not usually mentioned about living near a polluted river. Now, I didn't live as close as the people who inhabit the precarious houses along its shores—the people who get sick, who have diseased skin and constant diarrhea. But I lived close enough that it was part of my intimate landscape. And it's sad, yes, and unpleasant and frustrating. What people don't say is that it's frightening. The Riachuelo scared me. Its protuberances of animal fat, machine grease, and bottles formed fantastic creatures always just about to show themselves. On its shores I could only imagine horrible crimes, hands clutching on to the dry grass of the bank. I was sure that the abandoned factories along the river hid crazed murderers who used the hooks where cows had once hung to skewer the bodies of their victims.

■■■

Crossing the Riachuelo to go to the city was a terrifying and often daily rite of passage. What if the bus fell into the water? What if the bridge collapsed, and all the cars were offered up to the voracious water? If I was in my parents' car, we usually went to the capital by crossing the Victorino de la Plaza bridge, a beautiful structure painted white that was built in 1916. I would hide in the backseat, under the Renault 12's torn upholstery if I could, until we were safely on the side of the capital. If I crossed on the bus I just prayed until we reached my neighborhood, where floodwater was only pooled in dark puddles on the street corners.

4.

The first environmental problems were recorded at the beginning of the nineteenth century, when the city's slaughterhouses and meat-curing plants started to spring up. Argentina is famous for its beef, the best in the world, and for leather, gauchos, the pampa. For over a century, those animals were killed and processed on the banks of the Matanza-Riachuelo. Hence the name. In 1820, reports began saying that blood and viscera from the decapitated animals were reaching the river. Chronicles of the time talk about clots of blood that sank under the water, lending a reddish tone to the surface, like a biblical curse. From then on, there are news items as well of government orders for the slaughterhouses to be moved farther from the river. Those orders were published every year: from this we can deduce that they were neither followed nor enforced. When the epidemic of yellow fever broke out in Buenos Aires in 1871, the doctors declared that the most likely source of the disease was the stagnant water, the stench, the overcrowded people who by then were already living along the Riachuelo. Toxic people. The rich families moved to the north of the city to escape the illness, and they never returned. This theory has more prejudice than science, but the idea persisted, and after the epidemic the areas around the Riachuelo were always associated with poverty and poison, places no one wants to be, things no one wants to get close to.

5.

The Matanza-Riachuelo floods. My mother tells of inundations that lasted days: she would wait on the terrace of her house for the water to recede. I remember being shut inside with the hatches battened, looking out the window as the street turned into a black river. There were many times when I walked around my house with the water up to my ankles. These days it's worse. It rains more, harder and more often. After a flood, I have to carefully disinfect the patio. My mother, who is seventy-two years old now, often stays shut inside because the water keeps her from going out. In some neighborhoods, the kids go swimming in the streets as if they were pools—the rotten water no longer bothers them. This happens every time it rains. It's not an exceptional situation, and we're used to it.

6.

The river wasn't contaminated only by organic waste from animals at the plants that processed meat for export. In the twentieth century, the country started to industrialize, and the river's banks filled with small workshops that used heavy metals, like cyanide and bromine. Everything that came out of those small factories flowed into the Riachuelo. It's often thought that pollution is the result of evil businessmen and evil politicians, a double entity that rubs its hands together and cackles. That is a soothing idea for a clear conscience, but it's simplistic. The truth is that if there was never a consistent plan to control industry and slaughterhouses, it's because Argentina never had a political balance that could enforce it.

And there are phenomena associated with political imbalance and economic underdevelopment that contaminated the Riachuelo more than cows or cyanide. When the factories closed and

Argentina's deindustrialization began—a process that started at the end of the 1950s but that was conscientiously carried out by the dictator's generals between 1976 and 1983—it left behind abandoned buildings, empty land, and many fewer people circulating in the area. The impoverished and uninterested state didn't set foot in those desolate zones to enforce any regulations of environmental safety, and the Riachuelo's banks—where only the poorest people lived then, as now—became lawless places: trucks arrived day and night, backed up, and into the river went their full loads, or barrels of toxic substances, or rubble. No one stopped them: the destruction of the industrial economic network only made the lack of oversight worse. There were no more workers who arrived early to the workshops, or public transportation along the riverbanks. Today there is a governmental organization tasked with healing the Riachuelo. It's slow going. It's the first serious attempt at cleaning in two hundred years.

7.

In September 2002, a group of policemen who were drunk on power forced nineteen-year-old Ezequiel Demonty, who lived on the Riachuelo's banks, to jump into the river. They were after him for a false complaint of robbery, and they decided to torture him before they arrested him. The body appeared by the Victorino de la Plaza bridge, the same one I used to cross with my family when I was little. In 2014, near an offshoot of the Matanza river, seventeen-year-old Melina Romero's body was found. Her murderer and rapist left her in a garbage bag. The newspaper headlines said that she "didn't go to school" and "liked to go out at night." They often illustrated the articles with a selfie of the girl crying in the mirror, her eyeliner running, her cheeks stained with black tears.

8.

The Riachuelo's psychogeographists assure us that there are still beautiful places that could be used for recreation. They talk about a secret wetland where tortoises live, a beach called Puerto Piojo (Port Flea) that was closed down by the army but that can be accessed with permission: it was once used as a vacation spot for workers, decades ago. Psychogeographists are an organized group that raises money to recover public spaces. They make alternative maps. They travel the river in boats and sit looking at the abandoned factories. They say the ruins are beautiful at sunset, when the water reflects the blue hour of the sky and there are birds on the barbed-wire fences.

9.

It's not that the pollution comes from any intentional or ignorant apathy either. Every month, five hundred tons of garbage are removed from the Riachuelo (along with one hundred fifty sunken boats, and, in 2018, twenty cars). No one goes to the riverbank, and people use the river as a dumpster. The river basin, those streams that connect with other streams, is surrounded by very poor neighborhoods. These areas now flood twice a month, while the people who suffer are told that "it's been raining a lot," as if it were a misfortune and not a definitive change for which no one is prepared. There is no garbage pickup in those neighborhoods. There are no companies that come to pick up the waste. The trucks can't drive on the roads—they're made of dirt, when they exist; some of the neighborhoods aren't legal, they're squatter settlements that don't appear on maps, and no one is in charge. Nor are there sewers. People use cesspits, and they don't throw their garbage in the nearby streams that flow into the Riachuelo because they're evil or dirty or uneducated or apathetic. They have no other option, there is no other choice. Four million people without sewers or plumbing. They're just left out. The middle-class citizens who compost in the capital insist that they could organize, collect their garbage, take it somewhere; they forget that poor people are lacking in many things, and foremost among them is time. Time—to eat healthily, to move to a place where it doesn't flood, to be meticulous with their waste and separate glass from plastic—is very costly. It's not a matter of changing habits: it's a problem of development.

The river's greatest contaminant is sewage, which is why it has an enormous amount of organic matter. It's impossible for life to exist in the Matanza-Riachuelo today: the water doesn't have enough oxygen to support animal life. Soon, it will no longer support the lives of those people who live along its banks. With the new, intense rains, the flooding will be unstoppable. Where will the people go? Is there a plan for them? Over sixty years ago, the water rose so much that they took refuge on the terraces of ten-story buildings, and from there they used canoes. They rowed on a dark sea. The world underwater. It could happen again but no one believes it, or they choose not to believe, or they decide to deny the possibility, or they don't know how to solve the problem and don't have the money to do it. The Riachuelo is scary: it's a sick and wounded animal, a dead thing that lives and that hides a secret, sad violence.

DUSK

Lauren Groff

UNITED STATES

PERHAPS IT WAS BECAUSE THE WORLD felt tissue thin at the moment, as though if I moved too quickly I could poke my thumb right through it, perhaps because I had felt unable to leave my house for two weeks, but when I glanced out my window that afternoon and saw the girl thrashing on her back on the opposite sidewalk I understood in a dark and wordless part of me that she was having a seizure and that it was up to me to save her life.

I ran out the door. There was no time to worry about being seen in pajamas I hadn't changed out of for three days, or to marvel at just how artfully the girl's shirt had lifted in her twitching, to just under the bottoms of her breasts, revealing a golden sweep of abdomen so whittled I could see hip bones, rib cage, a diamond in the navel winking. I bent over her. When she felt my hands on her shoulders, she startled and her eyes opened, and she stopped thrashing and reached up to take out her earbuds. No, no! she said laughing when I asked if she was epileptic, I'm sunbathing. Here, she said, and put an earbud in my ear, and I winced at the intimacy of this thing so warm from the inside of her body suddenly inside my own. I heard the kind of pale techno that hasn't changed much in twenty years, since my own dissipated youth, when I routinely bought baby aspirin from men in clubs and waited, always in vain, for the world to dissolve and recompose itself into something better.

This was how I met Dusk. I knew the moment she told me her name that it was not something that a loving parent would bestow on a child, that she had carefully selected it for herself when she reached the age of rebellion. Her real name was Moira, which I would later see on the packages that came for her. She was very distinctly South Florida, which means, in our more puritanical northern part of the state, of a breathtaking wealth and materialism that showed itself to be highly advanced in Dusk. She was a college student but had a gray Mercedes so new there were still stickers on the windows. She had a tattoo running from the outside of her right knee to just beside her breast that was one of the truest works of art I had ever seen, and which had surely cost many thousands of dollars: a medieval sword so delicate and ferocious that its bearer could only feel invincible wearing it at all times under her clothing.

I handed back the earbud and didn't know what to say, so I warned her that the median strip was so overgrown that people just let their dogs' poop sit there without picking it up, and that her long and glossy black hair was threatening to entangle itself in all that mess. Thanks! she said and lazily reached up and tied it into a bun, and held her earbuds near her ears, smiling at me, waiting for me to go. It felt gross to stare at her—she was exquisite, it was hard not to—so I said, Welcome to the neighborhood! and returned to the safety of my house. All morning, I wondered at how someone like Dusk could have rented the house of slow disaster opposite our own, until later, when I remembered that after the most recent calamity, the owner in desperation had brought in a whole team of men with paint and cabinets and tiles and granite countertops, leaving behind the skim of perfection under which the termites still teemed and the windowpanes still rattled on a windy night. Dusk would only have seen the new-ness; her ilk was not trained in disintegration.

I, too, had once been young, and I had never believed that houses could hold disease in them until we moved into our own and saw the way the house opposite spread its disaster into its inhabitants. It had been built by the sister of the woman who had built our place in 1904; but her sister had simply stolen her care-fully thought-out plans, and after that, the sisters never spoke again, although their houses were breathing in each other's faces. The tenant who had lived there when we first moved in left his drugs out on the coffee table, which his girlfriend's cat ate and that night died a particularly terrible death, after which the girl-friend took a tire iron to his stereo and car. When he moved out he was catless, girlless, carless, songless, weeping. The next ten-ant was a beekeeper who went one day to the hives in a field he had rented right outside of Alachua, and found that the bees had either died en masse, or swarmed elsewhere, leaving him both poor and bereft. The couple who had lived there before Dusk had stayed for seven years, somehow bearing the weight of the house's disease, but they were almost as desperate as the house itself, two bizarre creatures of the night who had miraculously found love in each other. They woke after noon and began drinking beer and smoking endless cigarettes soon thereafter on the porch, which they'd turned into a kind of haven of thrift-store statuettes and plants others had given up on and set out on the curb, which they nursed back to life. They played their dollar-bin records with in-creasing volume until, most nights, I was released to get up as the clock hit midnight, after having simmered in my resentment for hours, and ask them to turn their goddamn music down, please. They pretended they couldn't hear me until I took a step toward them up the porch, and the man would stand up bellowing in his yellowed singlet and smeary glasses and shout, Don't you fucking come up onto our property! He was mostly paunch; I wasn't scared. But the girl would theatrically interpose herself between her man and me, saying, Honey, chill, the *homeowners* have to go to *work* tomorrow, making it clear that she thought the words *homeowners* and *work* were sneers. Eventually, he'd reach out a bare and hairy toe and turn the volume down. Thanks so much! I'd say cheerfully and go back across the street, flipping them off in the pockets of my robe. I feel pretty sure that they made their money by buying things in thrift stores, taking artful photos of them, and reselling them at a giant markup on the internet. In any event, one day the man's abused heart gave out and he died, and it was somehow shocking to find out that he was almost exactly our age, not yet forty, because he looked at least sixty. Over the next four weeks, his bereaved paramour slowly moved out, filling the back of a borrowed pickup truck and driving it away, heaping and driving, over and over again. No matter how many times she did this, she never seemed to have less stuff; there were the same piles the next day, then the next. I began to wait up for her at night in the darkness of my own porch, thinking that I would find her taking back inside the trash bags and bits of furniture that she'd packed that afternoon, a Goodwill Penelope unweaving the forward momentum of that day. My heart hurt for her then, because I could easily imagine her desperate hunger not to have to get rid of the life that she and her lost love had built together, to break it all by going to a new place, to allow the things they held to lose some of the ineffable spirit of the man that had bled into them during their stay in that house of disaster. Because if the seepage can go one way, from the material world into the human, from house to inhabitants, from the made thing to the makers, surely it could go the opposite way, human to material, from maker to the made. As proof, I submit that the sadness of

God at beholding her human creation has become our own sadness, our downfall.

Yet even hoarders, which is what I slowly understood these people had been, can eventually come to the end of their material possessions, and the girl was at last finished with her move. The landlord came in and out of the house swiftly with a stricken look on his face, and soon brought his troop of handymen, as though the successive disasters the house infected the tenants with were a grisly bloodstain he could just paint over. And into this refreshed version of the house came blithe Dusk.

I watched Dusk; she was endlessly entertaining. I waited to see what new wild outfit she would wear to the bars on the weekends, strips of metallic silk barely tied on. If I was still awake in the middle of the night, I'd peer eagerly into the dim porch light to see the person she came home with, and they were almost always the handsomest boys I'd ever seen. I cheered her on: anyone who was able to snare that kind of beauty with her body should delight in said body's wizardry. A month after she moved in, Dusk took off the porch swing and tipped it over the railing so it fell into the bamboo, where it stayed upended for months, then put in its place a hanging bed so that, if she was too drunk to walk herself into her house, the Uber driver could deposit her on the bed and not have to come in and inevitably get creepy with her. Some nights her outdoor bed would be so irresistible to weary passing homeless people that they'd climb up and sleep there, and in the morning, she'd bring out a Styrofoam cup of coffee and a microwaved egg muffin, and rouse them, and before they were even off the porch, she'd empty out an entire can of Lysol on the bed and call it a day. Sometimes, if she didn't especially like the boy she came home with, she wouldn't want him in her house and would seduce him al fresco, and because it was a swinging bed, often the attempts were hilarious, and from my own porch before I would flee inside out of decency, I'd have to muffle my laughter with a pillow.

I knew it wasn't right to spy on my neighbor, but I had little else to do. I would like to think of myself as a bohemian, a refusenik, an underminer of capitalism, a soldier in the war against the hegemonic superficiality and materialism of this current death rattle of the American dream, but I didn't have a job. Even a few months earlier, I'd fill my time with free Zumba at the senior citizens' center down the block, or with waylaying my children's teachers with ever-more-refined pedagogical questions, or with bird-watching. But a few weeks before Dusk moved in, I had gone out to the prairie every day to catch sight of my favorite natural phenomenon in Florida, the migration of sandhill cranes, with their vivid red necks and their rubbery honks and metallic whirrs. God, I loved them, all the raucous mob of them that spoke of plenitude and beauty for the sake of beauty. But day after day passed, the window of the cranes' season slowly closed, and I'd only seen a few of the birds at all. At last, a week past their migration season, it dawned on me that they wouldn't be coming this year. Maybe they wouldn't be coming ever again. Something terrible must have happened to them. And then I remembered one of the many hurricanes-of-the-century we'd been having with increasing frequency, two or three a year, and thought that perhaps the storm had found the birds in their nests, had blown them up and into the air above the Gulf, deposited them in the buffeting high winds where they flapped, disoriented, trying to find land, until one by one they dropped exhausted into the dark sea below.

It was this imagining that drove me into my house, and kept me there. It wasn't the thought of all the death that bothered me; I am from a morbid people who keep the certificates for their grave

plots framed upon their walls and believe the afterlife is an idiocy
that a four-year-old could poke philosophical holes into. It wasn't
the fact that soon human life will cease to exist on the planet; we
likely deserve it, after all. No, it was all the great suffering I could
smell on the wind, not simply human suffering for which we are
culpable as a species, though there will be a great amount of it
and the idea of children suffering was particularly acute; but
there was also the animal suffering, innocent suffering, a tsunami
of horrific pain rushing toward us, and I was powerless to stop it.
I was powerless to make anyone sense it and understand.

My husband urged me to clean myself up and leave the house,
he entreated, eventually became quietly disappointed in me, the
all-time extremity of his censure; my children asked me to take
them to the park but with such faux innocence, I knew they'd
been set up. But I wouldn't, because I couldn't. I was laid out flat
by future mourning.

I had the time to watch my neighbor, in short. As the days
cooled, Dusk's behavior grew more erratic. I began to be worried
about her. She didn't seem to be eating and grew even thinner;
she started to go out not just on Friday and Saturday, but sometimes even Thursday and Wednesday. Once, she must have driven
home drunk from a very particular kind of party, because in the
morning her car was parked half up on the curb, and the back
door was open and out of it spilled such a huge pile of Mardi
Gras beads in purples and yellows and blues that my children,
seeing it, ran out urgently and swam in the mass of beads on the
street like seals, and I found strings of plastic in their pockets for
a week. Once, three sleek boys drove up in a convertible, and
Dusk came out with her roller bag and sunglasses, and when she
returned a few days later, she was much tanner and still wearing
her bikini top but no shoes, and staggering.

I noticed a pattern; after Dusk's worst nights, when she wasn't mobile or speaking, and the driver dumped her already passed out on her outdoor bed, two days later, there would be a massive pile of boxes delivered to her house, probably from drunken binge-shopping after she'd woken in the early morning cold and dragged herself inside. I watched with horror as she'd rip open the boxes one after the other, and make a pile of stuff on the porch, then toss all the cardboard into the big black garbage container without breaking them down or putting them in the recycling.

Even though the end is nigh, I wanted to shout from my perch across the street, we don't have to hasten it! I couldn't stop thinking of the boxes, the trees slaughtered to make them, the trucks filling the highway carrying mostly paper and air and shit people didn't need, that caravan of death, that burning of dead dinosaurs releasing carbon into the atmosphere, heating us up, how the marketplace that conservatives beheld in slavish adoration somehow came up with the most profound inefficiency known to mankind.

The second time Dusk did this wild, greedy internet shopping, I was so agitated that I couldn't sleep, and at last rose, put on my slippers and went outside in the night with a kitchen knife, and broke down all her cardboard and stacked it neatly in the recycling bins. I also found a few unopened things that she'd ordered and decided she didn't want, still wrapped in plastic: a clock in the shape of a cat, a twenty-pack of protein bars, a purple dress still with its tags, that would have looked ludicrous even on Dusk's perfection, but that she'd spent two hundred dollars on. I didn't want any of it, but someone might, and so I stored her castaway things in my garage. I would donate it all, I thought, one day when my courage returned to me and I rejoined the world. Soon the pile was the size of my younger son.

By the fifth or sixth wild shopping binge, I began to long for the rude hoarders to come back; at least they understood the value in unwanted things. It was cold when I crept out to break down the boxes, and I shivered as I pulled them out of the garbage, and then I saw myself as though with the eyes of anyone who might happen by, and knew that I looked like a bag lady with my unwashed hair and holey pajamas and angry mutterings in the shadows. In one box, under a careless mess of plastic bubbles and still wrapped in tissue paper, I found a large necklace with a fist-sized dangling skull on it in a glowing rose-gold color, a thing Dusk hadn't even seen before discarding. Instead of adding it to the growing donation pile in the garage, I put it around my neck and felt, very briefly, both young and wildly sexy. It was so heavy, so ridiculous, it made me laugh. I kept the necklace on through my fitful sleep in the night, and in the morning, when I went into my children's rooms to wake them up for school, they both opened their eyes sleepily and grabbed at the skull in wonder. Downstairs, my husband was cooking eggs, and he said, Wow, that sure is a big old thing around your neck!

Dusk threw it out, I said. I love it almost too much.

He stopped cooking and went still, and looked at me, then said carefully, You're going through her garbage now?

Oh, I said, no no no, she never breaks down the boxes of shit that she buys and it agitates me so much that I have to go over there and do it for her. I'm just being responsible.

He carefully put the spatula down. So you pull her boxes out of her garbage? You wait until everyone's asleep and go to the neighbor's and pull things out of her garbage? I wonder if it's possible that you're a little obsessed with this girl? Like, you may be scaring me a little? Do you think this is normal behavior? Should I be worried about you?

No! I'm doing it for the environment! I said, and fled.

I felt stung, but after the boys left and the house was all mine again, a plan began to form in my head. I took the necklace off, and bathed, carefully washing my hair, and put on one of my nicer dresses, a long, white minimalist sheath, and hung the necklace on myself again, thinking that this way my body would be a gallery wall and she couldn't *not* see it. I would force the issue with Dusk; we would gently talk it out. I envisioned tears, me calling a therapist for her, because for the past few months, many of my friends had quietly sent me the numbers of their therapists.

So I sat on the porch with a book until midmorning, when Dusk came out with a cup of coffee, in her slippers, and I nonchalantly came out the porch door with my dog, who had been leashed and trembling in delayed anticipation for hours. Hey, I called out, and she squinted at me, and said, Wow! You look hot, sister. I didn't even know your hair was blond.

Yep, I washed it, I said. My dog, to whom all humans are a source of adoration, pulled us across the street, and Dusk kneeled and fondled my dog's head, and when she looked up at me, she said, That is like the most killer necklace I've ever seen.

I was nonplussed; I couldn't speak. I was prepared for anger, for shame, but in none of my projections did Dusk not even recognize the thing she'd spent a good deal of her parents' money on and tossed out without opening. My brain went into a loop, and I hardly clocked her when she said to my dog in a baby voice, You're gonna have a neighbor! Yes you are. Yes you are. My little puppy is coming today! And then, looking up at me, she said solemnly, I've adopted one of the dogs who had been orphaned by Hurricane Michael, it's like so sad. Their owners just let them wander out into the storm. And then they were like homeless. People can be so terrible.

And then she stood, and stretched her lean body like a terrific jungle cat, and poured the dregs of her coffee on the ground, and said, See you! and went inside.

When her words finally struck me on my way to the dog park, my agitation peaked, because a dog was not a necklace, not an ugly dress, a dog could not be tossed into the landfill if it displeased. Dusk could not possibly care for an animal, I thought; an animal didn't fit into the life of a hedonist. As soon as you own an animal, you enter an honorary middle age. You have to take care of the body of something else, not just your own beauty.

The dog arrived that afternoon in Dusk's arms, some kind of Jack Russell mix that snapped at my dog when she ran over and said hello. If a dog can wear an expression, this one's was constantly sour. It pissed all over Dusk's house so that she threw out her rugs, which in the night I pulled out and treated and rolled up and put a FREE sign on them, and they were snatched up by dawn. When Dusk went out at night, the poor dog barked for hours until I thought surely it would go hoarse or I would go mad. That first night when she returned at three in the morning, after six hours of the dog's shrill barking, Dusk must have done the wildest shopping binge of all, because a few days later, the pile of boxes in front of her door was the size of a small car.

And this was it; this was the breaking point. I waited until Dusk appeared in the morning light to practice her yoga on the porch. She gasped with pleasure at the wall of junk that the postman had built and said to her dog, It's Christmas! That is when I walked across the street, grim and sure.

Dusk, I said. We really need to talk.

Uh-oh, she said. You sound like my mom. What's up?

I am worried about you, I began, but she interrupted, saying, Oh. If this is about the partying, it's okay, I have a 4.2 GPA, it's all under control.

No, I began again, and she said, No, I see, I get it, I didn't think you were the puritanical kind but if you're scandalized by all the guys I bring back, whatever, like, I'm body positive and I love sex and like it's none of your business. My body, my choice! Also, I use the rhythm method, it's fine.

This made me pause for a long moment, but I started again, No, Dusk, it's not the sex, it's not the drinking. It's what the drinking leads to. It looks like you get drunk then buy a bunch of shit that you later just throw out.

Oh, she said. That's all? I mean, it's my money. I can buy what I want. Right?

But your actions have consequences for the world, I said. Every box that comes here puts a tax on the environment—

I was about to launch into a long and carefully prepared speech when she said, Ugh. She stood up very tall and put her hands on her waist. You're one of those climate change people. I should have guessed, I mean, you dress like one for sure. You do you, whatever, free country, but just so you know I don't really believe in climate change.

What? I said. It's not like Santa. Or God. It's not something you don't believe in. It's empirical.

Yeah, but, we'll be dead before it matters, she said. Like in a hundred years.

Wait, but, I began, no, the U.N. put the timeline shockingly soon, the scientists—

Yeah yeah yeah yeah yeah yeah yeah, she said. I mean, I'm not dumb, obviously I know what science is, but this is the way I look at it? Okay, so I'm sure that in my lifetime things are going to be impacted but like there are already too many people on the earth and the people who are going to be hurt are the ones who aren't really contributing anyway.

And she smiled at me, and there was something victorious about her smile, and I turned away because I had no words. I came into my house. I sat in silence for a very long time; I lay sleepless in silence when everyone slept around me, still stunned.

And, for the past week, Dusk has ignored me or made a face as she sees mine in the window. Far worse than contempt, her expression is one of profound pity. I have, in asserting my moral position, somehow lost my moral authority. I am now just another pathetic Old.

There is one small bright spot, though, and it is that since the moment when I failed with Dusk, I have become frantic with the need to leave the house, and I have begun to take my long walks down into the prairie again. I bring a bag with me, to pick up litter. It is stupid, but it is something; I am not doing nothing. The imperative for leaving is because that poor, small adopted dog of Dusk's barks and barks all day as soon as she leaves for her classes. He barks in a screaming pitch, without ceasing, in furious urgent need. I don't know how he finds the oxygen, how such constant barking doesn't make him pass out. But he continues; he is adamant; he will make us hear him; he insists upon it. In fact, there have been times when I've felt myself leaning forward, listening, and I feel in those moments that I am very nearly hearing what it is that he's trying so hard to tell us; there are times when I feel certain that he's telegraphing beyond language the things that he knows intimately, lessons his very flesh learned, and if I only listened hard enough and cared enough, I'd understand the story.

Perhaps he's telling us of that lost first life of his, so easy and beautiful and good in the little apartment over the sea, with his old, slow humans and his daily food from a can and his walks on the beach with the long-legged birds and the balcony where he could keep an eye on it all and smell the wind. And then one day the birds became raucous and fled, the beasts of the water went deeper or ran on their strange and stubby legs inland, the bugs found deeper places to stow themselves, the skies grew black and furious, and the terrible vast thing came ever nearer and ever darker from over the distant horizon. And the little dog barked, increasingly loudly, telling his humans to get out, to take him with them, but they did not listen to him, they did not want to leave their place, the careful accumulation of their things, their so carefully crafted life. And then the winds rose even higher and louder and the water gnashed and bit and drew up over the sand in its surge, then over the road, and against the building, and it was so loud none of the shouts of the humans could be heard, and he could feel the very structure below him weakening in all the water and the wind, slowly disintegrating, and with a smash the glass blew out of the sliding windows, and the wind was now a great bad beast in the apartment, and with its buffeting and roar it picked him up and threw him through the air, out into the storm, and this was the last of that life that he knew. His terror was so extreme he was frozen in the pile of rubble where the wind had blown him, and there the wildest blackest wettest loudest wind blew at him for endless time. And when he woke his whole world was gone, his people were gone, his apartment had been blown off the face of the earth and in its place was a snarl of rubble and death. This is what the dog would have told me, I feel sure, if he had the language, and if I had the ears to hear him, to heed the prophecy the god of dogs had chosen him to tell.

FROM TEOTWAWKI

Lars Skinnebach

Translated by Susanna Nied

DENMARK

One year I lived on sandworms
and lay down in the dunes
when the disco closed
when the border closed, the interpreters
killed immigrants
and put the heads
on stakes, I hid my
knives in the heather, laid
sliced-off lips on the hummocks
as a sign for others lost in it all
And when the ants came
I followed them down
underground where they lived
blocked their exits
and plundered their nests
and plundered their stores
minerals, eggs, and dust
minerals, food, and knowledge
and poured saliva into their saliva

SURVIVAL

Sayaka Murata

Translated by Ginny Tapley Takemori

JAPAN

"WELL, MISS KUMI SUZUKI and Mr. Hayato Sumikura," the survival-rate adviser said, and sighed. "If you do get married and have children, the probability of either of you reaching sixty-five is under thirty percent." His face was grim as he ran through the computer data.

Hayato and I were sitting side by side on the sofa in an office of the Tokyo City Survival Advice Center, holding hands. As I glanced at him, he turned pale and covered his face with his free hand.

"But that's—"

"It's a pity, but that's the fact of it. Of course you're okay, Mr. Sumikura. As a highly qualified professional member of the banking elite you are ranked A, so your survival rating is as high as eighty-seven percent, as long as you remain single. However, I'm sorry to have to say this, Kumi, but you're only ranked C-minus, and in fact if you remain single your survival rate is below twenty percent."

"Ah," I said listlessly.

The adviser glanced at me reproachfully, apparently sensing

my lack of motivation. "You're okay as things stand now. It's just if you have a child, you see. A child's survival rating depends entirely on the parents' income. I'm sure you're already aware, but these days if you want to live until sixty-five you need money. A child must enjoy the best medical care and live in secure housing in order to grow up to be an elite and earn a good salary. That's what's needed to come out on top in this battle for survival."

"This world is too cruel!" Hayato groaned.

The adviser nodded in agreement and went on. "That's why you need to spend a lot on educating your child from the start. You must send him to cram school when he is still an infant, make him take extra classes and raise him to have top grades, and then pay the fees for a top university. Then he will naturally follow an elite course to attain his own high survival rating. I hate to say this, but as things stand now, the prospects of your child surviving until sixty-five are less than fifteen percent."

"Fifteen percent! You mean his chances of dying young are eighty-five percent?" Hayato howled and buried his head in his hands.

"Ah . . . does sound a bit like he'd die young, doesn't it?" I said to him with a wry smile.

He looked as though he'd just been informed of his own imminent death. "Isn't there *anything* at all we can do about it? Some way to raise our child's survival rate to at least fifty percent?"

"Well . . . I hate to have to say this, but, as I said, the problem isn't with you, Hayato. So really, it's up to Kumi to get better qualified, acquire some practical skills, and get a job or two on the side. That's the way to improve the survival rating. Still, I have to say that in this day and age, it isn't easy . . ."

Seeing Hayato hunched over in desperation, I took the flask of saline solution I'd made at home that morning out of my bag.

It was hot in the office; being a municipal facility, they were probably cutting down on the air-conditioning. My favorite dress was already soaked with sweat and stuck to my skin.

After leaving the advice center we looked around for a cheap café, but unable to find anywhere we ended up in the lounge of a nearby hotel, an expensive option frequented by A's.

I took the wallet for our date money out of my bag and peered into it. Given the gap in our income levels, at first we'd always argued over where to eat on our dates or how to split the bill. In the end we'd agreed to put aside the same amount of money and use that to pay for our dates. I counted how much was left of this month's date allowance: five thousand yen. About enough for coffee.

"Shall we split up, then?" I said, just as our coffees arrived.

Hayato looked up, startled.

"It's the obvious thing to do, isn't it?" I went on, taking a sip from the antique coffee cup. "I would feel awful about you and our child having a lower survival rating because of me."

"Let's not jump to conclusions now. There must be a way."

Outside, people walking by the lounge's glass front were drenched in sweat. They must be C's, I thought. A's always got around by cab.

"My great-grandma always used to say that in the old days they had winter and fall. I can get winter, but what was fall like, I wonder."

"I have no intention of splitting up with you."

"Well then, will you give up on procreating? Can you imagine how awful it will be for our kid to be born a C?"

"But I—I do want to have a child."

"I'll be happy for you to leave your genes to posterity, too, Hayato. I'm fine with that. You should marry another A and live a good long life."

"But what about you, Kumi? Will you find another A?"

"No, I reckon I'll become a D. I've been thinking about it for a while now. I'll be fine."

"A D? No way!" he shouted.

"Keep your voice down! It's our last date, after all." I smiled, and reached out for his untouched cookie.

Through the window I saw a rescue team rush out to help a C collapsed in the heat.

■ ■ ■

I'd always had a low survival rating, ever since I was a child.

The survival rating was the probability of you still being alive at age sixty-five expressed as a numerical value. Nowadays just about all illnesses could be cured in childhood, as long as you had money, so the survival rating was roughly proportional to the salary a person could be expected to earn. The calculations also took into account natural disasters caused by global warming and earthquakes. But even then, if you had a high-enough salary you could afford to live in secure housing, so ultimately it didn't change the fact that the disparities in income and survival rating were practically equivalent.

Survival ratings were graded and written large at the top of elementary school reports. A survival rate of 80% or over was an A, 50 to 79% a B, 10 to 49% a C, and 9% or under a D. Instead of striving to do well in subjects like Japanese or science, children focused on improving their ratings. Many children burst into tears upon receiving a C or D on their school report. I always got C, but strangely I wasn't all that scared of dying. I merely thought to myself, *Oh, well, not long to live then*.

The classroom was enveloped in a strange feverishness whenever school reports were handed out and pupils saw the imminence of their own death in numerical terms. The teacher would desperately try to soothe hysterical children, saying, "Everybody calm down and listen, please. I'm sure some of you are quite shocked to learn of your low survival rating. But this is meant to help you to survive. It's really important to know what the reality is in order to survive these terribly difficult times. Study hard and try to improve your rating even just a little bit, okay? Everybody do your best now."

All the children threw themselves into studying and exercising as hard as they could. Since we were all desperately trying to improve our survival rating, it was even more difficult for those of us who'd always had a low rating to improve ours, however hard we tried.

I'd always been a C-minus with a grade below 30%. My Dad was a D, but he'd disappeared off the scene when I was still little. Mom had been informed at her workplace health check that she was a C. I'd always felt bad about her survival rating having been considerably reduced by being burdened with a child—me.

My best friend, Megumi, who lived next door, was lower than me at D, but she worked really hard and managed to get her rating up to B. Under her influence, I too studied hard until high school. We set our sights on becoming elites, and encouraged each other, saying we'd become healthy old women together.

These days the so-called exam wars to get into college equated to a war for survival, and we studied hard. But then one day, I wondered how long I'd have to continue doing this. Do well in my exams, get a good job, and make money. Get up early and stay up late studying, day in, day out, all for the sake of the survival rating. I was suddenly fed up with the lot of it: was life really all about survival ratings?

Once I stopped studying, my B rating plummeted. I didn't care. Rather than live my life controlled by the survival rating, I had the feeling it would be far more wholesome to accept my lot in life and die when my time was up.

Megumi urged me to change my mind, but I simply dropped out of the elite course and didn't even try to get into a good university. School fees were a waste of money, so I left school and took up a casual job in a family restaurant. It was there that I met Hayato. He was a student at a famous university in the neighborhood and came in every day to study. I would idly watch him studying hard, thinking how tough it was to be A-rated. I was shocked when he slipped me a love letter as I took his order for a coffee refill.

"But I have a much lower survival rating than you," I told him.

"Your survival rating has nothing to do with how I feel!" he said passionately. "I'm in love with you now. That's what matters."

I was kind of touched by his words, and we became lovers. Eventually he graduated from his top university and landed a job with a top company, while I carried on working at the family restaurant. I knew from the outset that my existence brought his survival rating down, and had resolved from the moment he declared his love that it would be a temporary affair.

The next day it was again so hot I felt as though I was being stabbed to death by the sun's rays. I opened my parasol, hung my flask of saline solution around my neck, and hurried to the municipal center for the seminar on Ferals. I got there to find it was packed.

D's were rarely able to hold down a job, and most of them went to live in the mountains as Ferals. I'd heard that in the past homeless people used to live on the street, but it was too hot for that now. The feeble perished, and only those who turned Feral survived.

When people turned Feral, their appearance changed, possibly as a result of adapting to the heat. Their mouths grew bigger to better capture liquids, their hands turned into paws and they went on all fours in order to be able to move quickly away from danger. And for some reason short white fur grew thickly over their entire bodies, covering their skin, so they no longer needed to wear clothes; when lots of them gathered in one place, they looked like a mass of wriggling white shapes.

The seminar was full of C's and young D's unsure of whether they were cut out to be Ferals.

"The key to surviving as a Feral is basically forgetting. You have to forget everything you have learned to survive in the modern world—your knowledge, language, everything. You must just live for the sake of living. This way you can attain a survival rating of one percent. Otherwise you'll drop below 0.0001 percent. Have you got that? You must forget these figures, too. Just focus on staying alive."

The speaker droned on and on about abstract ideas that I didn't really understand, and my attention wandered. I noticed some D's in the seminar were already beginning to sprout thick white fur, and I wondered whether it wasn't counterproductive for them to be there.

Bored, I fiddled with my phone and saw a text had arrived from Megumi: Why don't you come over to mine after the seminar? I'll come pick you up by taxi when it finishes.

OK, I texted back, then put my head down on the desk and dozed. The speaker didn't seem to mind much.

I began to hear loud snores here and there in the classroom. Whether it was simply because the seminar was so tedious, or whether it was the first step in transforming into a Feral, I didn't know.

■ ■ ■

"Seems like Shikoku's going to be the next area to sink. You know, the storms are getting so bad there's going to be a major crustal movement soon, apparently."

"Really? Then the rents around here will go up again."

The air inside Megumi's one-room condo was hot and stuffy. She wiped away her sweat, turned on the air-conditioning, and sighed.

"This is a safe area, but it's already the limit for a B-grade salary. I'll probably have to move to somewhere a bit cheaper."

Megumi's place was in a prime area occupied by a lot of A's. It was secure, on firm ground, and had a low crime rate. She had been grumbling for some time that even her tiny apartment was too expensive for a B like her.

"Oh, chicken—how unusual!" I exclaimed when Megumi brought out some yakitori.

"Well, it's synthetic meat, though. I just can't bring myself to eat cats."

With the heat, practically all animals had gone extinct, and now the only living creatures other than humans were cats and cockroaches. I'd have liked to see the elephants and cows and other animals shown in picture books, I thought.

Cats, cockroaches, and humans: come to think of it, that was also part of the battle for survival. I didn't mind which survived as long as some living creature remained on this planet. Some people weirdly regarded cockroaches as rivals and went around killing them, but if we all died out only plants would be left. Better we all get along, I thought.

"But I was really rooting for you and Hayato, Kumi. Look, lots of C's and D's that haven't yet become Ferals try to hook up with A's just in order to survive. I suppose they're simply doing whatever they can to survive, but it's pretty grim and I never really agreed with it. But you and Hayato are different, right? These days it's unusual to find couples who are together for reasons other than to raise their survival rating. That's why I was hoping it would work out for you."

"Well, I don't know about Hayato, but personally I always

thought of falling in love as a kind of hobby. I always thought that he should eventually marry someone who would raise his survival rating."

"Hey, Kumi, you don't take much interest in survival ratings, do you?" she said as she stuffed her face with yakitori.

I smiled awkwardly. "You reckon?"

"Yes. Why is it? You didn't even try to get a decent job after high school, and insisted on being a D. But you're easily able enough to get your survival rating up to forty percent or so if you put your mind to it. D isn't even one percent, you know!"

"Has it ever occurred to you that the survival rating is like a virus?"

She looked shocked. "A virus? What are you talking about?"

"Like, our survival ratings have taken over absolutely all our actions, right down to procreation and our thought processes. It's like we're being eaten away by countless invisible viruses."

I grabbed the remote control for the air conditioner and switched it off. "And it's because we're all controlled by our survival ratings that you're renting such an expensive apartment and keeping it cool. It really creeps me out."

"But Kumi!" Megumi said, stunned. "That's what life is all about, isn't it? Although I guess in some ways we have lost sight of ourselves by putting a numerical value on it. But survival is an animal's most basic instinct, right? Like, all creatures are controlled by their genes so that they continue their species. The only thing that's changed is that a numerical value has been placed on it and called the survival rating."

"You're probably right. But I still wonder. Once all the cats, cockroaches, and humans have died out, all that's left will be the survival ratings floating in the air. The infinite number of invisible viruses called survival ratings are the true rulers of this planet. Even after all life on Earth has died out, any new life-forms that come along trying to settle here will also come under the rule of the same survival-rating viruses, be controlled by them, and end up going extinct. The same thing over and over again, isn't it?"

"Kumi, you must be tired, saying things like that . . ."

"I'm sorry. You're probably right. I think I'd better go home now."

Megumi looked a little relieved, and checked the time on her phone. "I guess you're not used to going to seminars, and that one must have stressed you out a bit. Best you go home and rest for today. Sorry I called you up out of the blue."

"That's all right. I'm glad I got to see you one last time before I become a Feral."

"It's still hot out. Are you sure you're okay? Shall I get a taxi to take you to the station?"

"No, it's fine. I'll walk home," I said, shutting the door behind me.

■ ■ ■

To my surprise it was getting dark outside, even though it was still only about three o'clock.

Just then, someone tapped me on the shoulder. I turned to see Hayato standing there, dripping sweat.

"I've been thinking things over, and really wanted to talk with you again," he told me. "So I called Megumi and got her to bring you over here today."

So that was it, I thought. It had struck me as a bit weird when she'd suddenly invited me over for no particular reason.

The sky was really black now. It looked as though there was going to be a guerrilla rainstorm.

Mom had told me that they never used to get these weird sudden torrential downpours in the old days. They used to get heavy evening showers, but that rain was beautiful, she'd said. "How were those showers different from the downpours we get now?"

I'd asked her, but she just smiled. "Well, I've only ever seen them in movies myself."

Nowadays these unpredictable storms happened several times a day. And as soon as they started, young people all started having sex under cover of the rain. Nobody had the money to go to a hotel, and hardly any non-elites could afford to live alone, so the best way for a couple to be alone was in the rain.

Hayato was a little taken aback when I led him out into the rain. Being loaded, he'd never had sex in the rain before.

"Shall we go to a hotel?" he asked timidly. "There's lots of things I want to talk about, and doing it in the rain with the girl I love seems so . . ."

"This rain is my world from now on," I told him.

Finally he seemed to understand that it was over between us.

In the rain, the baking hot concrete cooled down a little, and the sun-scorched planet began to return to skin temperature. In the closeted world of the rain, all sound was shut out, and we could hardly see a thing.

We lay down on the warm concrete, and hugged each other close. Innumerable distant cries began to reach us through the rain—the voices of couples having sex like us, or maybe the Ferals.

As we embraced, I noticed downy white fur beginning to sprout on the back of my hands. Hayato was oblivious to this as he kissed me, pouring saliva into my mouth as though wringing out all the moisture from his body.

The downpour intensified. My body covered in downy white fur, I clung on to Hayato's rain-drenched skin. I briefly wondered what my survival-rating percentage was now, but that too gradually receded into the distance.

THE ASTRONOMICAL COST OF CLEAN AIR IN BANGKOK

Pitchaya Sudbanthad

THAILAND

THE CONDO SALESPEOPLE like to point out that the higher you live, the whiter your lungs. They'll tell you that less tainted air here sweeps freely above the smog that keeps Bangkok in a perpetual haze. Up this high, you can look forward to breathtaking views of color-saturated sunsets. The way the sunsets are described makes you think of ones seen after terrific volcanic eruptions. That view. Not every hundred years. Not even every decade. Champagne-worthy sunsets are yours every evening.

These are spectacular times for those who value great heights; you've looked it up. In the mid-1980s, the tallest building in Bangkok reached 33 floors; the tallest one now—just over thirty years later—has 70, with a 125-floor tower slated for completion by 2025.

The urge to build higher never abates, because the worshipful pray skyward. Before modern times, each pagoda built had to be bigger and more awestriking than before, and so must the new towers, reaching higher, beyond the earthbound sky, past the heavenly strata where the devas dwell—higher and higher—until the occupants of such towers exceed the possibilities offered by mere nirvana and arrive at the most holy realm of capital.

The air is so much purer here, those of this realm will remind you. They will, if it happens to be a clear enough day, invite you to take a break from the crisp AC air and step out to the balcony, where they will take a big breath and express disappointment if you don't do the same.

Depending on the weather, the view from the balcony might even resemble its digitally simulated depiction in the tower's sales brochure. The color of the sky doesn't look very far off from the gradient of sacred blue belonging to both night and day. Here, you're simultaneously waking up and falling asleep. You're like Vishnu dreaming the universe. Live in this tower, and the Gaussian-blurred city below is yours.

The depiction you saw in the sales material, however, had omitted the other buildings in the vicinity and erased the colonies of long-necked cranes turning and dipping everywhere. There were no other emergent towers shrouded in dust screen as if Bangkok were a colony of mega art projects, nobody doing calisthenics on a balcony across from you, and no one to watch you until it was your turn to watch them too. Rather, staring at the brochure, you were made to believe in the verdant spread of trees between low-rise buildings and shophouses, so that you might've wondered whether the condo building is in Bangkok at all or among a lost civilization's undiscovered ruins in a tropical jungle.

Perhaps, standing on the actual balcony, you'll think more about that lost civilization, and you'll start to wonder about its people. Who are they? How do they live their lives? You swear you can faintly hear them. They're alive in the bursts of car horns and the whooshing from the nearby highway. You hear them in the cries of scattered sparrows. You remember their impatience. They want to arrive everywhere as quickly as they can, and to do so, they'll work to collapse time itself and everything along with it.

You know the outcome. What the people of this civilization

instead live with is time stretched further and further, so that, stuck waiting to resume their motion along the grand roads and avenues they've paved across land and water, a minute comes to feel like hours.

You know what that's like. There are now almost 10 million cars and motorcycles in Bangkok. It took you an hour in traffic to get to the condo building. You passed the time thumb-scrolling on your phone through updates from friends and family you haven't seen in a while, because it would take hours to visit them across the city. At least you weren't riding a bus—one of those with permanently open windows that only bring in hot, smoky air. By virtue of hermetic privilege, you rode to the condo building in a taxicab, while motorcycle and scooter drivers breathing through surgical masks wove past your window. The city's pharmacists dispense allergy medication like candy. Every day, you check an app for the day's Air Quality Index. You know about a 2017 World Health Organization study of air pollution in Thailand; every one of the fourteen cities monitored exceeded acceptable safety standards, with an estimated fifty thousand premature deaths each year attributable to breathing to stay alive. Bangkok's average concentration of particles smaller than 2.5 microns was three times higher than the organization's safety limits. What can you do?

Almost everything in Bangkok eventually becomes smoke. You and your family learn to live with it: the fume clouds from cars and buses and scooters, but also the delicious clouds from skewered meats blackening on a clay charcoal grill, like the kind your grandmother used to cook; the pulpy smoke drifting across the pavement from where an old amah has squatted down to burn afterlife money to those gone; the gray wisp billowing out of a crematorium's chimneys towering over the temple ground.

At night, the citywide canopy of smoke and mist reflects the light of busy life. The sky glows like a dim lantern. There are no stars. The only constellations you see are made of high-rise windows twinkling blue and gold.

Soon, you return to gaze at these celestial bodies from below. You leave the sanctity of the building complex driveway and reenter circulation as a ground-walker. The heat is near unbearable, even after the sun has receded. The whole day's sunlight, trapped underfoot, makes its ascendant return from the hard concrete that seems to cover every square foot of the city. Where tall buildings form mountainous ridges, the heat's return is thwarted, and so it curls back to the Earth, caught in tormented limbo. Balcony air-conditioning units whirl over the heads of those lingering outside, who are topping up their data plan at the mobile phone shop or eating pickled mango at the curb, or leaning, exhausted, against the bus shelter in their white-and-blue school uniform—some fanning themselves with any suitable object, be it a folded newspaper or their own cupped hand.

For most in the city, there's little hope of escaping high above to look out at the hot haze while breathing cool, filtered air. You do the math in your head, and it's unlikely you'll be able to rent out the condo unit so that it'd pay for itself. The mortgage payments would amount to twice the likely market rent, which is already astronomical, considering the average salaries of even those jobs considered respectable in Bangkok. The gap only seems to continue to widen; relatives have suggested that you can always flip a unit for worthwhile profit in a year or two. In Bangkok, like in so many cities dead set on the track of infinite growth, a condo is not just a home; it's also a store of the unreal. Money is everyone's unspoken housemate.

You swipe the back of a hand across your forehead. The beads of sweat at your eyebrows save you from thinking any more about money. Rather, the heat makes you think of the day in April marking the beginning of the New Year and rice-planting season, when almost everyone young is out on the sidewalk with buckets of water, waiting to splash or get splashed. Pickup trucks rove the street transporting platoons armed with water bazookas and plastic bathing bowls. There are hardly any rice fields left in the city anymore, and the cleanliness of the water is usually very questionable, but you'd pay good money to get haplessly splattered right about now. You do feel yourself getting drenched—by your own sweat. Your clothes begin to stick to your shoulders and underarms. You wave your arms in wide, frantic arcs, trying to hail a taxi, but you're in central Bangkok and don't look like a tourist and easy mark. Each taxi passes by you, empty, the drivers shaking their heads or not even acknowledging that you're there. You at least head in the direction of a Skytrain stop. You're walking, or more rather wading through gelatinous, watery air that feels like it's about to boil.

Is it possible to drown on land? To drown is to be deprived of life-giving oxygen by its replacement with a fluid matter—water, of course, but why not also fumes? In Bangkok, sometimes it's hard to tell the difference between air and water and whatever lingering gases. The city's all a soup really—spicy on the nose and acidly sour with a hint of char; it's a taste that forces you to acquire it. You're again reminded of Thai Buddhist cosmology: the underworld you were told of as a child, where the sinful are made to endure a boiling in copper cauldrons. What have you done to deserve this punishment? What has anyone done but be reborn into this age? Here, water and smoke hold dominion. You're afforded no illusion of escape, unlike those in the sky.

Not long ago, in 2011, you saw what could happen when everything went wrong. The water's coming, everyone in Bangkok said helplessly, and it did, viciously—perhaps vengefully—washing over anything in its path. The airports shut down. Car factories sank. Entire neighborhoods turned into an unnatural sea. You stood outside your house and eyed with wariness the thin film of water that covered the road. Your toilet backed up, brimming with who knew what, and you had to pee into a bottle to avoid flushing. You kept the TV on all day and night for updates from parts of the city already overwhelmed. Who knew what could've happened even after you'd prayed for the higher entities and land spirits to keep the water from reaching you? Next thing, you could be watching the wall of sandbags you'd built prove entirely useless or maybe joining with neighbors to pry open a water gate you believed was keeping your home inundated to the second floor. You were either dry or drowned. It all seemed random, but you also hoped you lived close enough to central Bangkok, with all its important HiSo addresses and billion-baht buildings, for the water to magically flow elsewhere.

They've since told you that kind of catastrophe won't happen again. Measures have been taken. New barriers and drainage were built, and canals dredged. Next flood, no problem. You can trust them, you want to think. You can ignore observations that the streets still very often turn into canals and after only a day's rain. You can deny that the weight of all the newly built towers is helping to press the city downward, tugged even lower by subsidence from excessive use of groundwater underneath. Bangkok's sinking anywhere from three quarters to over an inch a year, as you've read scientists estimate in the papers. And no, the sea isn't rising, you say to yourself. The tides will let any flooding empty into the ocean. The water won't come again.

A taxicab finally stops for you. You happily hop in and let the air-conditioned air pummel your face. It's arctic cold.

A DOWNWARD SLOPE

Juan Miguel Álvarez

Translated by Christina MacSweeney

COLOMBIA

"RUN, RUN!" THE CRY BROKE the silence of the early morning. "Get out. The mountain's giving way!" It was the voice of a man who, from a safe distance, was witnessing a landslide that threatened to bare the foundations of a condominium. No one seemed to have heard him or taken notice of his warning; no one came out of the apartments or even appeared at the windows. But seconds later, after a sudden shudder, a ninety-foot gash appeared, leaving a building of a hundred apartments teetering on the edge of the chasm. Screaming, with the short-circuited cables of the street-lights exploding around them, the terrified inhabitants of the condo fled in all directions.

It was the second Tuesday in June 2019, and the Colombian city of Pereira had endured two weeks of torrential downpours. The lashing rain had occasionally eased off, allowing people to close their umbrellas for a few brief moments, but then it set in again for hours, as if unleashing a blood feud. In the offices of the state government it was calculated that during those two weeks more rain had fallen, and fallen more heavily, than in the whole of the previous two months. The authorities were worried because if it didn't stop, neighborhoods in the valley might be flooded and those on the hillsides washed away by mudslides.

There had already been fifty-four landslides in Pereira and the surrounding suburbs. Although one of these caused a single fatality, all the others had been minor incidents, that is to say approximately ten tons of soil and rock blocking a rural road, a footbridge falling into a creek, or a portion of the coffee crop washed away, nothing worse. So landslide fifty-five took them by surprise. The city had never before experienced such a deep, vertical, heavy fall from the mountain face: sixty thousand tons of red earth and Jurassic-sized boulders, plus trees and vegetation.

And while no one in the condo was harmed, the landslide left a tally of five dead and a dozen injured when the heavy load slid like an avalanche onto the highway connecting Pereira with nearby cities, crushing without warning the handful of cars and motorbikes that happened to be passing at that instant.

■■■

Pereira is a medium-size city located 185 miles west of Bogotá. With five hundred thousand inhabitants, it's the most populous city in the Coffee Belt, where Colombia's traditional crop has long been cultivated. Its topography is sinuous: the center of the city was built on low tableland, but the houses of the residential zones gradually spread up the adjoining hillsides. In fact, the greater part of Pereira's suburbs are on sloping ground, reached by winding roads that follow the undulations of the landscape.

The same happened all over the Coffee Belt; in the nineteenth century, cities and towns were constructed on ground stolen from the mountain range. As it was an agricultural area, the constant challenge was to cultivate the mountains in order to sow, gather in the crop, and take it to market. At first the campesinos transported their produce by mule along tracks cut into the mountainside.

Then came the railway and paved roads; tunnels were cut into the mountain and highways constructed. But each of those projects had its toll of landslides. It was as if the mountain range were crying out in pain each time it was pierced.

Today, despite all the technology available to civil engineers, the region still suffers from rockfalls. Whenever I drive through the Coffee Belt—and other mountainous areas of Colombia—the most common roadside warning sign is a vehicle beside a vertical surface from which rocks are falling. And there are stretches where the deterioration of the mountain is so plain to see—cracks in the surface, the earth scorched, overhanging boulders—that I wonder when the next landslide will be. And then I ask myself an existential question: "Am I going to have the bad luck to be passing here at the exact moment when the mountain comes down?"

■ ■ ■

There are no seasons in Colombia, but our calendar includes two periods of heavy rain: the first is from April to June and the second from October to December. Year after year the news stories of tragedies caused by rainfall don't change: a landslide here killing x number of people, a flood there that carried away y houses. It's as if we all know that every time we have heavy rain over a period of days there will be deaths and people will be left homeless, but no one has been able, or even tried, to prevent this happening.

The day following the landslide that left a condo hanging by a thread, the authorities had to attend to another emergency: the Consota, one of Pereira's most important rivers, overflowed its banks and flooded an adjoining neighborhood. The television images were heartbreaking: torrents of water pouring through the streets and bursting into houses. The inhabitants waded through waist-high water to reach the hillside, from where they watched, eyes brimming with tears, as the river swept away the contents of their homes: television sets, tables, beds, kitchen equipment, plus motorbikes and even one or two cars. Fortunately, there were no fatalities. Private citizens and the authorities began to supply food to the victims and replace their lost possessions.

In the condo, by contrast, the situation was worsening. Two days after the mountain fell down, all the apartments were evacuated. Many of them were already showing cracks and the concrete in the parking lot had fissures like those caused by an earthquake. Police officers and soldiers went from door to door advising the families to leave. It was midnight, and to avoid putting excess weight on the ground, with the risk of producing another landslide, the authorities prohibited the entry of heavy vehicles. So people were forced to carry their belongings on their backs. "Our whole world, gone," said forty-year-old Dagoberto Garcés, his voice tremulous and his eyes damp. "I've lost everything I've worked for all my life. My house, my savings, everything," said fifty-year-old Félix Hincapié.

A little farther up the mountain, the inhabitants of a poorer neighborhood were also told to vacate their homes. The landslide had been so devastating that it had affected the geological soil structure within a range of a third of a mile. The walls and floors of some of the homes in that neighborhood had cracks you could put your fist in. Unlike the residents of the condo—middle class with steady jobs—these people had nowhere to go and no money to start afresh. Many of them refused to leave: "Where are we going to go?" "I built this house with my own two hands and there's no way I'm going to lose it," they said. But, given the danger that the ravine might give way and bury the area, the authorities forced people to leave and then welded the doors shut to prevent them getting back in.

■ ■ ■

It took the emergency services two weeks to clear up the earth from the landslide, locate the bodies of the victims, and reopen the highway. Now, at the roadside, the twisted chassis of a cab can still be seen. For a whole stretch, mounds of dark earth are piled up among the vegetation. Above this cleared area is the enormous wound on the face of the mountain, as if a giant hand had struck it mercilessly. Water still springs from deep in the rock and falls to the ground in soft streams of mud and gravel.

The cause of the disaster remains unclear. Some experts maintain that it will be repeated in the near future. Climate change has meant that the sun is hotter and there are fewer cloudy days. The soil has been damaged almost beyond repair; then, when the strong rains come, there's nothing to hold that soil, and the water filters through to the rock and breaks it up from within.

Another point still to be clarified is the level of responsibility of the construction companies. Residents of the condo complain that they had been warning both the company and the authorities about structural cracks for months. And although they had never even imagined such extensive damage as that produced by the landslide, they had suspected that the construction was faulty. "Whenever we showed them evidence that something was wrong," explained Félix Hincapié, "they told us not to worry, that it was normal, that the condo wasn't in danger. And now, after that landslide, nothing can be done. We're all at rock bottom."

THE FLOODS

Mohammed Hanif

PAKISTAN

MANY PAKISTANIS WHO'VE not been directly affected by the floods are asking each other this question: Is it a punishment from Allah? Or is He just testing our faith? One of the many religious scholars who pop up on our television screens during the holy month of Ramadan was asked the same question last week. He shook his head and answered with the kind of hokey wisdom only TV preachers are capable of: If you have transgressed, He is punishing you. If He likes you, He is testing you.

Not everyone is reaching out for a divine explanation though. In southern Punjab, poet Ashou Laal linked the fury of the river Indus to our collective greed and corporate rape of the land. People have built roads, bridges, houses on the riverbed. And when the Indus returned after many decades, it couldn't find its old path. It went around like a mad dog sniffing for its old habitat and devoured everything on the way.

Between the righteous indignation of the faithful and poetic flourishes of folk wisdom, the reality might be quite simple— something we have lived through, only sixty-three years ago.

The images of old people on donkey carts, naked children perched over salvaged household items, cows and goats on the move kept reminding me of something that I had seen before but I couldn't quite place where.

Then a journalist colleague of mine, chasing the flood, arrived in southern Punjab, and reported back that the bridge over the river Chenab resembled a giant set that might have been erected for a film about Partition, when India and Pakistan were prized apart. A Partition set in Noah's time, I thought. He was obviously referring to the millions who have been on the move, mostly on foot; shriveled old men carrying their beds on their heads, women shepherding half a dozen children, grandmothers separated from their families, walking in a daze, toward a destination they have no clue about. (For many of them this is the longest journey they have ever undertaken in their lives.)

Like the 2 million–odd people butchered during the Partition, these people have rarely registered in the national debate and their faces have never been seen on our TV screens before.

It seems the land has ripped out its entrails and thrown them out for all of us to see.

These people don't live in picturesque valleys where city folk go on vacation. These areas are of no strategic interest to anyone because they have neither exported terrorism nor do they have the ambition to join a fight against it. Their only export to the world outside is onions, tomatoes, sugarcane, wheat, mangoes. The word "terrorism" doesn't even exist in Seraiki and Sindhi, the languages of the majority of the people who have been rendered homeless by recent floods. They belong to that forgotten part of humanity that has quietly tilled the land for centuries, generations of people who are born and work and die on the same small piece of land.

And this time there are 20 million of them.

What we don't realize is that these 20 million were poor but they were not starving. They come from a place where they could raise a whole family because they own a buffalo or a few goats. They were probably the last 20 million who lived off the land. And in the process fed us as well.

These 20 million are our invisible slave army.

When the world media reports on the tragedy it finds it difficult to leave behind a decade-long habit of linking everything to terrorism. The reporters look for a banned militant organization involved in relief work; usually some random men with beards will do. And we're told, in good faith I am sure, that if the victims are not provided with relief they might well turn to the Taliban. Our own politicians join the chorus. A friend involved in relief work in Sindh pointed out that a hungry person is not likely to ask your views on terrorism before accepting your packet of food, for the simple reason that his children are starving.

If this was a disaster movie the posters would include the young man swimming across a deluge with his rooster tied around his neck. A puzzled relief worker wondered aloud why the world would think that this man who has just swum across a raging flood would want to bring about a bloody Islamist revolution in a far-flung country that he's never heard of? Isn't it obvious that he just wants to save his chickens?

But this is no movie. That half-naked child that you see in pictures with his face covered in flies is not dead. Not yet. He has dozed off out of hunger and heat and exhaustion. When he wakes up in a little while he'll ask for what every hungry child in the world asks for. Surely everyone everywhere understands that language.

BORN STRANGER

Burhan Sönmez

TURKEY

People? . . . The wind blows them away. They have no roots.
The Little Prince, Antoine de Saint-Exupéry

I WAS BORN in a small Kurdish village of about three hundred people in the middle of a steppe in Turkey. There was no electricity. Daily communication with the outside world depended on the transistor radio that could be listened to only during news hours, to save its battery. It was the Turkish state radio—men and kids could understand it, since adult men learned Turkish during their compulsory military service at the age of twenty and kids learned it at the primary school that had recently been opened. The women were alienated, yet again. Kids would gather around men to serve them tea and get the benefit of listening to the radio. On one of those days, I remember, it was snowing outside, and the voice on the radio was talking about some strangers who created trouble in some faraway city. The word "stranger" was the point. We saw outsiders coming to our village as "strangers." And "we" meant the three hundred people of the village. That was the basic meaning of life in a vast, dry land.

Our conception of a stranger was like a coin; on the one side we felt deep in our hearts that we were obliged to treat them well and make them feel welcome, but on the other side we were vigilant because they were not one of us, so we could not be sure of them. It was told in Kurdish folktales, often based on versions of the tales from *One Thousand and One Nights*, that evil always came from outside in disguise. It might be a thief, a murderer, or a djinn. The wilderness around the village was full of foxes, wolves, and rabbits. Even they might look like something they were not. We did not trust the shepherds who came from nearby Kurdish villages and worked in ours either. We were aware that we would be seen the same way when we visited other villages. There we expected to be treated well, to be offered a bed to stay overnight and generous food, including meat. We were also ready for any hostility that might appear out of the blue. We all were strangers who lived in the same steppe.

When I left my family home at the age of seventeen to study law in Istanbul, I did not expect that it would take me quite some time to adapt to a big city. In Istanbul, everyone would ask each other where they came from upon meeting. Everyone was Istanbulite, but no one was of local origin. It was a metropolis whose society was under construction. I realized that I was a stranger in the city, that my existence was also under a new construction in my own country. In the city, the only thing that resembled my village was the snow. Istanbul's snow was heavy too. It was a couple of years after the military coup. When we were stopped at random police checkpoints, they would look at our identity cards and rate our being in their mind: which region we were from, which town, which ethnicity, and which religious background. You might be treated as "other" in many ways. If they could not find anything suspicious, then, if they liked, they would search for your political identity. That was the city of strangers who claimed possession of the city, all suspicious of others. Before long I became one of them.

When I left Turkey for the UK, in exile, I was still looking for a place on this planet to attach myself to for good. I reckoned that I was not alone. That it was an age of constant moving, displacing, migrating. As every Turkish village was gathering in Istanbul, now every country of the world was gathering in London, maybe because throughout the centuries London had spread its power to every country. The British had gone to every land to travel or to capture, and now people were coming to Britain to travel or to survive. I was there to survive. Having learned Turkish in primary school, now I had to learn English as a foreign language. "Say 'hello' and I will tell you your background," I heard soon after arriving. You didn't speak a language, but an accent. Accent was more than a clue to your identity—it hid your sorrow, your melancholy, and your hope. All were masked, no one could divine your dreams through your accent. There in London I had the opportunity of creating my own destiny. Reading new books, listening to new stories, meeting new people. That was construction too, I was learning.

About ten years ago I managed to return to Turkey. I went to my home village to spend harvesting time with my parents. It was a hot summer as usual. The village had gotten electricity long ago. Houses were lit by bulbs. Everyone carried a cell phone. Thanks to asphalt roads, access to the town was easier. But the population had dropped by a quarter. The life in a village was neither attractive nor sustainable anymore. Youngsters who had found a way left the village for work, and those who could not get that chance stayed. There were no foxes, wolves, or rabbits around. And the shepherds in the village were not from other villages but from a faraway country, Afghanistan. They worked for less than local people, but they too were given a place to sleep, and their food was provided by the farmer. While the village's youngsters went to European countries for work, their places were taken by those who came from Asia. The sun was moving from the east to the west while the earth was rotating the other way round. I asked myself how these people from Asia found a little village in the middle of nowhere, even though I knew from my own experience that the immigrants' wind could reach anywhere.

When I visited my parents a few years later, in the summer again, the population had decreased even more. The wheat and barley were less fertile. Peasants turned their hand to other products, like onions or potatoes, that could fetch more money but required more labor. That meant more people were wanted for work. Below the village were the tents of Kurdish worker families who came from eastern Turkey for the season. Daily wages were ranked in Turkey: men were on the top, women were second, children were third. Below them all were the Kurds. Kurdish labor was cheaper than Turkish labor in farming across the country. Kurds were "others." But in my Kurdish village, those Kurdish workers who came from the eastern regions were others to us too. We would call them Easterners, rather than Kurds like us. Because others could not be us. Then on the night of my first day in the village, I found out that there were even cheaper workers: Syrians.

In the cool breeze of the steppe one night, I was sitting in front of our house with some neighbors, sipping tea and talking about olden days. There was the sound of a tractor and its trailer rattling on the small hill, approaching the village in the dark. The neighbors said it was my cousin's vehicle, carrying Syrian workers from the potato fields. The tractor came and stopped by a barn. Workers got off the trailer in silence and went into the barn. The iron gate closed with a heavy, squeaky sound. The whole world was closed on them. I learned that the Syrians, who had left their country due to a war that had been fueled by others, including the Turkish government, now were treated like slaves.

They were equal only to animals, as they were not allowed to move around in the village nor stay outside of a barn. They were not only providing the cheapest labor, but they were also giving the local people the satisfaction of feeling above another social minority.

Around the same years the flies started to disappear. The steppe had always been full of black flies, which were a nuisance. Since the government had encouraged villagers to use new pesticides the crops looked better, but the environment started to transform. Nobody knows whether these new pesticides have had anything to do with the lately increasing cases of diseases like diabetes, cancer, blood pressure problems, and heart failures among villagers. The government does not support any research on that issue.

Life is not as simple as the philosophical quotes that we often apply to it in novels. Heidegger, the twentieth-century German thinker, would say that we all are outsiders, as we have fallen in this world. Or Ferdowsi, the tenth-century Persian poet, would say that we neither decided to come to this world, nor do we decide to leave it, we just have to live in it. But we still have the right to ask: What kind of life is this? That's the state of immigrants as outsiders. They don't know the place they have come to, and they are not known by people who live there. That's Heidegger's world.

In my first years in London I was seeing a neurologist, Dr. John Rundle, at the Freedom from Torture foundation. Dr. Rundle was helping me recover from an injury while I was trying to improve my clumsy English. Once I said, "You are constructing my brain, I am constructing my language." He smiled. "Both are the same." Since he passed away I cannot ask him anymore what he meant. I have to endlessly interpret it.

Yabancı is a Turkish word that translates to all these English words: stranger, outsider, foreigner, alien. They mean the same thing. Similarly we have a single word in Kurdish to cover them all: *biyanî*. As we travel across the world, words and their meanings change. They reflect the new situations of being that we have to face. In some ways life is as simple as philosophical quotes, so we draw them out in novels to grasp both the charmed and merciless fates of individuals. The wind does not blow the same speed everywhere. No land is equal to another. My village is smaller now. Wild animals disappeared. There is not much snow anymore. And I live in faraway places. A village abandoned like mine, a country torn apart like the Syrians', a geography disoriented like the westerners'. The old planet is being replaced by a new one. The question is on what basis it will be shaped and with which feelings its heart will beat.

IN THIS PHASE IN THE 58TH AMERICAN PRESIDENTIAD (UNITED STATES)

Lawrence Joseph

UNITED STATES

. . . in this phase of the American
    experiment acts of systemic
oligarchic thievery crushed
    into the body of a child in a chain-
linked cage in a row of tents
    in an old warehouse clutching
a copy of her mother's ID card; amped-up
    signs. Whitman's *To the States, To Identify*
the 16th, 17th, or 18th Presidentiad:
    "What deepening twilight—scum floating
atop of the waters . . . What a filthy
    Presidentiad! . . . is that the President?"
Precious, preening, blond cotton-candy hair,
    swastikas are his aura—capable,
very capable of changing into
    whatever he wants, he says, lips puckered,
his bombs, they're beautiful bombs,
    his generals, they're beautiful generals,

beautiful the word he uses to describe
    missiles he sells to Saudi Arabia and Israel.
His own hell, he owns it, in his own shit,
    feet of lackey weasels clamped
onto his pot-bellied stomach, teeth stuck
    in his puffed-up jaw. Equities levitating higher,
capital-captive carbon dioxide
    unleashed, prison construction
outsourced to Party-regular racketeers—
    no, we can't restore our civilization
with someone else's babies, no, they're not innocent,
    they're not people, they're animals
and we're taking them out of the country
    at a level and a rate like never before
into foster care or wherever—singsong voice
    almost a whisper, his eyes—are they eyes?—are dead.
And his Attorney General—is that his name,
    really, Ku Klux Kluxer III?—invokes not just law
but God's law, Paul, Epistle to the Romans 13,
    God's will, the divine order of things demands
government agents treat the poor like inventory,
    identities lost, irreparable damage to the structure
of brains. Hatred their brand, they love to hate;
    to make their money and to hate. Killing—
is jubilate a word? They jubilate at it. Killer
    robots, drones, artificial-intelligence-powered
ships, tanks, planes and guns, in air and on sea,
    under sea and on land, the future:
lethal autonomous weapons systems—LAWS—
    in this phase in the 58th American Presidentiad.

THE STORYTELLERS OF THE EARTH

Sulaiman Addonia

ERITREA/ETHIOPIA/SUDAN/BRITAIN/BELGIUM

THE STATE OF OUR EARTH is inscribed on refugee bodies, I think as I watch a group of weary, haggard, Eritrean-looking young men through the glass window of this Brussels café where I come to write.

The way they are dressed, almost in identical clothing—tight jeans, trainers, and leather jackets—and almost all with a Michael Jackson eighties hairstyle, convince me that they are newcomers. They remind me of myself when I first arrived in London in June 1990 and used to walk around wearing a coat in the middle of summer's scorching afternoons. Like a broken language, a mistimed dress sense is another hint of foreignness.

Remembering my own history of migrations, I want to look away but resist the urge to do so. Instead, I run my eyes over their bodies. I see the light of the desert in their eyes. The drought in their lips. I can almost feel the stories they carry inside like tsunamis rising with their heaving chests.

Refugees are the earth, I think, recalling Joy Harjo's poem "Remember" and the words "Remember the earth whose skin you are."

I exit the café but I don't head toward the young men. Instead, I try to observe them from a distance. I hear them talk in Tigrinya, a language that was once my mother tongue, before the change of countries, change of immigration status, uprooted my tongue and rerooted it here nor there, altering the way I speak, even more so when I started to plant new words of English inside my mouth like a British gardener growing exotic fruit in the countryside. To this day, some English words taste like strange fruit.

The young men huddle closer. I know from experience that many of us immigrants survive through group solidarity, because even a slight glow in the eyes of fellow travelers flickering to the wind of exile is enough to ignite the hope to go on hoping.

■ ■ ■

I had learnt from when I was a child and living in a Sudanese refugee camp that those fighting for or fleeing toward freedom often carry their own earth with them. I vividly remember the plays by the cultural troupe of the Eritrean People's Liberation Front (during the fighting for independence from Ethiopia), who came to our camp from trenches inside Eritrea that they had managed to liberate. When onstage to perform, the shiny, dark, and rough skin of their bodies looked infused with the taste of our country's earth. Adults watching these plays would weep when they hugged the performers, as if they were embracing their own soil from back home, inhaling the smell of their country's hills and valleys rising from the bodies of these freedom fighters.

And as I examine these young men and ponder my history, it seems to me that we, immigrants, migrate with a piece of our land. That while taking ourselves to a safe zone, we also seem to take a bit of our country along with us, as an ornament, or as memories etched inside us, so that the place we love might also experience some respite in a foreign place, away from the war and the wrath of an environment damaging our lands.

The earth, that red earth, yellow earth, white earth, brown

earth Harjo wrote about, is our skin and inside us wherever we go. The earth that bonded with our bodies as we journeyed through refugee camps, through the deserts, mountains, rivers, seas.

We are earth.

And so there should be no need to travel to the North Pole, to watch the ice flowing from mountains into seas to see the damage that has been done to the earth. It's all written in immigrants' bodies too, I think as the young Eritrean men disappear across the square, heading toward the street facing the statue of the Portuguese poet Fernando Pessoa. And as if words could soothe their invisible wounds, I think of Cavafy's poem "Body, Remember," and would so much want to recite it to them. But they vanish from view. I head back inside the café, slightly shivering, as the uttered poem, reminding a body of how much it was once loved, how much desired, slid deeper inside me.

■ ■ ■

I confess, until recently I saw the two issues, the fight against climate change and that of refugees, as totally disconnected. It wasn't so much that I denied climate change, but the notion of justice and equality—who caused this catastrophe in the first place—fed my doubts about making it my priority. Just how can refugees, while still engaged in an act of survival, of fighting past traumas as well as the new ones accumulated on our way to the safe places in the West, be expected to also find the time and energy to fight for what we are now being told is the single most important cause for humans everywhere—to save our planet?

I remember the numerous arguments my partner, a climate change activist from a white middle-class family in Belgium, and I had over the years—mostly when she complained about me eating too much meat, or wearing new instead of secondhand clothes. "Climate change is only becoming a priority for you in the West because you realize that life as you know it will come to an end," I recall telling her once in one of those heated debates.

"Of course that's true," she said, "but the real victims of climate change are people in poor countries."

As if I didn't hear what she was saying, I would go on a rant, narrating a segment of my life, my early years in London, in which I had arrived as an unaccompanied minor immigrant with only my brother, who was seventeen at the time. In those days, I was given only seventeen pounds by the government to live on every week. Without family support, seventeen pounds was all I had, with which I needed to buy food, a travel card to get to the college where I studied English for speakers of other languages, and medicine. I ate so little and lost so much weight that I was called "a walking skeleton" by my friends. I didn't have a penny left to eat meat and drink too much, to travel abroad and pollute the world in the way you did, I would tell my partner. She would reiterate her point about who, in an unequal world, suffered most due to climate change.

Feeling that my points were unheard, I would remind her too of my years as a child in the camp while she spent her childhood in an affluent Belgian town: "Saving the planet you destroyed is your fight and not mine. And just let me enjoy in peace a bit of what you always had plenty of since your birth."

She would shake her head. "But please remember it's your family back home who will bear the consequences."

My partner, whom I was accusing of selfishness, was in effect accusing me of the same. That not caring about climate change was a selfish act, because the people worst affected by climate change caused by rich countries in the West were not like me now living in Europe, but people in Africa. People like my mother and grandmother, who live in Eritrea, one of the poorest countries in the world.

I thought of my mother and grandmother, the two women

who brought me up. They had shielded me during the massacre of Om Hajar in 1975, after the murder of my father, and in the refugee camp in Sudan. The sacrifices of these women for me and my siblings I cannot describe. So here I was in a safe place in the West, while they were back in Eritrea, where more than half the population lives in poverty and where almost a quarter of the land is classified as hot and arid. Eritrea is now on the front line of the climate crisis. It is getting hotter, the rains are unpredictable, and the magnificent coral reefs on which sea life and local fisherfolk depend are dying off. The country is drying up, both literally, with the earth cracking dry like old powder, and metaphorically, with the population thinning as young people flee in droves.

The more I thought of my family back home, the scorching heat they faced, the failed harvests in the region, the decimated workforce, the more I realized that I was wrong not to connect the dots. I became determined to play my role in combating climate change, in my own way.

■ ■ ■

If there is a book in all of us, then there must be at least two in all immigrants. A book about us and a book about the earth.

In May 2018, I set up an academy to teach creative writing to refugees and asylum seekers in Brussels. Empowering refugees and asylum seekers to tell their own stories in a safe space was one of the things that inspired me. Being a refugee should not mean surrendering one's voice, or that there is no need for a "voice for the voiceless," because we all have our own voice and we all are capable of representing our stories. And the earth inside them is laid bare in these stories.

I could trace the time when I realized that the earth was intimately weaving itself in my body. It happened in the first few months after I came to the UK. My brother and I, who didn't speak English at the time, decided to move outside London, away from the immigrant communities, so we could befriend British people and learn the language more quickly. But English people in the suburbs of London chose not to see us, or have anything to do with us, let alone hear our stories. Feeling shunned by the society and lonely, I did a lot of walking then and found company, warmth, and humanity in the buildings, the streets, and the trees. Nature has ears and a heart, I discovered then. That's why when I encounter this woman on the streets of Ixelles talking to herself, I think it might not be because she is mad, but that because those closer to her have stopped listening, so she has decided to talk to the earth instead. Just like I did. Millions of stories of the lonely, of the dispossessed, of the poor, the hungry, the disadvantaged, the countryless, go unnoticed in the course of daily life.

And so I know that these refugees, like I once did, could walk and talk to the trees, but they could now also come to our class and write their own stories in their own voices.

The voices in the courses we have had so far come from Vietnam, Iraq, Somalia, Syria, Libya, Morocco, Jamaica, Eritrea, Ethiopia, Senegal, voices that got here via the U.S., via the UK, France, through the seas, the rivers, the desert, the air.

■ ■ ■

One morning, before I head to my academy, I have a brief discussion with my partner at the breakfast table. By now she has co-founded a citizens' movement in Brussels that campaigns for clean air.

Just as I changed my views on prioritizing the fight against global warming, she too understood the complexities that lie at the heart of climate change and inequality. "Action on climate change cannot be blind to social justice," she now tells me.

"Taking blanket policies that don't take social issues into account is a recipe for disaster. The revolt against the new environmental taxes in France and Belgium by the yellow vests, for example, is coming from people who are at the bottom and feel squeezed already. So poor sections of the society cannot just be taken for granted in combating this climate crisis. Immigrants in particular are going to have a double whammy, because while it is difficult to prove that people move as a direct result of climate change, the evidence is there that it is climate change that is now driving the destruction of their livelihoods. So, they shouldn't be asked to help solve the problem, but they surely are the main advocates for why people living here should be radically changing, fast."

I think deeply about her remarks. Refugees and the earth face the same marginalization, the same neglect, the same abuse. Refugees and the earth share the same story. And even a similar language is used to describe the fear around them both: "climate crisis" is now used more often than "climate change," mirroring the refugee "crisis" gripping headlines all over the world. The two crises, the two stories, are gathering pace together.

Yet, as I arrive in the class, I am still conflicted and burdened with the uncomfortable feeling that my students, mostly recent arrivals, have spent their life savings, gone through unimaginable journeys, only to arrive here in Brussels to be told that fighting climate change is not a luxury anymore, because no matter where you are, where you come from, no matter what your story is, you must roll up your sleeves and fight for this planet we all share, even if you didn't play a huge role in its ill health.

"How long do refugees need to recover before they engage in a fight to save our planet?" I ask one of our students during a coffee break, who is a Bedouin from Libya. "How long does a wounded body need to recover before it is ready to become part of a march for climate justice?"

From memory, he recites a poem in Arabic that conveys how he and his family never settled in one place, how instead they moved like the wind. How always standing up for the earth has been part of fighting for his existence. As he sits back, hunched over his paper with a pen in his hands, beginning the act of imagining new ideas, or reimagining old ones, I get a sense that his love for the earth supersedes everything else. That no matter what he will end up producing in this class where all of us come to imagine, perhaps heal and heal the planet with us, his story, like mine, is the story of the earth.

THE HOUSE OF OSIRIS

Yasmine El Rashidi

EGYPT

THERE IS A PLOT on the outskirts of Cairo, about twenty-eight miles from the city center, that is marked by a single palm tree and an overgrown hedge. On a good day, it may take forty minutes to reach there, but on most days, if it's not the crack of dawn or middle of the night, it can take several hours. There are checkpoints along the way—one manned by armed, masked special forces—and a part of the road veers right into a narrow, unpaved, two-way track, lined on one side with a deep and litter-filled trough, and the other by a dip into fields. Cargo trucks often swallow the path, slowing cars to a standstill, and on occasion, I've heard, pushing them over the rim.

I found myself on that fenced acre plot in the summer of 2018, standing by the palm, looking out, north. Before me, just yards away, stood three crumbling pyramids and the remains of a temple with its tomb. In the distance to the right was the Great Pyramid of Giza, and to the left, not that far, conceivably walkable if the heat weren't searing, Djoser's Step Pyramid—the heart of the Old Kingdom, dating back three thousand years. On a clear day, from that vantage point, nine pyramids lay in an apparent straight line across a stretch of desert. Once upon a time, the Nile veered here too.

It was a sense of exile and disorientation that had led me here, having recently moved from the house I had called home my entire life—a sprawling estate my grandmother had commissioned and built on the banks of the Nile, close to the city center, but far enough removed and surrounded by grounds to filter out and muffle its cacophony of sound. The house was both my grandmother's sacrifice and her dream; she had given up everything to afford it, and around it her whole existence revolved. It was a disposition, a constitution, I seemed to have inherited when I was born there myself, and to withstand the loss of leaving, I knew I would have to find a place to anchor myself in again. I would travel as far as I could from the plot of home, from landmarks and familiar sites, from everything that made the narrative of my forty years in and to and from that space. I would try to leave the city in spirit, without quite leaving its bounds.

I found a book-size, glass photographic slide of the Nile running by the pyramids as I was packing up the house; it was in the back of a closet, bundled in cloth, untouched for decades. I scanned the surface of Cairo using Google Earth. Hours a day, for weeks. Here it was (29.8985102, 31.2071975). The single plot that might accommodate me. If I could withstand the route, if I could acquire that piece of land, I intuitively understood, I could find home again. To my back would lie miles of the ever-expanding city—a tapestry of sepia, raw red brick, and the rare spot of green.

I called a friend, the Egyptian-Armenian artist Anna Boghiguian, to tell her I had arrived. Not in the literal sense, but once I was back at the apartment again, at my temporary setup in an old family building overlooking the house. I described the plot, the land, the view. Its history had been as marshland and mango grove. I told her I would plant all the trees and flowers my grandmother had many decades ago. The local miniature roses.

The olive and fig trees. I'd replicate our mango garden. I would create the form of the house like a sculpture, out of limestone, like the pharaohs did. This would become my occupation, not in a political sense, but as art, and a way of moving forward.

Anna understood. She encouraged the idea. "The only thing left at that point," she said, before hanging up abruptly, "would be to wait for death."

I drove out day after day, just to stand on the lot, to look out, to breathe, Anna's words still with me. It was true what she said, about waiting for death, both choosing something to devote myself to, and also, in some sense, giving up. It felt like the edge of the earth here, a place where life as I knew it ended, and a step into something other began.

On one of those afternoons, as I looked out of my window driving back into the center of town, the notion of death close, the vast expanse of sepia before me, the irrigation channel of Nile water to my left, I began to emerge from my stupor, and see what I'd been passing on my trips out to the coordinates of my future existence. The mounds of plastic mixed with silt heaped on the side of the channel. The empty lots that looked like piles of earth but were simply years of accumulated plastic fished out of the Nile and dumped in what space there was. The channel itself was like a wasteland. Plastic bottles of water, of Coca-Cola, of the Egyptian favorite, Fanta. You could hardly see the Nile. I drove along the channel, miles of it, never getting to the point where water emerged again. For as long as the water once flowed freely, plastic now permeated, forming its own surface and ground. I couldn't quite place whether it was the plastic that had driven farmers to give up on their crops and fill their land with redbrick buildings, or whether it had happened the other way around.

I wondered about the orchard I had planned on planting, and became a student of the environment—the soil, the water, the people who inhabited the land. The Nile was drying up—I heard this over and over—and the government was directing what water was left deep into the desert to serve wealthy gated communities, along with a new capital for the country flung into nowhere. Farmers in the area along the route to and from my fantasy future plot told me that the water had stopped reaching them long ago, and the crops they had subsisted on, like rice, were now impossible to grow—they required too much water. What about other crops? Corn? Wheat? They built buildings instead, thinking they could sell or rent apartments, but most of them, miles of them, stood empty. Did that happen to all the farmers, the trickle down of water until it stopped, or did they just copy one another, thinking it was a more lucrative idea? No one could quite answer or explain what had gone so terribly wrong. But water was expensive. This point everyone agreed on.

The once marshland, once mango grove was arid for yards down, deep into the earth. Neighbors had tried to grow crops and trees once indigenous to the land, but in the end, gave up and went with palms and rolled grass. My mango garden was likely an impossible dream. I was told that in the next thirty years, 15 percent more of the agricultural land would disappear to drought.

When my grandmother built her house, in the late 1930s, the highest summer temperature was 80 degrees Fahrenheit. During my last months there, as I documented sound and light, shadows moving through the space, footsteps and my mother's voice, time of day, the grandfather clock ticking and the temperature vacillating, it reached 109.

In the desert, on the line that marked to me where the life I had known ended and a future possibility began, we were talking, I was told, of five degrees higher. In the next thirty years, not only would more of the Nile be lost, more of the land, crops, but, I realized, as well, my plot might be uninhabitable. It's a matter of life and death, the keeper of the land told me. I wasn't precisely sure of what he meant, except to wonder if I would even still be alive in thirty years, and to understand that in coming to the edge of death, its very abode as the pharaohs believed the desert to be, I was being turned back. I wondered about the keeper, and the farmers, how resigned they were to their fate. When I asked about the future, the coming drought, the possibility of having to migrate as temperatures became uninhabitable, they all shrugged, and said it was in the hands of God.

A CALYPSO

Khaled Mattawa

LIBYA/UNITED STATES

—After the Mighty Sparrow

Their trawlers slurp
the fish out of the seas,
their breathing wipes

the clouds out of the breeze:
They fuck up the world,
tell you to stay home.

They move their border
to the edge of your town,
hire your brother and cousin

to keep you hemmed in:
They fuck up the world,
tell you, you can never leave.

Holes dug where used to be trees,
machines policed by thugs,
a Mr. Kurtz born every minute,

a local with imported degrees:
They fuck up the world,
tell you better not come near.

They send their old clothes,
old cars, stale processed food,
bankers like probation officers

chain you with the freedom to choose:
They fuck up the world,
always changing their slimy rules.

Like termite eating up metals,
grinding up animals and woods.
No more ivory, but human bones

plentiful almost for free:
They fuck up the world, fuck it again
until the world ceases for good.

CAVERN

Chinelo Okparanta

NIGERIA

THE WATER SOURCE, a borehole, was dependent on electricity. But NEPA was always taking light; there was often no water in the tank. Fuel scarcity made it so that all of the fuel lines were perpetually winding things, so that there was no way Emmanuelle would sit in all that traffic, waiting in line to fill up her jerry cans, a baby in tow, just so she could run the generator, just so that she could have light, just so that she could have some water from the borehole, just so that she could run the washer.

She could have done as so many of the other women she knew did: got on her knees and prayed to Jesus to bring back light, to make it so that NEPA never took light ever again. But she wasn't the kind to fawn over other humans. She wasn't the worshipping kind, the way other people she knew fawned over bare mortals like celebrities—2Face, Tupac, all the twos and Tus not worth worshipping in life. If she had stumbled upon Jesus in the flesh, she would have talked to him like any other person. Maybe on a bad day she would have greeted him with the normal polite sort of greeting with which everyone greeted everyone else and then walked right past him to go put the baby to bed.

Forget Jesus. A woman must take matters into her own hands. On days when there was no light, if it were her old, young days, she would just take a bucket outside and wash the clothes by hand with some Omo, and hang them up to dry out there in her backyard. But her back was always reminding her these days that she was no longer young, a searing ache every single day. Maybe from carrying Godwin's child—their child. How long had he been gone now? Months? A year? Didn't matter. Whatever the words used to quantify it, it all amounted to a very long time.

But today was her lucky day. There was light. The tank of water was full, and so the washer would run.

She left the laundry for a moment to peek into the living room. The news was still breaking. All day long, it had been breaking. Since yesterday, in fact. The banner on the television, like a broken record, read: NORTH KOREA FIRES INTERCONTINENTAL BALLISTIC MISSILE AS DONALD TRUMP MOCKS REGIME.

Nobody cares, she whispered to herself. Nobody cares. She would say it to herself, repeat it over and over again, until she began to believe that she didn't care, until she began to believe that the news was not fazing her. But even as the words were slipping out of her mouth, her head was racing, because: ballistic missiles.

Back in the laundry room, she poured in the detergent and turned on the washer. The baby was sleeping in a nook adjacent to the living room. A bare space with a crib and a guest daybed and a poster of Jesus hanging on the wall. This was where Emmanuelle now also slept ever since Godwin disappeared—in the baby's room. She could no longer set foot into the master, the room she and Godwin had shared.

From 1:00 to 3:00 P.M., the baby would sleep. Let her sleep. Her useless father gone, a useless husband gone. All she had now was Jesus, a baby, and a pile of soiled laundry.

Emmanuelle stopped again in front of the television. She switched the channel to the BBC. The world was surely falling apart. The BBC headline read: NORTH KOREA CONFIRMS "SUCCESSFUL"

NEW BALLISTIC MISSILE TEST. Another headline, from the *New York Times*: U.S. CONFIRMS NORTH KOREA FIRED INTERCONTINENTAL BALLISTIC MISSILE. ANOTHER ONE LIKELY. WIDESPREAD DESTRUCTION TO BE EXPECTED.

Her heart beat a little faster. She paced the living room. Through the open louver windows a soft breeze caused the curtains to billow. Godwin was gone, not a word from him, the baby sleeping, and the world was falling apart. Stupid countries fighting with one another. And what if the missile missed its target? What if, instead of blowing up the U.S., it hit and destroyed the whole of Africa, would anyone even blink an eye? Not a chance.

Africa, the reluctant guinea pig. The arteries of the world would simply go on pulsing without Africa, blood propelled through veins, no recognition of the missing heart.

Outside the sky was graying, clouds moving past. Inside, she paced again. The room smelled of clay. She imagined a mountain made of sand. Wet sand, that gray-colored scent that permeated the air in the moments before it rained. Drywall, Sheetrock.

How much longer before the clothes she'd dumped into the washer would be ready? So much dumping, the waste soiling all the clean things in life. So much effort to clean up the waste. The port of Eel Ma'aan, north of Mogadishu. Radioactive materials in Somalia. Toxic beaches in Nigeria. Agbogbloshie, Ghana. Nothing to be done.

Her cravings again. She could soothe them with a glass of ice.

In the kitchen, under her breath, she said a random godless thanks for light, without which the ice tray would be small pockets of liquid. She grabbed eight stodgily square translucent cubes, tossed them into her small wooden mortar, which she used for exactly this purpose: to crush the cubes with her pestle. She sucked on the ice one crushed bit at a time. The doctor had said it was the blood loss from the baby. She had now become anemic.

So many lost things: first, the love, then the man whom she had loved, then her blood, maybe now even her job (with the disappearance of Godwin, she'd stayed home on a never-ending maternity leave), and who knew, maybe also, soon, the loss of her entire country, and an entire continent.

The washer was spinning loudly, and she could hear it from the kitchen. Such a loud spin cycle. She should return to it, this new washer. She should check that she had not accidentally spilled detergent onto its sides. She should do a thorough wipe-down of it. Not that it mattered. When all was said and done, and she was gone, and the whole country was gone, North Korea would be the ones inheriting the washer. But for her sake, she would go clean it. For her peace of mind. A clean home, a clean mind.

In the laundry room, she sponged the sides of the washer, though there had not been any detergent stains on its sides. That old washer had been too soiled to save. Or maybe she had simply wanted to rid herself of it because it had been Godwin who had done the laundry, who had been so careless with it that when he'd left, and she'd finally begun to do the laundry herself, the stains and dirt had seemed insurmountable. No matter how much she wiped she could not wipe away the trickles of blue soap, the tiny lint-bits of dirt.

She swept the floor of the laundry though there was no dirt on the floors. She cleansed the light switch, the wall.

When the cycle was done, she took out the clothes, one carefully sought out article at a time, making sure that none of them touched the surfaces of the laundry room or the walls of the machine. She hung them each up on the rack to dry.

The rain had begun to fall, and with it still, the dense scent of Sheetrock. Her mouth watered. She craved. She tasted the weight of her cravings on her tongue. Sheetrock. Clay. Toothpaste. Ice. One temptation could serve as a substitute for all other temptations. One temptation could be made to occupy the same space as all other temptations. One single temptation could satisfy the hunger created by all other temptations combined.

Emmanuelle turned the knob softly, entered the baby's room to check on her. The baby was still fast asleep, her little pink-clothed self curled up in a child's pose. A tiny little lump of a human that should have united the family, that should have been the harbinger of all good things, that should have brought Emmanuelle and Godwin so much happiness. That was the problem with life. One never knew whence happiness would come, like the song went, just as one never knew whence happiness would slip away. She should not have laid the burden of her and Godwin's happiness on a mere baby. You cannot create a beautiful work of art and say, "Now you will fix all the problems in my world. Because I created you, my life will be nice and easy." Beauty alone does not fix anything. Where there was a mess, there will still be a mess.

Outside, in her backyard, the rain had softened the earth. She stepped out not far from the back door, where the slab of zinc lay. She lifted the zinc to allow herself to take in with her eyes the extent of the den, the depth and the width. The zinc cover had been the leftover from the patchwork roof of the boys' quarters, back when she and Godwin had been renovating the small backyard flat, back when they had made plans of hiring house help. All of this was long before the baby came, long before their relationship had started to fall apart.

Emmanuelle was a short woman, five feet two, and the hole was only a little deeper than shoulder height on her, but it was wide enough that she could stretch her arms wide, and even almost double her outstretched arms. She'd lined one section of the flooring with a polyethylene tarp, so that she'd not have to sit directly on the earth, and then she had spread one of her old wrappers on top of the tarp, to give it just a bit more of a homey feel. She'd set a small wooden bench in the bunker, which she had used as a storage shelf in that section. On the other, still-earthy, uncovered section of the ground, she set three buckets—two of them labeled and covered with a lid, and the third simply with a bowl in it, in very close proximity to four full barrels of water.

Had she known the rain would come, she might have waited until today—until after the rain—to dig and to do all of that energy-draining setup. But, in the heat of her fear, she'd done all the hard labor yesterday, almost as soon as she heard the news of the missile, which was almost as soon as the first reports of it had come out. She had dug for hours, the baby on her back, her old rusted shovel in hands, only stopping for water for herself and for nursing the baby.

Down the ladder she went into the dark and strongly smelling earth. She held a batch of garments in her arms as she climbed down the ladder's steps. These were the clothes she'd washed yesterday and then hung up to dry. Now they were dry. Now she was filling up the plastic tub that she'd set inside the bunker yesterday with articles: mostly the baby's clothes, a few of her own clothes—just a few knockabouts, nothing fancy. And when they'd worn and soiled them all, and if the world was still falling apart, they might as well go nude. Already, she had stacked up boxes of diapers in the bunker near her bench-shelf, where packs of Indomie and bags of rice and a set of three pots and gallons of water also sat stacked. Several cans of peanuts. Food and water were definite necessities, as were diapers, in this falling-apart world of launched missiles. As was her small battery-operated radio. As for the darkness of the bunker, she had three lanterns and half a dozen small jerry cans full of fuel stashed away near the bench. She'd endured the line last night just for these preparations. Just that once. She wouldn't dare touch the fuel even when NEPA took light again. She would simply embrace the darkness, the sacrifice she had to make to prepare herself and her child for the most frightening of futures.

Back again in the house, it was nearing 3:00 P.M. Soon she must wake the child or else the girl would not sleep at night. Also, the girl must be hungry by now. But then, she seemed so peaceful, lying there like a small clump, her little belly expanding and deflating with the rhythm of her breathing. Just a bit more sleep, Emmanuelle decided. Let her sleep some more.

The first thing that caught her eye after turning from the baby was that very painting of Jesus: brown-colored Jesus with a black lamb around his shoulders, a halo on each of their heads. Both gazing far left, into the distance. His clothes were beige, but he wore a purple ipele down his shoulders and across his body, like a proper Naija Jesus. Minus the wavy onye ocha hair, of course.

She stared at Jesus for a minute, which then led to ten minutes of staring, which then led to twenty. This beautiful, brown-skinned Jesus that hung upon her wall, watching over her and her baby. She thought of what he represented to so many people. His love for humanity, his soothing, saving grace. Was it not he who made the blind man see? Was it not he who walked on water, who exorcised demons, who turned water to wine, who brought back the dead?

She felt a numbness in her soul. So much numbness that she might as well be dead. A numbly racing mind. Could Jesus one day settle her numbly racing mind and bring her back to life?

When the anxiety was so much that she could no longer bear it, she knew what she must do to attain release. It was then that she called softly to Jesus, the way she always did when she was feeling this way. But instead of only calling, this time she lay on the bed, tied a sock around her mouth to make sure she did not make a sound that would awake the child. She lay so that she was facing Jesus, so that he could speak to her with his eyes. She brought her hands to herself, embraced herself by the arms, downward, lifted the skirt of her dress. Was it blasphemy? A sacrilege? She might have given it more thought, but the desperation in her heart, in her loins, doused her concern with such trivialities as blasphemy. What she needed was a release, or else she might very well go crazy, and what would become of the child with a missing father and a crazy mother? Drips of pleasure came as soon as she touched it, her fingers wet with relief. Slowly, the pleasure built up into something full, something massive, and she saw it in his face, Jesus encouraging her to continue to climb. Jesus, blessing her. Jesus, calling on her to embrace her humanity, to revel in the small pleasures of her being. She was almost there. Soon, she'd be there. A matter of seconds, and it would finally appear, her long-sought deliverance.

When the knock came, she swore it must have been Jesus coming to release her in the flesh. But the persistence of the knocking was like a wedge in the arc of her pleasure. Jesus could not have been so cruel as to have introduced a hard, cold, recurring obstruction of a sound just when she felt herself a mere step from her climax. She exhaled with deflation. The baby was turning a bit in the crib. Another tumbling, rambling knock on the door, and a woman's voice calling out her name. "Emmanuelle!" A pause. "Emmanuelle, it's me. Are you in there?"

She opened the door. Chinasa looked like a washrag, like a person who had given up on life, like a person who was trying to harvest the courage to live.

"What took you so long?" Emmanuelle asked, one hand holding the door open, the other reaching down to make sure the skirt of her dress was down as it should be, not exposing her thighs. The scent of herself was still on the tips of her hands, though she had quickly run into the bathroom and washed her hands before answering the door. She wouldn't have wanted her personal fluid all over the knob.

The clouds had moved away. The sun was shining down on them. A wind blew the postrain air into her nostrils. Sheetrock. Clay. Toothpaste. Ice. She craved them all so strongly again. Inside, the clothes were drying.

Chinasa moped her way into the living room, dragging her luggage along.

They had been planning this visit for some time. Two friends reuniting, in order to help each other to get back on their feet. But now, with the breaking news on the television, the original plan had been disrupted. Even with Chinasa's clear exhaustion from her daylong journey, eleven hours in an automobile (or had she in the end decided to fly?), Emmanuelle could not help but announce the change of plans right away, in order to get on already with the relocation process.

"We won't be staying in the house," she declared.

"What do you mean 'We won't be staying in the house'?" Chinasa asked, still on her feet, not yet having made it to the couch. "Where will we be staying, then?"

Already, Emmanuelle was helping Chinasa to zip open her luggage. "Only take the most important items. I have a list. Here," she said, extending the catalog of essentials to Chinasa.

Chinasa confusedly scanned the list. As if mechanically, she began separating her things.

After what could not have been any more than twenty minutes, Emmanuelle asked, "You have everything you need?"

How much could Chinasa possibly need? One or two knockabouts? A pair of slippers? A box of provisions? In all the time they had been apart—in all the years Chinasa had been in New York, and then in the three years after the redhead American man nearly blew off her head in that Jamaica, Queens, café, after which she'd been hiding out in Abuja with her mother, she'd surely learned that life was far more valuable than material things.

■ ■ ■

Emmanuelle woke up to the sound of the baby's crying in her little foamy cocoon of a makeshift crib. Their first day in the cave, and the crying was understandable: a cave home like this one would take even a baby some adjustment. The hollow was damp as with morning dew. Already, Emmanuelle's cravings were strong, so early in the day.

"Try to focus on the millipedes," Chinasa said.

"There are millipedes in here?" Emmanuelle asked.

Chinasa pointed to the corner of the cave, behind the bench-shelf. Emmanuelle tilted her body forward without moving, peered closer at where Chinasa was pointing, then threw her plastic slipper at it. Then she peered closer, her head bent forward so as not to hit the roof of the den, picked up the slipper. She stared at the millipede. The millipede was not moving.

It must have been the scent of the dead millipede that intensified her craving.

Above the bench-shelf hung a photo of Chinasa's family, who had stubbornly refused to take any protective measures, which had been the reason Chinasa'd made the trip all the way to Port Harcourt, so that she would have a chance of living, if not with her family, then alongside a friend.

At first looking at the family photo seemed to work. A distraction of unmoving proportions. But then again, the cravings. She picked up her baby, rocked the baby in her arms, licked her lips continually to try to settle the longing.

"Look, if you bite down on your index finger, long enough to pause blood flow, then just watch the blood return, you might forget all about the cravings."

Chinasa had come with a stash of burner phones—at least a dozen of them. Now, she picked one up and began tinkering with it.

· · ·

"Why didn't you even think to bring ice?" Chinasa asked, their second day in the cave. She was still niggling with her burner phones. "Mehn, it's no fun being stuck in a hole with a person as miserable as you."

"Are you daft?" Emmanuelle snapped. "Ice melts. Ice perishes. Only nonperishables allowed."

"And toothpaste?"

"No toothpaste," she said. She'd been afraid that in the fervor of her cravings, and without any ice to turn to, she might wind up eating all the tubes at once, poisoning herself to death. Better no toothpaste at all. Instead, she'd packed a large container of chewing sticks, the old-fashioned teeth cleaning way.

The phone in Chinasa's hand lit up. "Finally," she said. "My mother must be so worried. I need to call her and tell her I'm fine."

"It's not as if you needed all those burner phones to call her. What happened to your own phone?"

"What if he somehow tracked us with my phone?"

"What if who somehow tracked us?"

"I don't know . . . North Korea? The U.S. government? The café bomber?"

"It's him you're really worried about, isn't it?"

Chinasa nodded, a dejected, defeated look on her face.

"What if the world has already blown up, your mother and all, and everyone is dead already?"

That was a cruel thing to say, she realized, almost as soon as it had slipped out of her mouth. Chinasa stared at her with dumbfounded eyes and her mouth agape.

"It was just a joke. I'm sure your family is fine. It's the cravings . . . they get to me. I'm never more irritable than . . ." She opened a bottle of water and began drinking from it.

"It's true," Chinasa said. "I mean, it's why we're here, no? The possibility that everything will be destroyed, everyone except us."

They sat together in silence, except for the sucking sound that the baby made as she pulled on Emmanuelle's breast.

"My mother, after the café thing, she kept telling me that life goes on," Chinasa said. "The world, it keeps on turning. Find your old friends, rebuild your life. Forget New York. You need to learn how to exist in this world again."

"Good old Mama," Emmanuelle said. "You found me now, didn't you?"

An old friend she was. They used to be best friends during their primary school days at Federal Government Girls College. Playing Oga always together in their brown-stained uniforms and muddy sandals. Both on the Purple team for track and field. But that was much further back than three years. All that time they had lost touch. Somewhere along the line, rumor had it that Chinasa's family had relocated to Abuja and that Chinasa had since moved to New York. And then suddenly she was back in Abuja. And now, here in Port Harcourt. All of life was a circle. A circle hastened by a series of specific traumas. With all that circling and traumatizing, a person could not help winding up in a hole.

The baby still in her arms, she nudged the bench-shelf a bit to the side. The photo frame of Jesus that she had taken into the cavern with her now came into view.

Jesus, she thought. She saw the irony of it very clearly now. All this time, she should have been helping her friend to come out of hiding; instead she was goading her deeper into it, shepherding her deeper into her trauma-induced psychosis. Both of them sinking further together into the hole.

By the end of the day, Chinasa had still not succeeded in making any calls from her burner phones.

The twin bucket latrines, labeled "pee" and "poo," weren't at all full, but in the corner where they sat was a faint fecal scent emanating from them, also the faint scent of urine like near the market, near the panhandlers in their moistly dark, cemented crouching places. As for the baby's waste, Emmanuelle scrubbed out the solid matter from the diaper into the "poo" bucket, simply tied up the used diaper and tossed it into a large plastic bag. She might have to tie the plastic bags that lined the pee and poo buckets earlier than expected, Emmanuelle thought now. But what to do with the waste?

■ ■ ■

The smallest of the four water barrels on the opposite end of the bench-shelf was what they used. Emmanuelle lathered the small bar of Ivory soap, very barely, on her body in the corner of the den, then using the bowl, she scooped out water from the bucket and rinsed herself off. She'd filled the bucket only halfway, for rationing's sake, and certainly she would have loved nothing more than to lather up in some far more substantial way, but sometimes in life, there were sacrifices. Anyway, after two days of not having bathed, the abruptly fresh feeling from even only half a bucket gave her satisfaction, as if she had used entire buckets of water.

When it was Chinasa's turn, Emmanuelle filled the bucket halfway again. The baby had been the first to be bathed. Now she sat in her cocoon crib, making baby noises. As Chinasa lathered her body with soap, Emmanuelle said, "Biko, be careful you don't put too much soap. We only get half a bucket of water."

"Not even after two days of not washing? Please, if I need a little bit more water, is it the end of the world?" Chinasa replied.

"And when we run out? You will be the one to run out into the crumbling world and fetch us some more water?" Emmanuelle now sat cross-legged by the bench-shelf, chewing on her chewing stick.

Chinasa continued her bath in silence. When her bucket of water was down to the very last, she set the bowl aside, lifted the bucket and poured the entire remnants all at once on her body and declared her bath complete.

Then they sat together eating a bowl of Indomie noodles. Ordinarily, in order to improve the nutritional value, Emmanuelle would have poured some hot water over the noodles, then she'd have cut up some onions and tatashe peppers, without the bitter seeds, and maybe even some tomatoes into the bowl and cooked them along with the noodles. But instead, she had allowed the noodles to sit in a bowl of room temperature water and now sat eating the cold, hard, peculiarly wet noodles.

"Beans," Emmanuelle said.

"Beans?"

"Baked beans. I should have found some cans of baked beans. Beans are good for iron."

"You mean like American-style beans?" Chinasa asked. "I once had them at a diner back when I was there."

Emmanuelle nodded. "Yes, like American-style beans," she said.

Chinasa shook her head. "Not me and you," she said. "No palm oil. No pepper. No crayfish. All that sugar. Since when were beans meant to be sweet?"

"No wahala. Then you could have just starved."

They sat in silence, and after a while they began drifting in and out of sleep.

The radio droned on, and every once in a while, Emmanuelle scanned the stations for news on North Korea. Always the same. *Another launch likely. Destruction expected.* She stared at the stray beams of light seeping in from the minuscule perforations in the zinc roof. Good that there had not yet been another launch. She'd have to fix the perforations soon. She'd have to find a way to make their little cavern airtight. No sense in their being in a hole all this time when all it would take to kill them was a tiny bit of contaminated air.

When night began to fall, she had not yet come up with the best way to seal the gaps in the roof. Now that there was no longer any light seeping into the cave, she lit a lantern. Chinasa sat across from her glaring at her burner phones. The baby's breathing was a steady stream of muddy sand in Emmanuelle's mind. The kind of sand she'd like to allow to linger, and then to dance, and then to linger some more on her tongue.

■ ■ ■

"Aren't you wondering how long it will take for them to just go ahead and blow up the bloody world? Just blow it up and let's just be done with all of this nonsense?" Chinasa asked. It was the middle of the night and neither of them had managed to sleep. Only the baby was asleep.

Emmanuelle was holding Jesus to her chest, as she lay curled up in her little corner. "It isn't as easy as you think," she said, "to blow up the world."

"Then what are we doing in here?" Chinasa asked.

There was a silence.

She held Jesus tighter to her body. She fell asleep that way.

In her dream she was saying to Jesus, "Show it to me. I want to see it."

"Here?" he asked, his teeth slightly crooked but his body quite fit. He looked like a finely chiseled dark-skinned, redheaded worker who seemed a mix between a mason and an electrician, ruddy stubbles coloring his brown face. He was carrying a bucket of cement and a belt of side cutters, wire strippers, pliers, and a set of screwdrivers. Show me your very precious and private part, she pleaded with him. I want to see it. May I touch it? May I touch you?

"Here?" he asked. They were in the middle of a hallway in what appeared to be some sort of work building. He scanned the passageway with his eyes. "People will see. How about somewhere else? Somewhere a bit more private?"

But her office was crowded, like her mind. A woman was sweeping the sandy floor, and another was asking to use the phone.

She woke up slowly from sleep, not at first aware that she was still in her muddy little den, not at first aware of her hips gently thrusting back and forth, even as she lay in her fetal position. Involuntarily, the speed of her thrusting increased, a crescendo of thrusts. Soon, she felt a rhythmical narrowing, a pressure-filled constriction inside of her, and then a pleasure-filled explosion. She wallowed in all of it, for seconds, for minutes perhaps, the way the current coursed through her entire body. There were still remnants of the constriction, so taut, almost painful, even after the explosion, that she had to lay a finger, like a sheath, in the hollow space between the tip of her lips down to her fourchette. This soothed, just a bit, the residual pressure that had amassed. Only then did she remember where she was: in the middle of an earthen cavern with a friend and a baby.

She lay with her eyes closed, afraid of what she might see if she opened them—Chinasa watching her with disgust, with disbelief. Shock gripped her. Astonishment at herself, at what her body had just done in this crowded little den, more or less without her permission.

Just what had Chinasa seen? How much? From beginning to end? Did she see the initial gentle thrusts that sped and culminated in the shivering that overtook her body when she finally came? Her cheeks burned with the heat of embarrassment.

Why was she even in this stupid cave? The missiles, she remembered. The missiles. There they were again—her awful, unrelenting cravings. All the while, she'd thought only of the missiles. The aroma of the earth was somehow more fresh and strong smelling and alluring to her. Outside, it must have rained. There it was again, that scent, like Sheetrock, like drywall, the kind that made her mouth water. She thought of ice. If only she had the ice.

When she opened her eyes, she saw that Chinasa was facing away from her, toward the wall of the cavern, rather than at her. She felt a relief, but also a disappointment, because seeing Chinasa there reminded her of Fatu. Fatu, whose loss was somehow worse than the loss of Godwin. Fatu, who had come and comforted her after Godwin left, who had held her and kissed her and made it feel like her life was whole again. Fatu, who had promised to always be there because "in the end, we women have only each other." Fatu, who had disappeared just as soon as she had made that promise and was now somewhere in the U.S., doing God knows what. Emmanuelle cursed the day at FGGC that she met Fatu.

Perhaps Fatu was the straw that broke the camel's back, the reason for her compulsions, the loss that gave rise to her incessant wiping, her incessant cleaning, as if to purge away the things they had done together, the intimacies they had shared. Perhaps Fatu was the reason for this newfound appreciation of Jesus, the man. But now Chinasa had come, and who knew how much Chinasa could tell? What if she had seen everything? And heard everything? Because what if Emmanuelle had somehow accidentally called out Fatu's name while the pleasure coursed through her veins? What if Chinasa had only turned away with disgust after the fact? What if she had in fact been awake, only pretending to be asleep?

The anxiety was now too much to bear, and with it, the cravings. Life was an angle grinder, a diamond wheel, attempting to cut into the delicately porcelained perimeter of her heart, but she would not allow it to be cut.

She laid Jesus gently on the floor, then crouched down to the earth, began to scoop the earth into her palm. Jesus had somehow simultaneously released and failed her. She lifted the earth to her mouth, her tongue watering with longing. Just give in to it and eat the earth. No ice to soothe you any longer. Eat the earth and call it a day.

She was about to put it on her tongue when she realized her oversight. In a different world, she could simply eat the earth and be satisfied. Though of course it was not an act that a normal person should engage in, the thing of it was that the cure for her cravings in fact lay in the earth. But then, in this world, to eat the earth would be to poison herself. All of it was toxic waste. Eel Ma'aan, north of Mogadishu. The whole of Nigeria. Agbogbloshie. She had run right into the earth for salvation, instead of the other way. And then she had also called on Jesus. But Jesus had released her only so much: Jesus had not managed to rid the earth of those toxins. She sat up on her bed now and thought, Nothing to be done. Her eyes landed on her baby. Poor pitiable baby. There was hardly anything of real consequence to be done anymore, not even for a child. The earth was a sullied, crumbling wreck and all of it would go on crumbling. She began quietly to weep. For all the sullied, wrecked things of the earth that her baby must now endure, Emmanuelle wept.

THE UNFORTUNATE PLACE

Tahmima Anam

BANGLADESH

ONCE UPON A TIME, there was a girl from a terrible country. The country was battered by the worst combination of natural and human-made disasters: floods, cyclones, famine, war. The country was small and the people were poor. Every bad thing that could happen to a place would happen to that country.

When she was seven, she and her parents left the terrible country and moved to New York City. Her parents enrolled her in the UN school, which was called UNIS. At UNIS, the students were invited to take pride in where they came from. "What are you most proud of?" her teacher asked. The Australian boy said kangaroos. The Kenyan boy said Kip Keino, the marathon runner who had won Olympic gold in Mexico and Munich.

When it was the girl's turn, she had difficulty coming up with anything. Everyone still remembered that Henry Kissinger had once called her country a basket case, and that the image on the record of a famous charity concert for her country was of a starving child.

"Longest beach in the world?" she offered weakly, pointing to a photo of a scruffy stretch of gray-brown sand. Sometimes other children would ask her whether they had roads in her country, and what she did when cyclones and floods arrived. She had, herself, not witnessed either of these catastrophes, as her house was on the edge of a lake that swelled in the monsoon and dried up in winter, as it always had.

When the girl grew up, she attempted to make peace with this terrible country. *It's not so bad*, she told herself. *It's maybe, on the scale of things, somewhat unlucky.* But people often asked her the same questions about the floods and the cyclones. Then the world realized that something awful was about to happen to the entire planet. It was called, in turn, climate change, climate crisis, and then, climate catastrophe.

To her chagrin, the girl realized that her country happened to be unfortunate in this regard as well. Because it was located on the edge of the sea and made up of low-lying delta, when the sea rose, which it inevitably would, it would eat her country first. On the front lines of climate change, they called it now, because the world was different and basket case would've sounded too cruel.

As time went on, however, the girl came to realize that because of all the terrible things, her people had the ability to see into the future. In the terrible country, climate catastrophe had already happened. All the storms that would batter the rest of the world had already appeared on her coastline. The floods and the droughts and the cyclones—they were used to those. They had built shelters and learned to irrigate lands in unusual ways. They were people who were used to living with uncertainty, with the kind of expectation of disaster that the rest of the world would eventually have to adapt to. In a world divided between those who knew, and were therefore prepared for what was about to happen, and those who did not, her country was finally, possibly, a little bit lucky.

One day, at her son's school gates, a parent introduces her father. The father is a publisher, and the parent thinks, since the girl, now a woman, is a writer, they might have something to say to each other. "Bangladesh!" the man announces. "I call that the Unfortunate Place."

She smiles. *But we know things that you will have to learn the hard way*, she thinks. If she could speed back in time, she would have her younger self say to that class: Resilience. In the face of all that is unfortunate, resilience.

EVERYTHING

Daisy Johnson

ENGLAND

Open

I know of the box before it is given to me the way I know about everything kept out of my reach. I am ten years old and my mother is dying and the box is on top of the wardrobe in her bedroom. The only time she ever hit me was when she caught me reaching for it, her open palm across the back of my legs. The house smells of the pills the nurses crush beneath water glasses, the catheter that comes loose and drips across the floor. The box is dark stone with a small padlock on the catch. I sit next to her bed and read to her and it is impossible not to catch sight of it. We have not always seen eye to eye and she is angry with sickness, raging with dying. One day she catches me looking and closes her hand around my wrist hard enough to hurt. I sit very still.

It's yours now, she says.

The monitors next to the bed spasm and chirp, the nurse moves around in the bathroom, turning on the tap. Downstairs I can hear my aunt on the phone.

It's yours now. And if you open it you'll be sorry and I am sorry.

The nurse comes in and reaches over and taps at my mother's

fingers clamped around my wrist. My mother's face is bruised, softening. The nurse grapples with her fingers in silence and then I have my hand and I am running and I think: It's mine now, the box is mine.

My aunt lives out in the flatlands past Cambridge in a house with no stairs with a blind cat and no neighbors as far as the eye can see. She is fifteen years younger than my mum and smokes cigarettes out of the kitchen window, buys me jigsaws that we do rather than homework, works in a call center and comes home with glazed eyes and coffee-stunk breath. There is a tree the size of a small cathedral out the back of the house. A horse chestnut, she says, and the first autumn I am there we collect conkers by the sackful, line the windowsills, fill bowls and teacups. She loves that tree. The school I go to is smaller than the one at home and all the children have known each other forever. I learn the Lord's Prayer by heart and we say it four times a day, eyes clamped shut, uncertain how to do it, wishing and wishing. When I open my eyes some of the other girls are watching me, snickering behind their flattened palms. They trip me in the corridor and I go sprawling, underpants on show, skirt nearly to my chin, everyone watching. They drop the telephone my aunt gave me for emergencies into the fish tank. Their hate is wide sprawling, everlasting. You're not sick, my aunt says when I try to stay at home, her hand on my forehead, go get ready for school.

The box is on the bookshelf in the sitting room, just out of reach but not forbidden to me. One day when my aunt is at work I drag over a kitchen chair and heft it down off the shelf. It is lighter than it looks. I run my hands over the top and sides, the stone smoothed to fingerprints in places, the padlock a little rusty around the edges. I hold the padlock between my finger and thumb. I remember the things my mother had said to me about the box, not only as she lay dying but in the years that she was alive. I remember the feel of her hand across the back of my legs. I go into the kitchen and get out a knife from the drawer. I jimmy the lock, sawing and stabbing. I dig through my aunt's toolbox and pile everything that might work on the floor. I hack at the lock with a saw and a hammer and a screwdriver. It groans, nearly gives, finally lets loose with a crunch. I sit with the box in front of me. Outside there is the sound of the chestnut tree shifting, the noise of the birds who nest among the arbors, the rattle of squirrels skidding up and down. I think about school and how the other day they had cornered me in the bathroom and held my hand beneath the hot tap until the skin was red. I open the box, just an inch.

That autumn the horse chestnut tree gives us no conkers. I watch my aunt out the window, standing beneath its branches, gazing up. There is a smell to the tree that wasn't there before, mulch, ancient eggs, stagnant water, mildew, and oxidation. The leaves do not fall slowly but all at once, in the night, the branches weighing down to the ground, the trunk so soft that when we dig at it with our fingers whole chunks come away. There is a silence that wasn't there before. Nothing lives in the tree now and the tree surgeon that comes out to see it only stands with her hands on her hips and clicks her tongue sadly against the roof of her mouth. When the tree is cut down, dug up, the stump ground away, even the earth beneath is bad, the soil turned thin and infertile.

The mum of one of the girls at school gets a new job in Siberia and she moves away. The others seem less interested without her, even, once, wave me over at lunch so we can sit awkwardly together, grinning across the potato waffles and beans. They do not follow me caterwauling down the corridor or laugh at me in class or track me to quiet corners. The peace is quiet and unobtrusive and I do not entirely believe that it has come from the box. Although I do not quite believe the opposite either.

Open

Lancaster University is a concrete citadel on the hill. My aunt comes to visit and we sit in the campus café and eat pizza, drink watery coffee. There are twelve other people living in the same building as me and it is never quiet. I share a bathroom with the girl opposite, and her thick, dark hair clogs the drain, handprint smears on the fogged-over mirror. She is sick for the first year, sleeps a lot, appears groggily in the kitchen to microwave bowls of porridge and instant coffee. She gives me lists of things to buy from the shop across from our building: tampons, Müller yogurts, satsumas. Sometimes we sit in her room wrapped in the duvet and watch Jane Campion films until the night is gone and it is day again. She gets better in her second year and I see her out and about, spiky-heeled, wobbly, carton of fries beneath her arm.

There is a boy in one of my classes whom I catch sight of out of the corner of my eye, who stands out against the gray endlessness like a nail caught in wood. The other boys in the class are loudly opinionated, roughly shod with their facts, but he is quiet and grows red when called upon, hands twisting on the table, the six o'clock shadow over his chin and cheeks. I see him about campus with groups of people, at the center, smiling in a way he does not do in lessons. I have never really wanted anything the way that I want him. I do not know how to go about it. I am completely lacking in knowledge when it comes to this. I watch the way other couples get together on nights out or in class, the way they talk and mirror one another with their bodies, how they touch with ease and without the fear that I feel tangled up in the want as if they are the same thing. There is no way for me to connect with him. He has a large group of friends he is often at the center of and I sometimes see him with other girls, not holding hands but walking close beside one another, shoulders touching, faces turned close. I want to be certain and strict with purpose and vicious with action but I am not. Again and again I am not. A few times I pass him notes in class asking if he has a pencil or if he has read a certain book and he blinks at me and replies in tiny writing, monosyllabic phrases that take up so little of the page, as if even there he cannot share the space with me.

I begin to go out more in the evenings. There is a club with a winding line to get in and vomit on the bathroom walls and I brush my hair until it stands like a static halo around my head and I drink Vodka Red Bull at the bar and find people I only just know well enough to dance with and I keep him in my eyeline the way someone tracking an animal must do. I am ashamed of myself. Touching myself in the mornings with his face like a chilly ghost in the room around me, stalking him up and down the long pathway that connects all of the university, thinking about him more than I think about anything else: the essays I have to write, the people I could perhaps be friends with, my aunt's biannual visits, the trips I take home to see her. Days are days are days are days, only made spiky with interest when I catch a glimpse of him or have a class in which he—perhaps even on purpose—catches my eye. I think of the box but I remember what my mother said and I remember also—at the back of my mind like a bad dream—what had happened to the tree after I'd asked the box to help me before. I float through the days and my want is enormous—more enormous than I thought a woman was supposed to want anything—and he fills the entire horizon with his come-get-me body and his nervous hands.

There is a forest on campus where I sometimes go. The trees remind me of my aunt's horse chestnut before it died and the noise from the campus and the road is shut off there. I make sandwiches in the grubby kitchen and wrap them in foil and eat them beneath the trees. Sometimes I take off my shoes and dig my feet down into the ground so that they are entirely covered with the dirt and I feel the cold and the roots of plants and the insects that die in the earth.

One evening the girl whom I share a bathroom with knocks on my door. I am finishing off an essay and eating instant noodles. She is wearing impossibly high heels and red lipstick and says that she wants to go out and I should come with her. I finish the noodles and borrow one of her dresses and we do shots in the kitchen by the overflowing sink and then catch a bus into town. It is a Saturday and the whole university is lining up to get into the club. The Christian Union is there giving out cups of tea and flip-flops to the girls, who take off their heels as they wait. The girl talks about some friends she might meet later whom I'll like and how awful her essays are going and why she might not even go home for Christmas. There is a sort of awful, cresting frost in the air, lingering on our bare arms and legs. Something swings overhead and no one seems to see it but me, an owl perhaps, flat faced, razor-tipped wings. We pay to get in and then stand at the bar to order drinks, our elbows on the sticky wood. I look back over my shoulder at the bodies and I am not looking for him but when I see him it starts a jolt beginning from my toes and curling up the whole of me, ending like a fist in my mouth. Let's dance, I say, and tug her away from the bar. I do not know what I am doing. I am drunk. We raise our hands above our heads and drop our hair nearly to the ground and kick out our feet and shake our fingers. I have imaginings the length of a night. He comes up to me and we go to the bathroom and we bury one another in bodies that do not belong to us. We go back to his room and there is blood on his chin and on his fingers and on the white sheets his mother bought for him. We go into the forest and I wrap my arms around a tree and I do not know what he is going to do before he does it, the sound of our shouting exhaled and hidden by the canopy. The girl looks over my shoulder and laughs with her hand over her mouth and winks at me and points. I look. The boy has his mouth open and gaping on someone else's mouth, his hands beneath her dress, one of her legs draped up and over his hip. We go to the bar and we drink. The girl whom I share a bathroom with does not know how I feel about him but she accepts the shots and buys more and when I am so drunk I can barely see she comes outside with me into the chill and flags me down a taxi, which I am sick in the back of, and being sick sobers me enough that when I get home I shimmy the box out from under my bed and I open it just enough to slide a finger into it.

In the morning the girl knocks on my door. I have a hangover the size of a high-rise, but I get up and let her in. She sits on the side of my bed. Her eyes are red and she tugs at my duvet and tells me that something is wrong, something is wrong. She takes my hand and presses it down hard into the side of her breast and I feel it, large, a nodule the size of a flattened-out spoon. We go together to Accident and Emergency and I hold her hand very tight and we look at the woman with half her ear missing and a dog hidden in her handbag and the child red raw from screaming and the teenagers peering nervously back at us. I say: It'll be fine, it'll be fine, it'll be fine. But I remember the horse chestnut tree and I do not believe this.

They tell her she needs to stay overnight and I catch the bus home. The lights are on in the building, blazing, and I go tiredly into the kitchen and stand waiting for the kettle, holding my mug in my hand. When I turn around he is at the kitchen table, his face so unexpected for a moment I am uncertain who he is and then I understand and I go toward him.

Open

We buy a house with the money we've saved up. It is by the train station in Lancaster, on a hill with other houses tucked in close and a tiny wedge of a garden that we plant with daffodils and potatoes and coriander. We christen the rooms. His body still feels like something I have just discovered: the mole on his hip, the stray hair on his forehead, the scars from a tumble down a hill on his knee. It is still a secret glory to meet for lunch near where we work and take him into the bathroom and watch his face in the mirror. At the weekends we meet friends at the pub or walk along the canal until the city vanishes or spend all day cooking, drinking cider, listening to the local radio station. Small peace, endless serenity. This is what I pulled from the box. This is what I, grasping, tugged out with my fingers. I look up the girl I used to share a bathroom with on social media. She is hairless, eyebrowless, alive. I promise myself that I will never use the box again. I put it in the cellar, wrapped in a plastic bag, and I promise myself there is nothing else that I need. I do sometimes—it is true—go down and stand with the lights off and look at it not with my eyes but with something else that knows that it is there and sees it all the same. And I do sometimes—it is true—dream about it. I am in a boat and he is in the water, exhausted, not swimming but drowning, and I am holding the box so tightly that I cannot wrench my hands away to help him.

I turn thirty and we meet some friends at a pub on the river. It is cold and we drink warm cider and mulled wine, drinking quickly in celebration, eating fries from shared bowls in the middle of the table and talking over one another. One of his friends from university is there and I do not like him much. He seems to have stayed the same age while the rest of us have aged, seems not to have noticed that no one else goes out every weekend to the same club where the students go. He is drunker than the rest of us and starts making jokes about clocks and old women. I ignore him but he comes and sits next to me, taking up all the space with his legs flung wide and his arm across the back of my chair, his face close to mine. My partner is at the other end of the table and I try to catch his eye but he does not see me. His friend says: You're running out of time, don't you feel it? I stare at him. His pupils are dilated, his lips and teeth and tongue stained with red wine. Women are ready for childbirth as soon as they start their period. I stand up and move away from him, talk to a friend who has come late and is sitting on the periphery. I am shaking with anger but my friend distracts me with a story about her aging mother-in-law and when I look up again the man is gone and my partner is winking at me across the table, turning his eyes toward the bathroom.

It is a busy winter but I find the thought of the baby cropping up in places I did not expect to find it. My students are reading ecological fiction in class and they discuss loudly and with some fighting our responsibility and the pressure of overpopulation on the world. One of the teachers in my department brings her new child in and then gives her to me to hold while she goes to the bathroom. I have never held a baby before and the fear is vast. I remember learning once about the soft spot on the backs of their heads and I probe for it, rub my hand over the soft eiderdown of hair until I find it, a point of give. The baby opens its eyes and looks at me and I wait for some seismic feeling, a point of need or want the way I had felt with my partner, a surge of hormone in my womb; but nothing comes. Still I find myself watching closely the couple who live opposite us and have year-old twins, or people in the supermarket with raging toddlers tugging at the packets on the shelves or people in the swimming pool with their startle-eyed babies, fitted out with armbands. And I watch the way he sees them too, how he points to sleeping babies in strollers or held against their parents' chests, or rambunctious toddlers in the playground near our house, or even the teenagers who hang around the train station.

We stop using condoms almost without discussing the matter. The sex is different, thoughtful, almost disconnected. Sometimes I see my hands moving and feel a jolt, as if someone else has climbed into the bed and pressed themselves between us. I stop drinking and give up the occasional cigarette I would sometimes smoke while I drank and I take up walking along the canal every morning, almost before it is light, the going-off smell of the water, the lights on the canal boats moored to the crumbling concrete. There is no baby but still I can sometimes see it, in the spaces where we do not quite manage to touch, in the hesitations between sentences. It becomes something not that we want but that we must have, that will be there, that is set in stone before it is even possible. We talk about it as if it is there, in the next room, waiting for us to go in and care for it. I ring my aunt and tell her that we are trying and she sends a pack of old children's books that I had as a child, wrapped in blue ribbon and marked with crayon and my grubby fingerprints.

We try for nearly a year and then go to talk to the doctor. In the time we have been trying three of our friends have had babies or got pregnant and seeing them is like an aching wisdom tooth, always there at the back of my mouth. We are examined, and I know that both of us secretly think the other is the problem. I remember seeing him at university with different girls, his arms around them, and I imagine what he has brought into our house, an inability, a lack. Except that I am the one whose body it's supposed to live inside, the house, the apartment, the box, the holding pen. I dream of black rot and asbestos and fallen trees and burst pipes and falling roof tiles and clogged drains. I dream of the box wrapped in its plastic bag, wedged into the corner of the cellar. The doctor says that it will not be possible for us to have a child naturally, that he is sorry. We try IVF once and then again and again. Sometimes I come to and we are screaming at each other in the kitchen, mouths torn wide with rage, smashed glasses in a blast zone around our feet. Sometimes I come to and we have just had sex and he is in the act of turning away, the outline of his cheek and nose, the pressed-down line of his mouth.

He goes away for work and I try to keep busy, bringing home piles of work to mark, keeping the radio on loud, ringing a friend to come over for dinner. I work through the day, pausing occasionally for cups of tea or to go to the bathroom but otherwise continuing steadily, mindlessly. I make a big salad and flat bread for dinner with my friend, buy hummus and Halloumi from the shop on the corner. When I get home there is a message from her on the house phone: her daughter has come down with a fever and she will not be able to come. I keep preparing the dinner but it is different now. The voices from the radio are tinny and sometimes the words do not make sense, seem entirely disconnected from the sentences. The light through the windows has an odd tinge, almost greenish, as if we are buried beneath a canopy. I blaze in and out of existence, find myself uncorking a bottle of wine I do not remember buying, catch myself before my hand slips from the onion I am chopping and embeds the knife into my thumb, discover I am halfway down the cellar steps and have no idea how I got there. I hesitate. The box sends out a thrum that I feel in the ends of my fingers and the itching roots of my hair. I go down the last few steps and stand in the darkness. I dig my fingernails into the palms of my hands but it is too late, it is as if I have already done it, have already walked over to the corner and crouched down and uncovered the box and tipped it open wider than I have ever opened it before and pushed my hands inside.

It is possible that nothing means anything and that everything happens for no reason at all. I sleep for nearly twelve hours and wake up late. The house is very quiet. I have lost my phone and it takes a while to find it. I put the television on while I hunt and the noise fills the space around me, the colors on the pale walls. Something has happened. I pause to watch. It is at first unclear exactly what it is, only a pile of metal, green-coated people moving around, the news reporter. I turn the volume up. A train, not far from the city, derailed. My phone is down the side of the sofa. I have more missed calls than I have ever had before and I remember—as if it were someone else who had done it and I only hear after the fact—the way I had crouched and pushed open the lid of the box and crushed my fingers into the gap. I press my hands against my belly and I think I feel—impossible of course— the stir of movement. And I hold my phone and try to ring him but there is no answer. There is no answer.

Open

Every minute I am older than I have ever been and it has not scared me until this moment. I go up the long hill to visit his grave and I talk to Iris—my lovely, fierce daughter, Iris—on the phone every other day and I sit trying to feel when it will come. Some days are worse than others and I cannot even find the energy to close the curtains in the sitting room or go up the stairs to the bed that I have slept in for nearly fifty years. Iris sends postcards from Peru and Chile and Hawaii and Mexico. I feel the living beat of her even from so far away and I tell myself that I will never open the box again, I will never open it again for her. A van brings meals-on-wheels that all taste the same and that I am losing my appetite for. I move the box around the house hoping that I will forget where I last put it and that'll be the end:

under the bed, in the cupboard beneath the stairs, down at the bottom of the garden in the shed with the lawn mower. I forget where I have put my glasses and what day it is but I never forget where the box is. It has a weight I feel in my sleep, pressing down on my chest. And I know that, really, it will not be long before I open it again. After everything that has happened, after all I have done; I will look inside the box one more time. I will take everything from it. I will take and take and take and take until there is nothing left.

THE FUNNIEST SHIT
YOU EVER HEARD

Lina Mounzer

LEBANON

A LONG TIME AGO, about a decade after the end of the war in Beirut, I lived in a huge, crumbling old house by the sea.

Every foray into the heart of the city—to work, to the supermarket, to the cafés on Hamra Street—meant a trudge up a steepish hill. Not so steep a climb as in, say, Lisbon or Istanbul, but enough to make it uncomfortably obvious whether you'd been keeping in shape or not. One early morning after a hard rain, I was making my way up the hill when I saw a line of traffic stuck behind a stalled car and heard the frenzied shouting of men.

And then it hit me. The fell-you-where-you're-standing stench of shit. One of the sewer drains had overflowed, blasting away its manhole cover, and a gleaming brown waterfall cascaded down the hill. It took me about a minute to understand what was happening: what this had to do with the stalled car, why there were about fifteen men gesturing hysterically, half of them yelling at the poor, broken-down driver to "Push on! Push on!" and the other half careering down the hill, warning the other cars to "Go back! Go back!"

The car's tires, you see, couldn't get a grip on the asphalt for the slimy effluence underwheel. They spun and spun in place, emitting an agonized whine, churning out fecal matter as the men screamed, and women craned their heads over windowsills and balcony railings, adding their own horrified shouting and instructions to the commotion. Occasionally there was a mighty string of curses as one of the men got too close and got splattered, perhaps with the remnants of the very same meal he had consumed at his dinner table the night before, and then unloaded into his toilet that very morning. The private became public in spectacular fashion. It was horrifying. It was hilarious. It was basically everything a great poop joke should be.

After watching awhile from a safe distance, I took a detour up another hill, giggling the whole way.

At the time it seemed mere punch line, not prologue. A self-contained anecdote unconnected to anything deeper, telling only of itself.

■ ■ ■

The fifteen-year-long Lebanese civil war officially ended in 1990, and soon afterward, the reconstruction project began.

The common wisdom at the time, repeated wearily by taxi drivers and shopkeepers, was that the warring parties had finally realized that there was more money to be made through peace. A massive private holding company bought out the entirety of the downtown area—which had been the front line between the two divided halves of Beirut—promising to build a shiny new city out of its ruins. One that would look very much like the old one, with its romantic, pale-yellow mandate-era buildings, but better and more modernized. For a single private company to acquire so much prime land—most of which still technically belonged to the homeowners and shopkeepers and businesses who had waited fifteen long years to reclaim their holdings; some of which was public property and belonged to the municipality and hence the people—required certain zoning and property laws to be rewritten outright. There was very little outcry, except from those who had been swindled out of what they owned, and saw the shares they were given in the company in exchange as poor compensation for their loss. At the time, everyone was invested, either financially or emotionally, in seeing the war come to an end, in seeing a future finally emerge out of the rubble of its past.

Downtown Beirut went from blasted wasteland to massive construction site overnight, with individual lots encircled by steel fences, upon which were digitally rendered images of the buildings that would sprout there, the apartments they would house, and the people who might live there (the vast majority of whom were inexplicably blond). There were also always a few lines of copy richly proclaiming the virtues of these soon-to-be dwellings. Some variation of "exclusive private luxury in the heart of the city" or else "luxurious private exclusivity." Really, the most the copywriters could be bothered with was to scramble the order of these words, occasionally also throwing in promises like "haven" and "retreat" and "elegant" and "singular views."

A general amnesty had been agreed upon as part of the peace accord that ended the war. All was forgiven; no one would be prosecuted or held accountable. The old warlords became the new government; private contracts replaced contract killers; the new city would leave the old war behind by erasing every last trace of it, by the cosmetic overhaul of its ruins. The holding company's slogan, etched into the hundreds upon hundreds of cement barricades erected to mark the limits of its empire, declared Beirut "an ancient city for the future." A rebranding of the old national myth: Beirut, the phoenix, the city that had been destroyed and rebuilt seven times over the centuries, would once more rise, glorious and triumphant, from the ashes.

(Some things that were accidentally exhumed during the re-construction process: mass graves, weapons caches. These were brief blips in the news, immediately buried, or rather, reburied.)

But as anyone with even a minimal grasp of how stories work can tell you, you can't just move forward into the future without some reckoning with the past. Otherwise that shit's just gonna come back to haunt you.

■ ■ ■

Beneath every city, its underground twin. Its dark heart; its churning guts. This is no metaphor: I'm talking about the sewer system. A network of pipes connecting to every shower drain, every kitchen sink, every toilet, disappearing a household's dirt and grease and vomit and urine and feces down the gullets of small pipes that flow down into the ground, that then feed into bigger pipes, and ever bigger pipes, all our shit merging: the or-ganic, fibrous roughage of the rich, the nutrient-deficient poop of the poor, and all the middle-class crap in between, all demo-cratically flowing together in a single system, ideally powered by gravity, ideally leading to the great bowel of a treatment plant meant to, well, treat all this waste, turn it clear again, so that it can be safely dumped into rivers and seas.

Alongside this system, another one. The storm-drainage sys-tem that receives a city's rain and rushes it back from whence it came. A rhythmic cycle, biblical in nature: from river to river, lake to lake, sea to sea. This water is also used to feed the ground-water supply, some of it piped back into wells and tanks. Soil absorbs rain, feeding it into the root systems of crops and flowers and trees; asphalt, concrete do not. As such, streets must be designed to be ever so slightly convex, so that rain may flow to either side and rush down into the storm drains meant to line every one of them. Streets also ought to be kept clear of garbage, not just for aesthetic purposes, but because this water picks up pollutants and trash along its journey and brings them back to our crops, our waterways, our homes. Storm pipes are bigger than sewer pipes: the deluge from above is faster and more powerful than any faucet, any flush.

Ideally, a proportional amount of money is invested in maintaining this invisible city in such a way that it keeps pace with whatever is taking place aboveground. As the population grows, so, too, must the sewer network. As the rains change, becoming rarer, or else more brutal, so, too, must the stormwater system keep up, with storage designed to compensate for the deficits of the dry season, or more expansive pipes to accommodate the assaults of the wet. In some places, these two systems, circulatory and digestive, are combined, both supplies detoxified by the same organ before being released. In others, where they are not, their networks must be kept strictly separate throughout, and any rupture can be as serious and poisonous as poop somehow getting into your bloodstream. Ideally, in both cases, the treatment plants actually work, and the sewage is not just dumped as is into the sea.

■ ■ ■

In that heady first decade and a half after the end of the fighting, before the massive car bomb that would kill the former prime minister and twenty-one other people besides and plunge us into a new era of national strife, there were many who continued to believe that Beirut's face-lift meant that the infrastructure of the old war, too, was being dismantled and renovated. I was of that generation who were too young to have helped make the war, and who now felt old enough to participate in unmaking it. We felt innocent of the past, and therefore not doomed to repeat it.

I remember an immense sense of freedom—we had grown up

confined to an indoor world, to interior corridors and under-ground shelters, and now all we wanted was to roam the city end-lessly, to cross its sectarian lines again and again, no longer hindered by checkpoints. Every meager public space was ours for the taking. We clambered over the railings of the seaside Cor-niche to sit on the moss-slippery rocks and feel the spray of the waves on our faces. We picnicked on Ramlet el-Baida beach, the only public beach in the city, undaunted by the garbage strewn on the white sands—used condoms and used needles, plastic bags and rotting food waste—because there were also paper-winged moths and candy-colored butterflies, a riot of green plants and small, pink flowers, all watched over by the nodding heads of bulrushes, and on clear, windless days, when the sand lay still along the seabed, hundreds of translucent little fish nipping and darting in the filtered sun. As for the fishy, sewagey smell, well—that was just the smell of the sea.

One night we took supplies of wine and beer down with us, as so many others did. Drunk, we ran into the waves stripped down to our underwear beneath the moonshine sky. I remember splash-ing around giddily, then leaping away, screaming nervous laughter when I imagined something might be brushing against my legs.

Sometime later an architect friend showed me a satellite image that had been taken of Beirut, in such high resolution you could zoom in on the dense patchwork of tightly packed blocks and see the individual rooftops of buildings, see who could afford satel-lite dishes and who still kept pigeons. The image had been taken from space, and so from space you could see the two dark lines on either side of the Ramlet el-Baida beach extending out be-neath the deep blue of the sea. Outfalls of raw sewage flowing straight into the water; you could literally see our shit from space. When I swam there I had been afraid of sea monsters lurking beneath the waves. I did not know that the things I should have feared were much, much smaller, measured in parts per million; monsters of our own making.

■ ■ ■

The reconstruction did not stop at the downtown area, it did not stop at reconstruction. More and more buildings are being torn down to make way for towering behemoths that have made the city unrecognizable. There is less of the sky (they cast long, stifling shadows), less of the sea (they block all views, often all access), less of the earth: none of the plans for this new city include parks, include public squares, include spaces for those who cannot afford entrance fees to the private, exclusive luxuries being built all around us. The streets are filthy with construction debris; the din is constant, maddening.

Nor do these plans include any real overhaul of the other city that lurks beneath our feet.

And what we have beneath our feet is a rotting, disintegrating, barely functional sewage infrastructure. Some of the pipes date back to the 1940s. No one knows how old it is. It is notoriously difficult to get any clear "whole network" maps from the municipal offices; many activists—many of them nonpartisan urban planners and architects—have tried. That there is a decided lack of access to information is already a type of information about what sort of city we live in. In the news, it is occasionally announced that engineers have been called in to reroute old systems, build pumping stations at the different outfalls, revamp old treatment plants or build new ones. But the pumping stations remain silent; the treatment plants as well. Running them costs money, eats into profits, withholds the reward of generous bribes for the municipal authorities. Also, there is the fact that the city's sectarian divisions, its original rotten infrastructure, extend all the way down into the underground. There are squabbles about who should host the treatment plants, how to route the sewers, through whose area. Each refuses, literally, to take the other's shit. So they send it to the only place that has always taken our unadulterated shit without complaint: the sea.

However, here's the thing: it is not merely the city changing at an alarming rate. Every year now it rains less—but harder and harder. In a few days the sky will dump down half the annual average in one ferocious storm. The soil, parched from a long, seething summer, cannot handle the violence of the deluge. The water does not feed the crops but washes away the very soil that sustains them. The soil can find no purchase—the trees that once held it in place are fewer and fewer. The mountains, too, have become unrecognizable; the bulldozers have carved great quarries into their sides making way for new developments, the exposed red soil like an angry wound from afar. When it rains that hard the streets flood; people drown in the refugee camps or else are electrocuted by the exposed wiring that turns streams into liquid lightning.

When it rains that hard the sea becomes invisible in the distance; the horizon is a single gray wall of water from earth to sky. It is not hard to imagine that the sea itself is falling upward, roused out of its bed to roar vengeance down upon us: the poison of our shit, our garbage, our waste, the collective punishment of our carelessness both innocent and deliberate having mutated it into a monstrous thing.

■ ■ ■

In 2017, the real estate giant Achour Development broke ground on yet another new luxury seaside resort—right on Ramlet el-Baida beach. Civil society activist groups and local NGOs had been campaigning for years to save the city's last public beach from private development, stepping it up desperately in those last few months: demonstrating, holding press conferences, filing lawsuits against the municipality, loudly warning of irrevocable damage to the social and natural environments. The president of the Beirut Order of Engineers and Architects compiled a report detailing every violation that had been undertaken to allow the construction to go ahead, including the illegal sale and rezoning of land that had been classified as unbuildable, the erasure of the limits of what is, by law, considered the public maritime domain, and the outright forgery of permit material.

None of it made a difference in the end. There is a long precedent here of bulldozing over the laws, of rewriting them to suit private interests. Today, the ghastly, oversized monstrosity, unironically and unimaginatively named Eden Bay, dominates one end of the beach, smugly looking out over the water, its back to the city.

The copy on Eden Bay's website reads, in part: "This luxurious retreat by the sea boasts exquisite accommodation, superior amenities, unmatched hospitality and the exclusivity of your own private community in the city." In all the intervening years the copywriters have learned no new tricks. Why should they? They know what the rich need, what they have always needed: to live in Beirut without living in Beirut, to float above its filth and rot in their own private bubbles, enjoying their singular views, untouched and untouchable.

But what, you might ask, did they do with the outfalls gushing raw sewage into the sea just yards away from Eden Bay's superior amenities?

Why, they did what any shortsighted, profit-minded, cartoonishly evil corporate villain might do.

First, they stoppered that shit up with concrete. Then, they rerouted it into a storm pipe. And then the rains came.

■ ■ ■

In November 2018, I was away from Beirut, briefly, for work. One morning I woke up to find a deluge of WhatsApp messages from various friends and relatives, all forwarding the same few videos. There had been a terrible storm. At one point, hail the size of fists had fallen. In one of the videos, shoppers run screaming as it smashes into the courtyard of a fancy mall. In another, a woman holds up a plastic chair she had on her balcony, so punched through with holes it looks like Swiss cheese. There are brutalized cars, felled trees and electricity poles, a man waterskiing on the northern coastal highway, mudslides in the quarries. The last was of the boulevard overlooking Ramlet el-Baida beach. The water was almost hip-deep if the drowned cars parked on the side of the road were anything to measure by.

But it wasn't water: it was shit. Exploding so forcefully up from the depths that the sewer covers danced atop the flumes, like in a cartoon. Yes, Eden Bay, and all its enablers, had caused a literal shitstorm.

Every so often, beneath the sound of rushing water, you could hear the groans of the man who had taken the video. At one point he giggles in disgust. No one, it seems, can resist laughing at a poop joke.

■ ■ ■

In every home, there is a place of horror, a place in which we must daily encounter the fate none of us can escape. I'm talking about the bathroom, more specifically, the toilet. The toilet, whose gaping maw is supposed to lead things away from our bodies and from our homes, to flush them away and carry them to some unknown place, to keep the shameful secret of our body's vulnerable materiality hidden and thus manageable.

Occasionally, however, it fails to do so. Who among us hasn't endured that moment of flushing the toilet and then, with dread, watching the water not go down as it should in one mighty swallow of the cistern, but rise up, slowly, trembling at the lip of the toilet bowl, threatening to overspill? It is the stuff of nightmares. Not because of the prospect of having to clean that shit up (though there is that, too). No: it is the true, actual stuff of nightmares, where meaning disintegrates, where some ancient, terrible thing emerges from the shadow world. An archetypal monster forged of the life-giving material of the real world, but twisted and transformed to reveal the awful truth that lurks always just beneath its surface. Which is about that which awaits us all in the end: not the sterile nothingness of death, but the horror of putrefaction. These bodies we inhabit, the cherished bodies of those whom we love, they will not only die, they will rot. Until they no longer even resemble something that was once alive.

Turns out the great cosmic joke of existence was a poop joke all along.

■ ■ ■

And so here we are, at the end of this history, in a city rotting from the inside out, for all the peeling, plumping, pulling, and rejuvenating treatment that has gone into its face. It looks, now, like any other aging city, desperately trying to ignore the inevitable reckoning of nature and time. Its glamour shots, taken from the sea to lure in tourists and investors, show a stagger of gleaming, ever-higher, brightly lit buildings rising up from the coast, but they can no longer blot out the real city behind the facade, the corruption beneath its surface.

Because we who live in it are drowning in our own shit. We're swimming in our own shit. We're eating our own shit perpetually now, as it flows back untreated into the groundwater, as it contaminates our crops and seeps into our wells, coming back out of our faucets and gushing over our faces, our bodies, and then back down into the drains, down into the pipes beneath our feet, a rhythmic cycle, biblical in its vengeance.

Perhaps the truest sign of unbridled, irrevocable disaster is when the figurative becomes literal, when the destruction is so large scale it erodes the distance between fact and allegory. The metaphors we use to take a step back from reality, so that we might see it better, become the actual reality we have to contend with. The border between this world and its underground twin collapses, and we have to live with the monsters of our worst nightmares. All that shit we tried to hide, forget, ignore is out now, flooding the streets for all to see. We've all made this shit together. And it is only cataclysm that reminds us of the most obvious corollary: we're all in this shit together.

As such we have arrived at a place where a poop joke can tell the story of a whole city, a whole planet. A poop joke in which the teller is no less than nature itself, trying to relay a moral lesson in a format that even the stupidest among us should have been able to understand, if only we'd stopped laughing and listened instead: If you don't deal with your shit, well, the joke's on you.

MACHANDIZ

Edwidge Danticat

HAITI

THAT SUMMER IN HAITI was the hottest I could remember. My husband and I and our two daughters were visiting my mother-in-law in a small town in the country's south, where we spent the long, scorching days watching World Cup soccer and showing my husband's U.S.-born niece, who was in Haiti for the first time, the sights. Suddenly a whole new generation of both our families, from the millennials to the preteens, wanted to visit Haiti, and they were telling us that they didn't want to visit "Resort Haiti"—which we were not that familiar with anyway—but they wanted to see what they were calling "the Real Haiti," or as real as we, their diaspora, living-abroad relatives could show them.

My mother-in-law could always be counted on to provide a rustic experience. One of the three bungalows on her property—the one we usually slept in—had a thatched roof. Behind our bedroom was a much smaller room where we showered in plastic buckets with water we pumped ourselves from her well. For a more luxurious bath, we could walk down to the river, which my husband's niece did in the most elaborate white ruffled

two-piece bathing suit that anyone in my mother-in-law's village (and probably on most American beaches) had ever seen.
At night we peed in chamber pots if we were too scared to walk
out to the latrine in the dark. The foods we ate were mostly
pulled from my mother-in-law's garden, or had been traded for
other foods from her neighbors' gardens. When we were served
chicken, it was likely that we had met the bird earlier in the day,
which led to my husband, who'd spent his childhood summers
in the area, being the only one eating those meals in their entirety.

Our niece took all of this in the way young people absorb
anything these days, with her smartphone. She texted, Snap-
chatted, Instagrammed, and Facebooked everything to her boy-
friend in Miami, her nine siblings throughout the United States,
and her hundreds of social media followers. She was the only
person we knew who was neither watching soccer nor complaining about the heat.

We did our best to stay one step ahead of the heat. There was
the river, which was crowded with local bathers every afternoon.
We also drove out to the beach, but we could not go in the water.
Most of the beaches on the southern coast of Haiti were covered
in red tide, a form of toxic algae that made the beaches look as
though millions of dead brown leaves were either bobbing on the
waves or had washed ashore. The combination of the algae and
the human-produced waste—plastic and foam containers being
the most prevalent—made it impossible to even approach the
beach, much less swim.

After our niece returned to Miami, we devoted ourselves
more fully to watching the World Cup games in the backyard
of a neighbor who happened to have a television and was charg-
ing people the equivalent of a quarter to watch each game. The

World Cup was an obsession in our area, as it was in the rest of Haiti, where the Brazilian team is a perennial favorite. There were Brazilian flags everywhere—on cars, motorcycles, and homes—not because Brazil had led MINUSTAH, a multibillion-dollar, decade-long United Nations peacekeeping debacle in Haiti, or because thousands of Haitians had migrated to Brazil during the past decade, but because most Haitians claim Brazil's soccer team as their own and many were hoping that the Brazilian team would win a sixth World Cup in the last sixty years.

One scorching early July day, we drove to the home of a family friend in Port Salut, a beautiful coastal town about thirty miles from where we were staying, to watch Brazil face Belgium in the quarterfinals. So many of our friend's neighbors had come to watch the game that he pitched a makeshift tent in front of his house to accommodate us all. When the match ended and Brazil lost, scoring only one goal to Belgium's two, the young woman sitting next to me began sobbing. I thought she was a superfan who was overcome with grief at the loss, but as she rocked herself she said, "What am I going to do with all the machandiz?"

She'd been hoping that the Brazilian team would make it to the finals, she said, and had gotten a high-interest loan to buy Brazil-related merchandise, jerseys, flags, and bracelets, to sell. Now the items would be practically worthless, and she was deep in debt. Her anguish was a reminder that the fate of some of the poorest people in Haiti is linked to factors far beyond their control.

Port Salut felt like a graveyard when we left it that evening, and not just because of the disappointment over the World Cup. During Brazil's final match, the Haitian government had announced that, in order to ensure that the country would qualify for low-interest loans from the International Monetary Fund, it was substantially raising the price of gasoline and diesel. Even the price of kerosene, which was used to light most homes in the Haitian countryside, was going up by 51 percent. We only heard the news on the drive back to my mother-in-law's, when we began receiving messages from family members and friends advising us to get off the roads to avoid running into roadblocks that had been erected in protest. We encountered nearly a dozen on the way, most of them made from piles of rocks and flaming tires and being guarded by anxious young men, some of them armed.

After fleeing one roadblock where a man was shooting in the air, we retreated to a back-road riverbed where we encountered a young moto-taxi driver, who while explaining why he and his friends would not let us through, detailed how the sudden gas hike would chip away at the life they were struggling to build for themselves and their families.

"We want a future, but they keep snatching it away," he said.

Twenty-four hours later, the government announced that it was reversing its decision on the gas hike. Days of nationwide protests followed nonetheless. Haiti's president, Jovenel Moïse, made sometimes scolding and sometimes pleading speeches on television. His prime minister resigned. A new government was formed. But a lingering flame of anger remained. Or, at least, was rekindled.

A year earlier, a Haitian Senate report had detailed how, between 2008 and 2016, funds that had been accumulated through Haiti's participation in Venezuela's oil-purchasing program were misused, misappropriated, or embezzled by government officials and their cronies in the private sector. The Petrocaribe agreement, which Haiti signed over a decade earlier, allowed the Haitian government to buy oil from Venezuela, pay 60 percent of the purchase price within ninety days, and then defer the rest of the debt, at a 1 percent interest rate, over twenty-five years. This debt has grown to almost $2 billion over the past decade. The Haitian government controlled the sale of the oil and was supposed to use those funds for social and development projects, including sanitation and health, at a time when ten thousand Haitians had been killed and nearly a million had been affected by a cholera epidemic that was introduced by the United Nations troops, particularly a group from Nepal. The funds were also supposed to be used to build infrastructure and grow the agricultural sector—the supposed specialty of Moïse, who had nicknamed himself Nèg Bannann, or Banana Man, during his presidential campaign. The funds could have been used, too, for education, one of the stated priorities of Moïse's predecessor, Michel Martelly, whose government had added a $1.50 surcharge on each money transfer to Haiti from abroad to finance free and universal education. (These funds, totaling millions of dollars a year, remain mostly unaccounted for.)

The pilfering of the Petrocaribe funds has been a concern in Haiti for years, but it wasn't until the sweltering summer of the Brazil quarterfinal loss and the gas hike protests, when a Haitian writer and filmmaker named Gilbert Mirambeau, Jr., tweeted a photo showing himself blindfolded like a kidnapping victim, holding a handwritten cardboard sign reading "Kot Kòb Petwo Karibe a???" ("Where is the Petrocaribe money???"), that these grievances began spreading widely online. #KotKòbPetwoKaribea became a popular hashtag, and other Haitians posted images of themselves inspired by Mirambeau's. Anticorruption street protests became larger and more frequent, culminating in massive demonstrations on October 17, 2018, in cities in Haiti and throughout the Haitian diaspora.

I attended a march of around a hundred people in Miami's Little Haiti neighborhood, where, between chants of "Where's the money?" and "Catch the thieves," the protest leaders were already talking about their next outing, on November 18. That date would mark the two hundred and fifteenth anniversary of the Battle of Vertières, the last major conflict fought before Haiti won its independence from France, under the leadership of, among others, the Haitian founding father Jean-Jacques Dessalines, whose death was also being remembered at the October 17 protests.

In a commemorative speech delivered near the site where Dessalines was assassinated, President Moïse promised to fight corruption at the highest levels of power. But it seemed unlikely that his government would perform a satisfactory investigation into the missing Petrocaribe funds—a probe that could implicate himself, his predecessor, and their friends and colleagues.

Right before the anticipated November 18 protests, I was in Haiti for the thirtieth annual meeting of the Haitian Studies Association, an organization made up of scholars who study Haitian history, religion, and culture. While at the conference, I kept hearing about a massacre that had taken place in La Saline, an impoverished neighborhood on the outskirts of Port-au-Prince. When I turned on the television in my hotel room at night, I kept seeing the corpses of men, women, and children, some covered in dried, caked blood, and looking as though they had been hacked with machetes. Interspersed with the images of these cadavers were testimonials by mostly young men recounting how a police truck filled with uniformed officers wearing ski masks, and other officers in civilian clothing, had entered the neighborhood—a stronghold of the Petrocaribe protests—and had shot at everyone and everything in their path.

At that time a notorious gang leader was on the loose with a 2-million-Haitian-gourdes bounty, the equivalent of nearly thirty thousand U.S. dollars, on his head. These young men said they thought that the police were looking for the gang leader, but what they saw were police officers indiscriminately opening fire with machine guns or going into people's homes and dragging people out into the streets. Later Haitian and international news outlets and human rights associations would report that between twenty and seventy-five people, including food vendors and pass-ersby, had died. The residents of La Saline believed that the num-bers were much higher. They were also not convinced that what they were calling a massacre was a result of neighborhood gang warfare, as the Port-au-Prince police chief and many Haitian news outlets were reporting. They were absolutely certain that the killings were an orchestrated effort by the government to keep them and their neighbors from participating in the Petrocaribe protests.

The November 18 protests went on anyway, in Port-au-Prince and throughout the country. The protests were so feared by the gov-ernment that President Moïse did not travel about eighty-five miles north of the capital to the historic site of Vertières, where the day's pivotal namesake battle had taken place. This had been an obligatory visit for previous Haitian presidents, yet Moïse did not make the trip. Instead he laid a wreath in front of a monu-ment related to the day, at the national museum in Port-au-Prince. In the prerecorded seven-minute national address that followed the wreath-laying ceremony at the museum, he urged Haitians to "wake up."

"The time for fighting is over," he said.

The Petrocaribe protesters, many of whom were also calling

for his resignation, disagreed. In some parts of Port-au-Prince and the rest of the country, roads were once again barricaded with burning tires, boulders, and rocks. Still the protests were generally peaceful.

The Haitian government got its gas hike anyway. In early 2019, one of the country's suppliers refused to deliver fuel to Haiti because the government owed it close to $80 million. Because Venezuela, dealing with its own political and economic crisis, was no longer providing discounted fuel to Haiti, the Haitian government was now buying from the U.S. market. The limited fuel supply led to a shortage that brought the price of gasoline to $9.00 a gallon in a country where, according to the World Bank, over half the population of 10.4 million people survive on less than $3.00 a day, and over 24 percent on less than $1.50 a day. Massive, countrywide protests continued through nine consecutive days in February.

From her home in the south, my mother-in-law constantly told us about sheltering in place during the protests, then about the very long lines at the gas stations and the spike in transport and food prices.

"And once the price of food and other machandiz go up, they never come down again," she said. "People will never catch up. It will be more debt, more children not going to school, more and more inequality."

My mother-in-law's use of, among others, the word "machandiz" reminded me of the young woman from Port Salut who'd been so anguished after Brazil lost the quarterfinal match in July, because her Brazil-related merchandise had suddenly lost its value. As I'd watched her cry, it felt to me as though she were crying not just for herself, but for all of Haiti. Listening to my mother-in-law explain how many of the young moto-taxi drivers in her area had trouble finding customers who could afford their new higher prices, I thought of the men who'd stopped us at that riverside shortcut on that scalding July night. I couldn't stop thinking about them and so many others who were constantly having their dreams snatched away. How would they and that young woman continue to survive?

RECORDING IS HIS PRIORITY:
On the Photographs of Lu Guang

Ian Teh

CHINA

> If you want a picture of the future, imagine a boot stamping on
> a human face—forever. —GEORGE ORWELL, *1984*

IN 2005 IN CHINA'S INDUSTRIAL NORTHWEST, a factory worker,
his young face partially obscured by black grime, looks back in-
quiringly at the photographer taking his picture. I know this because if I look closely into the worker's face, in the very blacks of
his eyes, a lone reflected figure, Lu Guang, stands looking

directly at him. The award-winning photographer gained international acclaim turning his unflinching eye on those marginalized in Chinese society, covering sensitive issues such as "AIDS villages" in Henan and industrial pollution. In the footsteps of the great American photographer Eugene Smith, whom he claims to seek inspiration from, Lu makes work that confronts us. As he has said in the past, "Recording is my priority. And of course, I want to solve problems."

A year later, thousands of miles away in a northeast industrial town, I watch coal being fed into a large furnace; giant machinery helps fill multiple cavities from the top of a platform, filling each available space via a funnel. Each slot is an oven designed to cook coal and turn it into coke, fuel modified to burn at higher temperatures for the production of steel—essential raw material for China's skyscrapers and its ever-expanding megacities. Clouds rise as hot coal, cooled rapidly in water, emits a searing sound and a rising plume engulfs workers and buildings nearby. As it reaches rain clouds high up, wind currents blow the vapors east and west, north and south, causing the toxic mass to shift and change, mimicking its innocent cousins before traveling to unknown lands. Back on the ground an entourage of Range Rovers, luxury four-wheel-drive vehicles owned by coal-mine bosses, leave a cloud of gray-yellow dust in their wake. They drive between the metal structures of this large industrial complex, past the coking plant and the steel plant, before turning the corner to exit into the surrounding countryside.

Yellowed grasslands in the far north of Beijing were once populated with grazing sheep and their herders. The rich coal seams and minerals lying beneath these rolling prairies brought mining, and with it, terrible pollution. When the wind blew, smoke and dust from an industrial plant would drift across the

grasslands where herders had grazed their flocks; these animals would fall sick and often die. These vast windswept grasslands have been home to pastoral nomads for thousands of years, but in the end the smoking factories pushed them out, leaving in their wake hundreds of concrete sheep and cattle—a tragic memorial, recorded by Lu, and installed by the local government in an effort to resurrect its pastoral past.

When I first saw Lu's environmental images, circa 2010, I had for some years been making a series of long solo expeditions exploring China's vast industrial crescent, the factories and mines and ruptured lands that dotted the vast expanses of the country's north and west. I was exploring the roots of China's industrial machine and the costs that accompanied it. I saw a dream of a nation, not only the state's ambition for global recognition, but the individual dreams of the many migrant workers who helped build today's China. They were cogs; their desire for a better life meant leaving poorly paid farming jobs for better paid but often more dangerous industrial jobs. This transaction, mixed together with an abundance of coal, helped propel the country forward. The immense scale of this nationwide operation was turning the countryside and its towns into some of the richest and sadly the filthiest in China. The cost was borne by the environment and the people's health. These interconnected themes occupied me for years. In my work I was attempting to answer whether these economic advancements were worth the human and environmental cost; Lu's images, in contrast, in their granular depiction of the human and environmental sacrifice, of all that has been laid to waste, leave no ambiguity. His images do not question the value of market reforms that lifted 800 million Chinese from poverty since the late 1970s; they are instead a heartrendingly persistent reminder of the suffering it took to get there. In a 2015 presentation he made at the Water Philanthropy Forum, his images of industrial pollution left the audience in shocked silence.

In early November 2018 on a trip to Urumqi to lead informal workshops for local photographers, in the resource-rich province of Xinjiang, he was detained. The Chinese province today is better known internationally for confining up to 1 million Muslim Uighurs in internment camps and using high-tech surveillance to monitor its people as part of its alleged antiterrorism policy. No news has been heard from him since except that he was detained—without any charges.* Some years ago he talked of a photograph

---

* At the time of writing, it was reported that Lu Guang had been released after nearly a year of detention in China. The news service Voice of America reported that the photographer's wife, Xu Xiaoli, announced on September 9, 2019, that her husband "has been home for several months," via Twitter. The article went on to say that Lu Guang "is believed to be under surveillance on a residential bail-like release, according to Wen Yunchao, a New York–based former political commentator and family friend."

of his depicting a farmer squatting in a field, outside a village affected by chronic industrial pollution. Villagers would often petition local authorities in these places because of the dramatic rise in illnesses. Lu remarked, "One of my photos, shot in those cancer villages during 2008 to 2010," at the height of the regime's Harmonious Society policy, "shows a government slogan on the wall, 'first time illegal petition, admonition; second time illegal petition, detention; third time illegal petition, reeducation through labor.'" For now we won't truly know Lu's purpose for his visit to Xinjiang; we could look at his past to surmise his intentions, but why bother when we need only look at the state's policy toward those who have persistently challenged the status quo. The writing is, after all, on the wall.

EL LAGO

Eduardo Halfon

GUATEMALA

WE CALLED IT El Lago. The Lake. As kids, growing up in the Guatemala of the 1970s, we probably never even knew its name—Lake Amatitlán. Nor did we care. It was only a winding half-hour drive from the city to my grandparent's chalet on its shore. We spent most weekends of my childhood there, jumping off the wooden dock, learning to swim in the icy blue water, digging out old Mayan pots and relics from the muddy bottom, paddling out on long surfboards while little black fish jumped up through the surface and sometimes even landed on the acrylic board. Gently, we'd nudge them back in.

Early one morning, we all woke up to two indigenous men floating facedown by the wooden dock. They were naked and bloated. Guerrilleros, my father said, his tone far from compassionate or even sympathetic. Guerrilla fighters, probably from one of the surrounding villages. I was still too young to understand that the military would dispose of some of their enemies there, dumping the dead and tortured bodies into the lake. A few weeks later, my grandparents sold the chalet.

■ ■ ■

My father now had a personal bodyguard. I got used to falling asleep at night to the patter of gunfire. The civil war between the military and the guerrillas, which had been taking place primarily in the mountains, had escalated into the city. One day, in the summer of '81, the military fought a faction of guerrillas just outside my school, in the Vista Hermosa neighborhood. The teachers hid all of the children inside an old gym, and we stayed in there for hours listening to the rattle of machine guns, and the earth-trembling explosions of tank mortars, and the hum of military helicopters in the sky. That same night, as my brother and I were getting ready for bed, our parents told us they were selling the house, and we'd soon be leaving the country. We did. We fled on the day of my tenth birthday, to South Florida. I quickly and effortlessly forgot Guatemala, forgot my native Spanish (English just took over), I even forgot about the lake. Until years later, sometime in the late '80s, while on a vacation trip back, I met a girl.

She was a year or two younger than me, and from one of the wealthiest families in the country. Old money. Plantation money. We met one night at a party, and the following afternoon she picked me up in a black Suburban with tinted, bulletproof windows. We both sat in the backseat, smoking some of my first cigarettes, while her chauffeur—armed with a .38 handgun— drove us thirty minutes along the meandering road to her family's chalet by the lake.

Everything inside was abandoned. The sofas and tables in the house were covered with pieces of heavy, cream-colored canvas. There were no chairs to sit on, no dishes in the kitchen, no sheets on the mattresses, no glasses or bottles in the bar. All the windows were draped with black plastic bags. But as deserted and forgotten as the chalet was, when we walked outside I noticed that the lake looked even worse.

The water was no longer a deep, beautiful blue, but a murky brown. Scum and garbage drifted on the surface. There were no people anywhere. No one swimming or sailing. No one boating. No city kids spending their weekend there. No locals fishing out Mayan relics. I looked around and suddenly realized that all of the other chalets in sight weren't just abandoned—they were decrepit, falling apart. Ruins and vestiges of another time.

It was late afternoon. The volcanoes were now barely visible in the distance. I could hear the chirping of bats flying close to the water and just above our heads. As we stepped onto the wooden dock, I was taken back by the stench of something rotting or decomposing. I quickly understood that what was rotting or decomposing was the lake itself. I said something to her about the awful smell, but she just giggled, took off all her clothes, and jumped in.

■ ■ ■

I was driving to the ocean. Or trying to. I had recently turned twenty-five years old and had come to the realization that absolutely nothing in my life made any sense.

I'd been back in Guatemala for almost three years, after having graduated from college in North Carolina. I had been living in the United States for over a decade, as a student, always with a student visa, and when my studies ended, so too did my tenure there, and I was forced to go back to a country I didn't know anymore, to a culture I didn't understand, to a language I could now barely speak. I attempted to settle in, working as an engineer, in construction, but was overwhelmed by a feeling of extreme frustration, of profound angst, which only kept getting worse. *Desubicado* is the word in Spanish. Out of place. Or misplaced. But misplaced emotionally, spiritually, not just physically (I wouldn't stumble onto books and literature and writing until a few years later, which probably saved me).

And there I was, in my car, running away from something or

from everything, trying to get to the ocean on perhaps the worst day to do it. Most of the roads out of the city were blocked for security reasons, because of the ceremony taking place downtown later that week: after thirty-six years of war, the military and guerrillas were finally signing a peace accord. The country was already teeming with international observers, foreign presidents, dignitaries, journalists. I was forced, then, to take another route out of the city: the winding, all-too-familiar road that went by the lake.

Even that road, however, as I discovered when I got there, was blocked. Not because of the peace-signing ceremony in the city, but because of a large mob of local onlookers that had gathered next to the lake. I parked my car on the median and got out.

The entire shore was a blanket of dead silvery fish.

■ ■ ■

He was still there. He had never left, back when everyone else did. His chalet, although old and weary, remained standing, and he was there standing with it, every weekend. Like a captain who refuses to abandon his sinking ship. Or like one of those Japanese soldiers who wandered around for decades, in uniform, looking for the enemy, because nobody remembered to tell them the war had ended.

He'd been my pediatrician, in the 1970s. Then he also became a renowned medical anthropologist. Now, as I turned forty-five, he was my son's great-grandfather.

We were lying in two beach chairs next to each other, in front of the lake—he, as always, and notwithstanding his ninety-plus years, in a slim Speedo—while we waited for the volcanic water in the hot tub to cool down a bit. He'd just finished telling me about his kidnapping in the early '80s by a group of soldiers, who apprehended him one morning just outside his clinic (the waiting room, I recall, was always crowded not only with wealthy Guatemalan kids, but also with the very poor and indigenous, whom he treated for free). The soldiers jostled him into a military jeep and drove him to the barracks. One of his sons and two of his daughters were guerrilla fighters, in hiding, and the military government of Efraín Ríos Montt—who would later be tried and convicted of crimes against humanity and genocide—wanted information on where they were. He didn't know. He couldn't tell them anything, and didn't, despite brutal and prolonged torture. After thirty days, and because of strong international pressure on the government, especially from the Red Cross, he was released.

Next to me, in his beach chair, he kept glancing at his black digital watch. I knew why. No drinks before noon.

The lake in front of us was a thick green. A pea-soup green. It seemed emptier, smaller. Its putrid smell was now everywhere. I asked him about the lake's current condition. He'd been there for over half a century. He'd been a witness to its rise in popularity as a weekend destination, and its subsequent downfall. He'd seen the construction and destruction of all the chalets on its perimeter. He'd seen its blue, pristine waters turn green and thick and foul. He'd seen all the little black fish disappear.

It's in the last stages, he said. Two main causes. First, years of runoff from all the chemicals and pesticides used by the surrounding agricultural farms. And second, untreated sewage and industrial waste coming downriver from Guatemala City, an estimated half a million pounds of sediment per year. It is suffering from hypertrophication, he explained, which is the excess of minerals and nutrients and is the reason why the water turned green with algae. And it's also suffering from siltification, the pollution of water by particulate terrestrial clastic material. He was speaking clinically, without emotion: a doctor talking about his patient. He said that, ultimately, it all came down to human and institutional neglect. He told me that experts foresee the lake drying out completely within a few decades, the long-term effects of which will be catastrophic for the ecosystem of the entire region. And meanwhile, he went on, the indigenous people here have lost their livelihood, their main source of income, not just their vacation homes. He sighed. He stood up slowly, almost painfully. Half grinning, he said that the bar was now open, and went off to the house to fetch us a couple of whiskeys.

I stayed there, lounging in the beach chair, looking out at the green waters before me, trying to think back to the midnight blue they once were. The sky was cloudless. The sun on my face felt warm and pleasant. In the distance, on the opposite side of the lake, I could just make out part of what had been my grand-parents' chalet. The red-tiled roof, the front yard leading down to the water, some eucalyptus trees I'd helped plant in the black earth by the shore, the rickety wooden dock. And seeing the dock I suddenly remembered—word for word—the secret prayer I used to whisper before jumping from its edge into the cold water. Like an incantation. Like some sort of magic spell. I was afraid of discovering in the water the floating dead body of my father's older brother, or he who would have been my father's older brother. His name was Salomón. He'd drowned in the lake when he was five years old, next to the dock, but they never found his body. Or so they told me.

THE SONG OF THE FIREFLIES

Gaël Faye

Translated by Sarah Ardizzone

BURUNDI

I'VE BOUGHT A PIECE of forest as a present for the children, and we've built a cabin on it so we can sleep there. I recently came across this sentence, in my father's handwriting, on the back of a photo from 1988. In the slightly blurred image, my sister and I are sitting on our father's knees, in front of a simple wooden shelter. My father had just acquired a hill at the entrance to the village of Musigati in northwestern Burundi, on the edge of the Kibira National Park, the largest and most ancient forest reserve in the country. Musigati was a tiny commune at the time, situated in a valley, its only public spaces a modest local-foods market and the occasional small shop. In the abundant wilderness of the surrounding hills, dwellings were few and far between.

Since the nineteenth century, Burundi, a land of hills and agriculture, has become one of the most densely populated countries on the African continent. Demographic pressure has shaped the landscape across significant parts of the territory. Indigenous species have disappeared and plant life has declined, due to the combined pressures of cattle herds, bushfires, and tree felling for construction and charcoal, as well as the cultivation of lands. Which explains why my father didn't think twice about buying "a piece of forest," when he stumbled across the Musigati region. If he fancied himself as Henry David Thoreau, he had found his Walden. A little less than forty miles from the capital, Bujumbura—where we lived— there still existed a wild region, almost virgin to the stamp of mankind, and to the famous "progress" grandly trotted out in the political rhetoric of the time.

At the end of each school week, we would clamber into my father's battered pickup truck for a four-hour expedition along the dusty, bumpy road to Musigati. My father's plot was a hill of several hectares, covered in dense vegetation and home to considerable wildlife, including birds, rodents, and reptiles. A path led all the way to a clearing at the top of the hill, where we had erected a wooden cabin without doors or windows, covered with a simple straw roof. Inside, we slept directly on the beaten earth floor, in sleeping bags.

At nightfall, we enjoyed heading off on foot, following the complex tangle of paths that interlinked the dwellings on the hillsides. On moonless nights, in the darkness of this region without electricity, the paths were lit up by a multitude of fireflies, suspended like supernatural garlands from the plants. It seemed to us, back then, as if a thousand fires were setting the night and forest aglow. When, for an instant, I held a firefly in the palms of my hands, I would boast to my father that I had caught a star. Today, the memory of that nocturnal sense of wonder, offered by nature on the hills of Musigati, still conjures up the deep enchantment of childhood.

In 1993, following a violent coup d'état, and the army's assassination of the first democratically elected president of the republic, Melchior Ndadaye, the country fell into a terrible and bloody civil war. Musigati wasn't spared and numerous massacres took place in those surrounding hills. The village was transformed into a camp for displaced persons. Armed Hutu groups withdrew into the Kibira forest to fight the regular army, principally composed of Tutsi. The road to Musigati became dangerous, with the rebels planting antitank mines, and ambushes occurring regularly in the region. And yet, despite the risks, my father continued to head to his hill every week.

The war lasted over ten years. The country was subjected to a trade embargo, while periods of drought affected many areas, leading to terrible famines. This was the case in Musigati. I can recall my shock in 1998, when I stood opposite a group of children suffering from kwashiorkor, with their bleached hair and potbellies, staring at me with keen deep-sunk eyes.

In 2005, following the peace accords under the aegis of the Tanzanian and South African presidents, Julius Nyerere and Nelson Mandela, the country regained a fragile peace. Development projects were launched left, right, and center. A tarmac road linked Bujumbura to Bubanza. Overnight, Musigati found itself one hour from the capital. Electricity was brought to the region and the population exploded in a matter of years. Increasing demographic pressure forced the countrymen to cut back the Kibira forest a little more each day, and this in turn exacerbated soil erosion.

In recent years, the political rhetoric about progress and democracy has slowly given way to talk of global warming and its consequences for the country. Burundi is being affected by increasingly prolonged periods of severe drought, as well as violent episodes of torrential rain that cause considerable damage. The rise in the temperature of Lake Tanganyika has led to the disappearance of local fish, while malaria has now reached those regions of high altitude previously spared. In addition, scientific reports suggest that the average American—irrespective of social class—emits as much carbon dioxide as over five hundred Burundians; yet the consequences of climate change weigh far more heavily on countries such as Burundi, where populations are particularly vulnerable, than on the big emitter countries in the northern hemisphere.

Today, Musigati has become a provincial town. The forest that used to cover my father's hill has been cut down in favor of manioc fields. Wherever the gaze rests, nature has been domesticated. At night, the halo of artificial lights has replaced the fireflies. Those glowing insects have disappeared and no longer illuminate the way for nocturnal walkers. For thirty years, Musigati has contended with wars, epidemics, famines, and poverty. In this remote village, in one of the poorest countries on earth, each day is a struggle for survival. The disappearance of the fireflies is a nonevent for its inhabitants, a paltry phenomenon compared to the demands of daily life. In 1975, in an article in *Corriere della Sera*, the Italian poet Pier Paolo Pasolini wrote: "In the early sixties, due to air pollution and, above all, in the countryside, due to water pollution . . . , the fireflies began to disappear. This phenomenon was swift and searing. Within a few years, there were no fireflies left."

The disappearance of the fireflies from my childhood is a silent metaphor for the climatic upheaval creeping up on us, its footsteps so stealthy we can still feign not to hear them. These upheavals threaten life on earth and its ecosystems, foreclosing the future of humanity, and imperceptibly destroying the poetic song of the world.

THE RAINS

Ligaya Mishan

HAWAI'I

IN THE EVENING it started to rain, pooling in the backyard until the earth couldn't swallow it anymore and the grass went under, a jade gleam like a rice paddy. Then it started coming in, finding the weakness under the sliding doors, seeping and spilling so gently across the white tile of the living room, almost apologetically, because it had nowhere else to go.

In Hawai'i, it rains almost every day, but for the most part gently, at the edges of waking life, early in the morning and again at night, what the weather reporters duly describe as passing windward and mauka (mountain) showers. When it does fall during the day, you can usually see it before you feel it, dark clouds massing in a corner as the rest of the sky stays that ridiculous blue, a color impossible to prove to anyone who doesn't live here. It can feel like rain is a place apart, with borders; you can drive out of it in a minute—walk out of it, even, by simply crossing to the sunny side of the street. The ancient Hawaiians had more than two hundred names for rain, as documented in the book *Hānau Ka Ua* (2015), by Collette Leimomi Akana with Kiele Gonzalez. Among them: kili noe, misty and fine, and kili 'ohu, mistier still; kuāua, windless; 'awa'awa, cold and bitter; apo pue kahi, the rain after a loved one dies. Sometimes a storm rolls through as if too busy to dally. Sometimes there are no clouds, just drops far apart and fat as tears, while the sun keeps going, untroubled, too above it all to care.

And sometimes the rain is forever and everywhere. Our house, on the eastern side of O'ahu, had always held firm, through lashings of hurricanes with Xs of masking tape on our windows, through flash floods that swelled out of the concrete canal built to hold it in, up on the hill between Haleola and Anolani and snaking down the valley. But now the living room was breached, and my mother, who turned eighty this year, was alone; I was in New York, six hours ahead and useless. After my father died nine years ago, she said it seemed to rain harder. She'd bought a pump for the backyard, and when that gasped and failed she'd bought a second one. The handyman who helped her around the house with leaks, jammed light switches, and obstinate appliances had just put in a new drainage system. She called him now and he promised to head out to the rescue. Ten minutes later he called back: Kalaniana'ole Highway was a river, cars abandoned in water a foot deep, flashers pulsing. The city had shut it down. Nobody could get into the valley, or out.

She went in search of towels, stacks of them from a hoard of decades, some so brittle and stiff they seemed less likely to soak up water than to float on it. (To me, a few of them still bore a faint whiff of our dogs, long dead, who'd slept on them at night in the hall—although my mother told me that was impossible, since she'd cut up those towels for housecleaning rags long ago.) First she tried to cram them under the doors, hoping to stanch the flow, but it was insistent, biblical; so she laid them out in a patchwork on the floor. By now the water had risen over the rug, lapping the legs of the furniture. She couldn't move any of it by herself—her hands were rigid from arthritis—so she stood on the step that marked the threshold of the room, taking stock, maybe even saying good-bye, consigning it all to rot. I'd worried about that step as my mother got older, so easy to slip and miss, but those were necessary inches now, holding the water at bay. She dried her feet, went back to the bedroom, closed the door and fell asleep. She said, "I just had to surrender."

■ ■ ■

My mother is at once a worrier, which is my inheritance, and something of a fatalist—or, more precisely, she is a believer: she trusts that God will see her through. This was not her first disaster, and not even her first disaster that year. Three months before, on January 13, 2018, at 8:07 A.M., the Hawai'i Emergency Management Agency had sent a statewide alert to every cell phone and TV screen, announcing an imminent ballistic missile attack: "SEEK IMMEDIATE SHELTER. THIS IS NOT A DRILL." Tensions had been running high between the United States and North Korea, which is less than five thousand miles from Hawai'i; from the Tongchang-ri launch site, an ICBM outfitted with a nuclear warhead could reach the islands in less than twenty minutes.

When I was growing up during the Cold War, air-raid sirens were tested on the first working day (to me, school day) of every month. It was a distant wail so familiar I barely registered it, and only as a reminder of passing time. At some point in the nineties, the sirens stopped; perhaps everybody envisioned a world suddenly at peace. In 2017, they started again, to my Californian husband's dismay on an otherwise serene Christmas visit. It hadn't occurred to me to explain, or that one day the warning could be real.

At 8:45, another alert came through. The powers that be had quickly determined this was a false alarm—apparently the wrong message had been clicked on a drop-down menu—but took thirty-eight minutes to share the delightful news with everyone.

I was in New York, in my own life, ignoring the world, so by the time I heard about it, the crisis was over. My mother didn't even call. She texted: "Missile attack siren! Early this morning. What was I supposed to do? 15 min to prepare for death?"

She never told me how she spent those thirty-eight minutes between life and death. I asked; she evaded. And when the flood came three months later, on the night of April 13, she said much the same thing, with a shrug in her voice: "I couldn't stop it. There was nothing I could do."

■ ■ ■

A few hours after the flood began, the water receded, and the rain, which had been falling at a rate of two to four inches per hour, slowed and ceased. The drowned towels were so heavy my mother couldn't lift them; her housekeeper, who came twice a month, made an extra trip to help her hang them in the yard. She sent out the rug to be cleaned, but a stain persists, as do stray marks around the legs of chairs, like a nipping at the ankles. For days afterward, she saw waterlogged furniture dumped all along the side of the highway, and knew that she was lucky: the water in the house had run clean and left no mud. ("I didn't even have to wash the towels," she said.) Elsewhere on O'ahu, there had been power outages and mudslides. The government took weeks to clear over eight hundred tons of debris. Acres of crops in Waimānalo were lost. Students were displaced from a mud-ravaged school on the makai (ocean) side of Kalaniana'ole. My beloved 'Āina Haina Library, where I malingered for much of my childhood, was so severely damaged it didn't reopen for a year.

Far worse was visited on Kaua'i, the storm's second destination. On the island's North Shore, 49.69 inches of rain fell in twenty-four hours, according to a gauge at Waipā Garden, which was verified by the National Climate Extremes Committee as the new record for twenty-four-hour precipitation in the United States. In total, 54.37 inches fell, most of it in three ruinous bursts: just under 20 inches in seven hours on Saturday, April 14; another 18 inches in five hours after midnight; and 8 inches in a little over two hours later that morning. People paddled surfboards down roads under six feet of water to help with evacuations. Cowboys rode Jet Skis to lasso buffalo swept into Hanalei Bay and stranded on the reef.

The farmers may have suffered most. Taro patches, representing close to 85 percent of the state's crop, were choked with silt, making the plant's bulbs go loliloli (spongy)—no good for poi, the sticky lilac taro paste that is a local staple, its texture measured by how many fingers you need to lift it to your lips: one finger at its thickest, three if it runs. Within a month, restaurant suppliers were complaining of shortages and likening taro to gold. It was more than that, a link to Hawai'i's past, before contact with the West, when the islands were self-sufficient and poi was eaten by the pound—up to fifteen pounds a day in some tales—keeping the people alive. To understand taro's importance in Hawaiian culture, you must know that it was present at the creation: When the Sky Father's first child was stillborn and buried, taro rose from the grave. The second child, the little one whom the elder taro had to tend and protect, was us.

■ ■ ■

Have the rains grown heavier since my father died? I still remember the New Year's Eve flood of 1987, up to seventeen inches of rain in some parts of east O'ahu, forcing the evacuation of thousands, with hundreds winding up in emergency shelters. My father recorded the aftermath with his video camera, walking the valley, panning over sideways trees and the brown torrent in the canal. He ended each clip with the old radio communication code *Over*, as if he were sending a message, although to whom, I'll never know.

Living on an island—on what is technically the most remote island chain on earth, more than a thousand miles from another country, more than two thousand miles from the nearest continent—we'd always been aware of our vulnerability to the weather, attuned to the possibility of disaster. Both of my parents were children during the Second World War, my father in England and my mother in the Philippines, and they took that memory of survival as a guide: much of the stock in our larder was in cans or powdered form. We had matches and flashlights at the ready lest a hurricane cut the power. I did not live next to a volcano, or at least not an active one, a fact I found tiring to repeat to boys at college on the mainland. (Their come-ons tended to feature either volcanoes or little grass shacks.) But on the Big Island, Kīlauea has been in constant eruption since 1983. In April 2018, one of its craters collapsed; a billion cubic yards of lava were later expelled—enough, as noted in a report by the Hawai'i Volcano Observatory, "to fill at least 320,000 Olympic-sized pools"—burying thirty miles of roads and more than seven hundred homes. Ash-white vog (volcanic smog) often drifts to the other islands, a veil over the sky that turns into a photo filter at dusk, bumping up the reds and golds and turning the sky bruise purple. You might have trouble breathing, but the sunsets are beautiful.

We learned about tsunamis at school, the deadliest smashing into the Big Island on April Fools' Day in 1946. Tsunami warnings had their own siren, a long steady blare, unlike the banshee oscillation that would greet a missile. When I briefly lived in an apartment by the ocean—not quite on it, but able to see a sliver of it from the window of my tiny, makeshift bedroom, cordoned off by a curtain from the living room—I checked the tsunami evacuation zone map at the front of the phone book to see how far I'd have to run if a wave hit. (Just across Kapiʻiolani Park, it turned out.) The only tsunami watch I can recall from recent years was not long before my father died, after a magnitude 8.3 earthquake off the Kuril Islands, northeast of Hokkaido, Japan. He and my mother packed up the car and drove around the corner to the next street up, supposedly all the higher ground they needed. They parked and waited, and when they got tired of waiting, they drove home.

■ ■ ■

This was just the way things were, and yet. In the violence of that April's rain, a number of scientists saw not an aberration, but the future. Temperatures are rising, as they have been all century: In May, twenty-seven record highs were set or matched across the state; in the first two and a half weeks of June, another eighteen. The trade winds are shifting, too, northeasterly turning easterly and weaker, less effective at cooling. A warmer atmosphere means more moisture in the air, feeding clouds for future storms, and less moisture in the soil, so it dries out faster—paradoxically leading to less rain and more rain at once, longer periods of drought and more abrupt, catastrophic storms, born of "disturbances," as the linguists of weather call them, and "increasing instability." Sea levels are rising, which may make the tsunami evacuation zone maps moot. We're told to expect more freakish "rain events," more extreme weather, like the storm in February that brought waves cresting 60 feet, wind gusts up to 191 miles per hour, and snow on Maui, at an elevation of just 6,200 feet.

My mother was right. It has been raining harder.

■ ■ ■

Later, when we talk about the flood on the phone, she corrects me, as she's done a hundred times: it wasn't the living room that flooded, but the dining room—after I left home, she'd moved the dinner table so that guests could have a view of the garden, her opus of many years' labor. But in my memory, we ate in that room only on special nights, huddled over folding TV tray tables, watching the Olympics, maybe, or *Murder, She Wrote*. I still come home expecting the living room, my living room, and when confronted by the new arrangement I don't know where to sprawl or curl up with a book; the front room, theoretically the new living room, gets less light and is haunted by the specter of the upright piano in the corner. (I never practiced enough.)

I can't seem to adapt to the new house inside the old one. And it keeps changing, like the island itself. Come December, in the car from the airport, I'm again surprised by the heights of buildings and the houses inching ever farther up the mountains, more each year, a game of Monopoly gone amok. I think, I can't stop it: my mother's daughter.

Even as I write this, a flash flood warning is once again in effect on Oʻahu, in June, historically a dry month. I read the news on my phone in the morning, New York time: rain falling at a rate of up to three inches per hour, the wettest June day on record, flooding, power outages, road closures, three people struck by lightning. A disturbance.

It's too early to call my mother, and by the time I do, the rain in the valley has stopped. She is fine. It rains every day in Hawaiʻi, she reminds me. *Over.*

THE WELL

Eka Kurniawan

Translated by Annie Tucker

INDONESIA

AS A CHILD, Toyib was fond of a girl who lived on the other side of the village, named Siti. In the mornings, he would sit in front of his house waiting for her to appear on her way to school, which was in a neighboring settlement. Together they would walk along the footpath that unfurled beside the open expanse of paddy fields. Sometimes other friends came along, but the best was of course when it was just the two of them.

Then, one night, Toyib's father fought with Siti's father. The fight ended with Toyib's father slitting Siti's father's stomach open with a machete, leaving him collapsed on the ground with his guts spilling out and blood pooling in the grass near the village floodgate. Siti's father could not be saved, and Toyib's father fled into the jungle. He was on the run for two days and nights, but the police gave chase and easily captured him.

There were no more walks to and from school for Toyib and Siti. There were no more large, flush rose apples picked from Toyib's garden and saved for Siti. There were no more gifts of little chicks from Toyib to Siti, so she could watch them grow until it was time for them to be slaughtered and cooked the night before Eid. Siti didn't want to see Toyib anymore, or anyone else in his family. And Toyib didn't have the courage to face Siti, her mother, or her little sisters.

■ ■ ■

There had once been a spring on the ridge, which flowed into a swamp filled with mangroves. When the water was abundant, the swamp deepened into a clear pond. Geese flocked there, and at night it flickered with fireflies. In the dry season, the swamp would recede into a mud wallow where buffalo jostled about. It was this spring that made Toyib's father and Siti's father lose their senses, one drawing his machete, the other his scythe. One put in his grave, the other in prison.

From the spring flowed a channel, which then split into two. Each branch flowed to a network of paddy fields, one on either side of the village. In the past, children would swim in that channel, with its ever-flowing current. The men would look for fish in the small inlets, especially eels and catfish. The women would forage for mussels and clams to feed their children, which helped them grow up hale and hearty.

But that was before. In recent years they had watched as the pond more often stayed a wallow. Rain rarely fell and the dry season lengthened to eleven months out of the year. Of course, there was only a small amount of water that now flowed through the channel, and even less of it reached the fields. That small amount of water still had to be shared, and so, right where the channel branched into two, they installed a floodgate.

As might be expected, disputes now broke out more frequently between the owners of the fields on either side of the village. Tempers flared more easily when the harvest no longer yielded much, and the villagers could see their children were no longer growing up hale and hearty. The smiles evaporated from the women's faces, and the wisdom leaked from the men's eyes. This all reached its peak in the fight between Toyib's father and Siti's father.

■ ■ ■

Four years and eight months, that was how long Toyib's father stayed in prison, after his sentence was reduced for good behavior. By the time he was released, Toyib was already an adolescent, fifteen years old. His father told him how, in jail, he had learned to repair motors—for cars, motorbikes, tractors, chain saws, lawn mowers, all kinds. He had become so skilled that the prison guards often asked him for help. He had been paid for his work, and he had been saving the money all this time.

"I always think of my dear friend," his father said. "When we were kids, we went out looking for firewood together, stole mangoes from Old Hajji's tree together, and guarded the village together. I still don't understand how my eyes clouded over and my blade took his life."

Toyib watched his father's eyes well with tears.

"I want to give his family all the money I earned in prison. You're good friends with Siti, aren't you? Would you like to take it to them?"

Toyib didn't have the heart to say that he was no longer friends with Siti, that he had never spoken with her again after the incident. Instead he nodded, ready to bring her his father's money.

■ ■ ■

At that time the channel no longer had any water in it at all, and the spring had shrunk into a small mudflat surrounded by a widening swath of dry earth. The mangrove trees first grew stunted and then slowly disappeared. The ones that remained began to rot. The fields were left barren, as the villagers would only plant them if there was a good chance rain would come. Sometimes the rain was in fact accommodating, even though the resulting harvest never made them smile, but more often than not their efforts were in vain.

One by one, people began leaving the village. If they didn't move altogether, to settle somewhere new, they went to the city to look for work. Those who stayed behind were left to endure the daily search for water.

Now the only source they could rely on was a well in a valley behind a small mountain on the far side of their settlement. That well was the umpteenth hole they had dug, the only one that gave water—and that was after they had dug almost sixty-five feet down.

Siti had the responsibility of fetching water for her family, which now was just her mother and her two younger sisters. Every morning, she would climb the small mountain and descend into the valley with an empty bucket, and then return home hauling a bucket full of water on her back. Toyib did the same thing for his household, but as long as his father had been in prison he had always taken pains to avoid Siti.

Until that afternoon, when he met her at the well.

■ ■ ■

They looked at each other, their emotions in chaos. Even at their young age, they could see the suffering of the village etched into each other's faces—suffering from the tragedy at the spring, suffering from the fields that lay fallow, the livestock that had been lost, and the interminable exhaustion of having to haul water every morning and afternoon. Above all they could plainly see the longing for each other that they each fruitlessly tried to hide.

"How are you, Siti?"

"Well. And you?"

"Stronger than a leopard."

Toyib wanted to make her laugh like he used to, but the girl barely lifted the corners of her lips up into a smile. Instead she bowed her head, looking down at the bucket near her feet, which was already full, and the small pail with a very long rope used to draw water from the well. Toyib felt so awkward that for a moment he could say nothing more, but seeing the girl move as if about to lift her bucket, he decided to voice his intentions for meeting.

He told her about his father's return, and the matter of the money. Toyib reached into his pocket for the small bundle of cash wrapped in newspaper, secured with a rubber band. He offered it to her. He didn't know how much was inside, his father hadn't told him. He just knew it was all the money his father had saved in prison.

Siti looked up at him. Two small furrows appeared in her cheeks. She shook her head and said, "No."

The girl walked away with the pail full of water tied onto her back with a cloth whose pattern was fading. Toyib stood at the mouth of the well, with the bundle of money in his hand, watching her go. The bucket on her back wasn't big, but still she stooped under its weight, staggering down the slopes of the hill along the rocky footpath. With such a small bucket, who knows how many times she had to go back and forth for water every day.

Toyib was lost in that reverie when he saw the girl stumble. Then one of her feet slipped on a pebble or some slippery grains of sand, and she lost her balance. Toyib cried out, but he couldn't stop anything. The girl's body was twisted, pulled down by the heavy pail of water on her back. She fell to the earth, and went rolling down the hill, drenched, before her hand managed to grab the branch of a bush. She lay there, her now empty bucket thrown out of her reach.

Without saying a word, Toyib ran to help her up. There were

scrapes and cuts on her arms and legs. He wanted to embrace her, to take her in his arms and carry her home. He almost did so, but the girl drew back and looked away. Toyib caught sight of her tearstained face. As he reached for her, Siti ran off down the hill without a word, without looking back.

Toyib was left alone. He didn't realize that a number of villagers, who of course had also come to draw water from the well, had seen it all. They just looked on silently, knowing everything and not needing to interfere.

Toyib took the bucket the girl had left behind, went back to the well, filled it with water, and carried it to her house.

■ ■ ■

After that day, villagers often saw the youth carrying a yoke hung with two pails full of water from the well to fill the water trough at the girl's house, going back and forth until it was full. The creak of the bamboo pole straining on his shoulder sounded shrill, splitting the silence of the hillside. He did it at dawn, when people were returning from the prayerhouse, before he went to fetch water for his own family. Day after day.

He did it without saying much. He knew that Siti knew what he was doing. He could sense her watching him through a crack in the bamboo wall of her house—her gaze upon him was a palpable fondness mixed with poignant grief—but she said nothing. Toyib took her silence as agreement, so he kept doing it, as a sincere obligation. Then one day, the feeling suddenly vanished. He was uneasy the whole day. The next morning, when he came again bearing the yoke, he could tell that warm, sad glance was truly gone.

After he filled the water trough, just as the first rays of sunlight appeared, he approached the front door and knocked nervously. A middle-aged woman stood before him—Siti's mother.

A little awkwardly, he repeated what he had said to Siti about his father's money and, of course, his father's regret. The woman smiled and invited him to come in and sit down.

"I know your father never meant to do what he did."

"Please take it."

The bundle of money had been once again prepared, and this time, despite some initial hesitation, it was received by Siti's mother. Toyib was happy—at least this would lighten his father's burden of guilt, and ease the day-to-day burdens of Siti's life with her mother and her little sisters.

Then he asked, "Where is Siti?"

The woman asked in return, "You don't know? Didn't she tell you? She left for the city two days ago, to stay with a relative. To look for work."

■ ■ ■

He still filled the trough at Siti's house every morning for years, pouring out the water he had drawn, along with his feelings of unimaginable loss. Every afternoon he would go stand on the parched and crumbled earth of the dry fields, look out at the browning hills, and ask himself what kind of curse had struck the village to make him and everyone here suffer so.

With his father, he cared for three goats and a cow. They had owned these for a long time, and used to have more, but had sold the rest off one by one after his father was put in jail and the yield of the gardens and fields became truly erratic. While waiting for a rainy season that never seemed to arrive, they had to go to the farthest reaches of the forest to look for any remaining grass.

Every morning, after hauling water for Siti's house and his own, Toyib would set out, carrying a sickle and an empty basket. His father would join him around midday, after trying his best to water their garden plot, planted with cassava and tubers. His father would tell him how the elephant grass used to grow all around the outskirts of the village, and the goats and the cows could just be left free to graze. Toyib didn't remember that time, maybe it was already too long ago. All he thought about was how to keep the remaining goats and cow alive.

He was now past twenty-one years old. For the first time, his father suggested Toyib propose to a young woman from the next village. Toyib immediately refused, without even considering it. Four months later, his father volunteered again, to propose to two different girls on Toyib's behalf, but he still refused.

In those days, Toyib's father could see his son's withering morale—once he almost hacked off his own leg with a scythe. He would stand in the middle of the forest staring into space, next to an old teak tree that had lost almost all its leaves, without finding any grass. His father knew there was no girl Toyib wanted, except the one who had left for the city and hadn't yet returned. Siti.

"When I was in prison, the guy who taught me machine repair worked in a garage. Right before my release, he came to me and said that if I wanted, I could stay in the city and work for him. I've been thinking about this the past few years, since there's nothing left for us to do here. We can sell our goats and our cow, to leave your mother and younger brother with a little money. I've decided. I'm going to go, and I invite you to come with me."

His father saw a flashing gleam of hope in Toyib's eyes.

The hope of finding Siti.

■ ■ ■

Soon before their departure, rain fell without warning. Toyib hesitated, because rain meant the chance to sow rice in the paddies or plant their garden. The grass would grow in a few days and that would give the goats and cow a chance to fatten up. But his father said, rain like this won't fall for long, it won't be enough for the rice to grow big enough to harvest. He insisted it would be better for them to go to the city and work in the garage. His father didn't want Toyib's hopes of meeting the girl to be swept away.

But the rain kept falling the following day, even heavier, and the day after that. Toyib tried to discourage his father, as they looked out at the downpour pelting the rocks. Still his father, who knew how much it hurt to be so far from someone who lit up your life, was unmoved and said they would go.

"Your mother and your little brother can plant the rice. If the rain really does continue and everything gets better, we can always come home. We can buy other goats and cows—we can buy kids and calves even, and you can fatten them up. But meanwhile, we will go to the city and work in the garage. Look around—there are no other sons or daughters your age still holding out in this village, except for you."

His father's words made Toyib's yearning for Siti grow stronger.

■ ■ ■

That day, the rain had been falling for three days and nights, in a torrential flood. The storm was truly like nature venting some incomprehensible rage—after the long drought that had lasted for more than a year, it was as if the sky was suddenly and all at once unleashing all the water it had been withholding.

They had been ready since morning. At first they were hoping the rain would dissipate toward midday, but it gave no signs of letting up—instead, the storm gathered force. Outside, the rain had turned the world white. Occasionally they could see something go flying past—maybe a coconut frond, or a goat pen. His mother tried to convince them to postpone their journey until the following day, but his father was convinced that the next day, and the day after that, there would be no difference.

"Better we leave right now."

They put on their worn raincoats, holes patched with pieces of used tarp. They tied their small pack of clothes up tightly and wrapped it in plastic. They covered their shoes with crinkly grocery bags.

To go to the city, they had to walk through seven settlements before reaching a main road. There they could take a dilapidated old bus to the nearest small town, one and a half hour's journey away. In between the sixth and seventh settlements, there was a river that had at one time been very big. Even though now, with its wide banks, the remnants of its size were still evident, the water that flowed through it was more the level of a small ditch. If the people in the valley got their water from the well, they usually brought their goats and cows to this river.

After walking through the driving rain, the father and son now stood on the riverbank. For the first time in years, they saw the water in the river surging wildly. The thundering and threatening brown waves bore whole palm-tree trunks downstream. They were stunned, but didn't have much time to watch the turmoil.

There was a simple suspension bridge connecting one bank of the river with the other, its deck made from spliced bamboo and its handrail from a thick wire. The bridge was now swaying back and forth violently, as the waves of the river, only one fathom underneath, rose up in voracious licking tongues. Father and son froze, their hands clutching the wire rail, each with one foot stepping hesitantly onto the slippery deck.

"Father," Toyib said.

"Let's go. Many people have crossed this bridge."

As soon as he spoke, Toyib's father advanced, his hand still holding tight to the wire rail. Two steps. Three steps. His body was tossed back and forth. Toyib checked to make sure his pack was fastened tightly to his back, forced to follow after his father. The journey felt never-ending—with every step, the bridge before him seemed to stretch out longer and sway higher. Then there was a rumble of thunder that reverberated on and on, seeming to gather force, and then something struck them—a powerful cyclone wind. Now the bridge didn't just sway, but undulated. Both father and son were thrown into the air. Toyib held on tight to the wire span. When he looked over, his father had slipped, but was still clinging to the bridge's bamboo base.

Toyib screamed and screamed for his father. Now he could only make out a dim shadow behind the dense curtain of falling rain. Then the roiling wind came again, trying to flip the bridge. Toyib felt himself flying through the air, then plunged underwater. His hand clutched the wire rail even tighter. Who knows how much river water he swallowed before he was once again lifted into the air, but only for a moment, before the wind slammed him back down underwater. That was when he realized the bridge had torn loose. He would only survive if he could keep his arms and legs wrapped tightly around the wire and haul himself up out of the water.

In a battle with death, he did it. When he was finally able to reach the pier on the river's edge, the bag he had been carrying was gone. And his father was gone too.

■ ■ ■

When he was twenty-five years and seven months old, he heard that Siti had married someone in the city. He heard it from Siti's mother, who now lived alone, since Siti's two younger sisters had followed her to work in the city. Toyib himself now lived with only his mother. His younger brother had also gone to the city, working at the garage his father had been heading for. As for his father, his corpse had washed ashore in another village one week after having been swept away in the storm.

The news of the wedding truly destroyed Toyib, so that when

his mother advised him to marry a girl from the next village, he agreed although he didn't even know her.

Not much changed in the village. The spring was not replenished. The dry season still lasted longer than the rainy season, which now came and went as quickly as a night-blooming flower. The hills got browner and more arid. Prospectors came and convinced the villagers to sell the remaining trees. It was easy money. The trees disappeared, and that made water increasingly hard to find. Because water was increasingly scarce, when they tried to replant, the seeds were increasingly reluctant to germinate. Nobody, including Toyib, understood how to break this cycle, until finally everybody stopped trying.

Toyib had sold their goats and cow years ago, and with part of the remaining money he bought three new kid goats. He still went out looking for grass, now farther up the river, walking for almost half a day. He still fetched water from the well every dawn, for his house and Siti's. The well had been redug, deeper this time, in a search for the receding water.

One morning, his wife asked him why he had to keep filling up the water trough in someone else's house.

"Because I've been doing it for many years and I will keep on doing it for many years to come. You don't need to meddle in your husband's affairs!"

He felt the urge to slap his wife's face, but instead he went out to fetch their goats some food.

■ ■ ■

In the small city, ever since she first arrived, Siti had been working at a modest food stall frequented by laborers and minibus drivers. She cooked, washed dishes, and served the customers. And that was where she met her husband, a driver. The first time they met, he flirted with her. Siti just smiled, because the food stall owner told her to smile. After seeing her many times, the driver asked whether she wanted to be his wife. Siti didn't want to, but the driver kept asking. Almost a year later, finally her defenses were worn down. Siti didn't want to go home to her village, so she asked her mother to come for the simple ceremony.

And so, they were married. The newlyweds lived in a row-house apartment that had only one bedroom, a living room, which also served as a place to store all their kitchen things, and a small washroom, the water for which had to be purchased in large jugs from a truck. They dug a water pump, and didn't have to go anywhere near as deep as for the well back in the village, but the water that came out was fetid and muddy—they used it only for washing their dishes.

Five weeks after the wedding, there was an incident. A woman appeared with her five-year-old son, looking for her husband. When Siti's husband appeared, the woman flew into a rage, slapped him, and dragged him away. That was when Siti realized she had married a man who already had a wife. She couldn't say anything, she just tried to continue on with her life.

The man still visited her occasionally, usually at night after driving his minibus, slipping into her bed. Then Siti heard he had been in a bad accident—his two legs had been crushed, and had to be amputated. Another minibus driver told her about it.

Siti began to think more and more of returning to her village. She had been saving up her money for years, above all because there wasn't much else she could do in the city. Her domestic situation was more like the sad hovel in a fairy tale than a happy palace. If she moved back to the village, maybe she could go to neighboring settlements that were still fertile and buy bananas, coconuts, papayas, or cassava from farmers, to resell to folks back home.

Finally, she spoke to the food stall owner, saying she wanted to quit. In the days leading up to her departure, her husband arrived, dragging himself along. In their little house, the man confessed that his first wife had divorced him. Siti had no choice but to bring him back to the village with her.

■ ■ ■

After Siti returned with her husband, Toyib no longer hauled well water to her house—he knew his place. But since Siti couldn't rely on her husband to do it, she once again set out with an empty bucket tied with cloth. After dawn prayers she walked to the well, intending to go to the villages where bananas, coconuts, papayas, and cassava still grew, later that morning. Of course, there at the well, she met Toyib.

Their meeting was so awkward that at first neither of them said anything. Siti drew water, filled her bucket, and put it on her back. Toyib did the same, lifting it onto his shoulder. Siti walked home in front, with careful steps, because she didn't want to slip and fall like the last time she had walked along the footpath.

But at their next meeting, after drawing water for their buckets, neither immediately made to leave. They stood across the well from one another. At first they were still quite uncomfortable, but all that melted away once Toyib asked how Siti was, and she replied, and they began to ask and answer each other, discussing many things.

Siti already knew about the death of Toyib's father. Toyib almost said how it had happened when they were headed for the city in search of her. Apparently, time had smoothed over many things—Siti said she had accepted the loss of her own father. You see, everything was parched, but when the rains came, the river overflowed with wrath. You and I don't know why all that happened. Maybe we, too, have been ravaged by anger. But it's not just you and I who have suffered, everyone has. You see, there are no more young people in this village. They drop out of school and go to the city. Become servants, become shopworkers, become parking attendants. You know not even cassava wants to grow in our fields.

Without knowing why, Toyib then asked, "Are you happy with your marriage?"

Even though she was a bit taken aback at the question, Siti replied softly, as if she had been wanting to say so for a very long time: "No."

That honesty, in turn, made Toyib fall silent. He longed to approach Siti, take her hand, even embrace her. But all they did was simply look at one another, still separated by the well.

"And you? Are you happy with your marriage?"

"No," said Toyib.

■ ■ ■

When his mother died, the house became a miserable place for him. Toyib had to live alone with his wife, who would occasionally ask, "You're meeting Siti at the well?"

His answer would be an outburst of anger: "You think I should stop going to the well? She has to go there like everyone else, and I have to go there just so you can rinse out your mouth. Understand?"

And they did keep meeting at the well and talking every day, before anyone else arrived. Those were the most beautiful moments they had, alone with the sky turning a gentle violet in the east. They often talked dreamily. What if nature had been kinder to them. What if the long drought hadn't come, and hadn't lasted. If the spring hadn't dried up, their fathers wouldn't have fought, machete and scythe. Siti wouldn't have had to go to the city, and the flooded river wouldn't have gone on a rampage, taking Toyib's father away.

"You know," Toyib said—he couldn't keep it in any longer—"I love you."

"I love you too. I always have," Siti replied. She smiled, bent her head, covered her pail and tied it with her faded cloth, then squatted to place the bucketful of water on her back. She held on to a wood stump, pulled herself up to stand, and then walked away from Toyib before he could say anything else.

■ ■ ■

Not long after that, the well dried up again. The remaining men in the village tried to dig deeper—one yard, two, five yards more, and they still didn't find water. Meanwhile, they went farther to fetch their water, all the way to the river that had swallowed Toyib's father and now had receded back to a trickle, sharing their water source with their livestock and who knows what else. For days they dug the well deeper, finding nothing but hard stone.

They gave up on the well. But even so, every morning Toyib and Siti would go there with their empty buckets. Standing across the well from one another they chatted like usual, as they had in the days when there was still water. There were so many things they wanted to discuss, sometimes night and day all they thought about was what they had said that morning. They would only finish their conversation when the light in the eastern sky grew brighter. Then they would leave the well and head for the river together.

Of course, many knew about those meetings, but chose to mind their own business.

Then one night, Toyib awoke and his wife was gone. He asked his closest neighbors, but they didn't know where she was either. The news quickly reached one house and then another, so that by first light, the alarm gong was sounding. The people searched here and there, before realizing that there was the same urgent rhythm coming from the other side of the village. Siti's husband had also disappeared.

Toyib sent someone to his wife's natal village, thinking maybe she had returned to her parents' house. But no, she wasn't there, and this made the news and the search spread. Then someone said that if Toyib's wife and Siti's husband had run off together, they wouldn't have been able to get very far, considering Siti's husband's condition. It was early evening, and they went back to searching in the hills around the village.

Just before Maghrib, the villagers found the missing pair. Sprawled together at the base of the dried-up well. With no trace of life and no parting message.

■ ■ ■

Of course, Toyib and Siti never went back to the well. And bearing his unremitting anguish, Toyib finally left the village. He joined his younger brother in the city, never to return.

A BLUE MORMON FINDS HIMSELF AMONG COMMON EMIGRANTS

Tishani Doshi

INDIA

after Cavafy

It's uncertain why they're here.

Pretty sure it's the same old sob story—
      no food in the fields, government gassing their kids,
            neighbors throwing bombs on their homes.

Shall we go down to the shore and save them?

They have such short lives,
      such unpronounceable names.

Wouldn't it be better if they stayed put?

Do they watch clouds or collect shells? Can we know?

So many die along the way.

Think about their lives in far Bombay—
    subsisting on the undersides of leaves,
        trying not to get shot in the head
            while hanging upside down from a tree.

Think of Nabokov, that crafty taxonomist,
    filling notecards with their habits—
        "The Original Climate Refugees."

I spoke to one—a Blue Mormon.

Do you know how difficult it is to be so beautiful? he said.

Stuff happens to beautiful creatures. It's unsettling.

All those nets and hours in glass jars,
    all those snot-nosed boys playing pin the specimen.

Did I mention they have a fanatical approach to breeding?

Sometimes, the Blue Mormon complained,
    when we don't get enough food we emerge as dwarves.

This is distressing.

How to explain there are no perfect conditions?
    There's always too little rain or too much.
        Someone's bound to give you a bad TripAdvisor
        review.

But why all this swarming across highways in lemon
    ribbons of heat? Why cluster around hilltops and lakes?

Why not gather less visibly in locations less elite?

Goes without saying they'll seduce our old parents
            and get them to sign off the property deeds.
                        Our wives will soon be kneeling at altars
                        of ixora.

We must proceed with caution.

Maybe we could give them wristbands or pin
            yellow stars to their tails. Maybe we should build fences
                        or draw crosses on the winglike doors of their tents?

In America at least, they fix them with sensors
                        so they can monitor where they go.

We must think about the environment.

It's too soon to talk of deportation.

Certainly it would be barbaric to separate
                        children from their parents.

How shameful the aberrant Blue Mormon is,

shrugging off his feathery vest,
            singing his sad song of asylum.

Do you think I'd be fleeing unless I had to?

And with these common emigrants?
            They're just insects. But me? I'm different, can't you see?

FALLING RIVER, CONCRETE CITY

Billy Kahora

KENYA

I REMEMBER THE FIRST DEAD BODY I saw. It was a wet thing, a giant tadpole with a fishy mouth, squashed face, and the eyes blearily half open. I was eight years old and we lived in Buru Buru Phase 1, the default description of which was still "middle-class estate." The Kenyan 1990s economic downturn was yet a decade away. There were regular car and house upgrades by our neighbors. Many new white Toyotas. Burglarproofing and metal gates. A new coat of whitewash every year.

During the school holidays all my friends and I wanted was to escape the newly white, uniform, two-story maisonettes with their orange-brick roofs, to roam far and wide outside Buru Buru in what was still wilderness. Back then, in the mid-1980s, there were dik-dik antelopes to hunt. Or to chase and chase and never get near these quicksilver creatures. As inept as we were, we once managed to catch a rabbit and it was because we were with one of the older boys who knew how to use a catapult. Mostly we found arurus, a kind of small pheasant that can fly only short distances before it tires and lies on the ground beating its wings. We roasted these over an open fire. The land-grabbing and unchecked development was still all to come. The long and short rains still followed the predictable announcements by the Kenya Meteorological

Department guy on the news. During the April school holidays, after the worst of the long rains, we would go swimming instead of hunting. Once the sun came out in the late morning one of us would shout "Kanaro" and we would troop out of the estate. The storks that always came after the rain flew high above us in the sky and younger children sang koko-mia-koko at them. Kanaro was the large sewage culvert just outside our enclosed lives, built to wash away our waste, our baby shit. Flooded by the Mathare River, the water came up so high that it covered the "HFCK" etching on the side of the culvert, and this became our swimming pool. HFCK stood for Housing Finance Company of Kenya, the state housing parastatal, which had borrowed money from the Bank of England to build Buru Buru. Prince Charles even came on the train to open Phase 2 of Buru Buru in 1982. This royal recognition made Buru Buru more than just a new middle-class estate—the dailies started calling it the largest residential housing development in East and Central Africa. Surrounded by what had been the African section of colonial Nairobi and now rougher lower-income estates, Buru Buru, like everything west of Uhuru Highway, was Babilon and we were babies.

The discovery of the giant tadpole ended our Kanaro swimming for good. When the police came to pick up the body we overheard them laughing, and the words "Mathare" and "changaa" as they wrapped the body in a blanket. Beyond Kanaro was dense arsenic-green bush into which we never dared to venture. From my bedroom window the bush was even more ominous and at night it became the stuff of my childhood nightmares, a land of ogres. But beyond the bush was Mathare, what would become in the 1990s a collection of slums, eventually housing over half a million people. When Dad, Mum, my younger brother, and I left Buru Buru every weekday morning to go to Nairobi Primary, formerly Prince of Wales School, west of Uhuru Highway, Babilon proper, we drove past the mud huts of Mathare. Our Toyota passed men trudging in the dust and women washing babies and clothing outside of doorways. Before my formal lessons in school, Mathare was the cautionary tale of that morning exodus: this is where you would end up if you didn't work as hard as Dad or Mum. We came to understand that you ended in those places around us if you were lazy in school, smoked bhangi, or liked to steal things. Jericho, Jerusalem, and Bahati had once been the African sector of colonial Nairobi. Dandora, Umoja, and Kariobangi, which were newer and different, we saw as just as bad. I remember meeting two Jericho boys on one of our "hunting" expeditions. We were at least six of us but the two came up to us with a confident bounce that our own Buru parents would have shouted at us for. We all froze, trying to decide whether to run off. The taller one came to each of us, staring us down. I remember the chuki in his face and almost peeing my pants. When I was a bit older I realized that he blamed me, us, everybody, for his life. Once we'd cowered enough the other boy went through our pockets and took all our shillings. So, every morning inside the car, listening to our parents' sound track, peering through the windows we felt chastened, happy that we were inside; safe away from the boys we saw who looked like our Jericho tormentors. I could also smell and feel the river going past Mathare and I was glad I did not live near it. By the time we reached school on the other edge of town, in what had once been the European side of the city, we would cross bridges or drive alongside a natural decline that sloped down toward more water in less dire circumstances. At school, the shamba had a clear stream in which we happily played boats without any of the dangers I thought we'd left behind every morning.

■ ■ ■

The main thoroughfares of Nairobi are oriented along its three rivers: Nairobi, Ngong, and Mathare, which form the Nairobi

River basin and which all flow into the east of the city to join Athi River, ultimately draining into the Indian Ocean. If the Mombasa-Kisumu railway line is Kenya's spine, the complex Nairobi River system is the capital city's nervous system. The water is not as visible as the Thames in London or the Congo in Kinshasa, but it is everywhere, which is, in a sense, nowhere. This is because the site on which Nairobi was founded was itself once mostly water, a wetland. The Maasai called the larger area Nakunsoleton, "the beginning of all beauty," before the British came. Early English traveler Ronald Preston described it as a "soppy landscape, devoid of human habitation of any sort, the resort of thousands of wild animals of every species." When the Mombasa–Kisumu railway arrived in Nairobi in 1899, it became mile 327, and with time the land was reclaimed to start the city.

■ ■ ■

After Nairobi was declared the capital of the colonial protectorate in 1907 and planning started for building, ordinances were made preventing habitation on each side of any river for over half a mile. The river thrived and was channeled into the Ngong, Nairobi, and Mathare waterways; but a network of streams, rivulets, and seasonal creeks in the city also developed. For the longest time the land around the river and any wetlands were respected. It was out of this respect, heshima for nature, that emerged all the unspoilt areas of my childhood. This is where the butterflies and chameleons of that time thrived. My primary school lessons about the water cycle—rain, trees, streams, and ocean—were tangible. There were even media reports that a leopard stalked the wild bush in the area. But between my boyhood in the 1980s and teens in the '90s, the river and the greenery shrank and concrete took over. A flagging Kenyan economy, partly from structural adjustment programs, brought more rural migrants into the city, to places like the Mathare and Kibera slums. Conditions were so dire that the unimaginable started happening in these settlements. Without proper facilities came flying toilets. Many would just shit in a plastic bag and throw it as far away as possible. As the city grew, its industries went unchecked and the dumping choked the river further. All heshima was gone. By the time I was in my preteens, Kanaro would stop flooding (there were now many swimming pools in the city anyway and the kids did not miss it). A few years after I saw my first dead body, we moved to Phase 5, the shiniest and brightest Buru Buru. I forgot all about Kanaro and Mathare. When I finished high school and went back to Phase 1 to visit a girl I had grown up with and still had a crush on, I was shocked to see that Mathare had grown beyond the river into my childhood playground. Babilon had receded and the wilderness of my childhood nightmares had become Kiambiu. Throughout the 1990s this became a pattern along Nairobi's river valleys, with land that was once protected filling up with such informal settlements. Corrupt administrative chiefs and city council bureaucrats had started off leasing out parcels of land to rural-urban migrants, creating squatter cities shored up next to the river.

■ ■ ■

In October 1997 it started raining and did not stop till February 1998. We were told that El Niño had come. Before that the long and short rains had failed for a number of years and it felt like the Rain Gods were playing catch-up. Giant culverts all over the city filled up and then the smaller ditches. Then, even the dried streams became rivers once again and it was as if Nairobi were going back to the swamp, Nakunsoleton, but this time around it was without the beauty that the Maasai had observed more than a century earlier. All the things that the city was fast producing as waste were one with the water. Maybe a decade earlier the city's drainage system would have prevented flooding, but now it was clogged with garbage. And so the water rose and filled the roads, and in the lower parts of the city houses flooded. Even parts of Buru Buru.

After El Niño, I left Kenya like many of my generation, unable to think of a future in Kenya, and returned in 2005, now a journalist. Back in Nairobi, I found myself in Mathare on assignment for an environmental magazine. By then the ubiquitous plastic bag was a national disaster. Everyone had given up on the river. Described as the national flower, the plastic bag sprouted everywhere. Mathare was now officially the second biggest slum in Nairobi, an ideal space to observe the plastic bag in full bloom. My guide took me to a kiosk not far from the Mathare River. We ordered some tea, and the proprietor asked whether I wanted *garatathi*—a plastic bag. The guide reacted to my puzzlement with a grin; in Mathare, milk, he explained, comes in plastic bags and is so diluted with water that tea with very little milk was called *garatathi*. So I nodded, yes, tea with very little milk, like the English drink it, would suffice, and the proprietor walked outside, whistled, and shouted, "Njoki." A girl appeared carrying two clear plastic bags with very watery milk. The proprietor handed over some money. I could not get over that image of milk in see-through plastic bags. Bags that took 5 million years to decompose. Bags that had become flying toilets. In the Buru of my childhood, milk had always been delivered by *lorry ya maziwa*, the milk truck. And of course, the milk packs came with a stamp of reassurance—Kenyan fine print that stated that the milk had been pasteurized.

Seeing milk in clear plastic bags made me think about the river and it all felt to me like the loss of my childhood. The plastic bag milk had no licensed stamp, had clearly not been tested with a lactometer. I walked past huts in Mathare with my guide, thinking of the years between milk in packets and plastic-bag milk and a smell grew in my nostrils. And so we slowly came to the river. It looked like tar and smelled like shit. I remembered the giant tadpole. That bloated man had probably been drinking at this very spot and then had fallen into the river and washed into my life. There was little chance that the sluggish thing before us would wash anything downstream. Now along the river there were countless drums spewing black smoke and breathing fire, a crude gin distillery. There was an acrid smell. Changaa, my guide explained. The local gin was Mathare's most lucrative product. I learnt that the demand had risen so much that its makers added formaldehyde (used to preserve dead bodies in the city mortuary) to increase its potency. Changaa's biggest risks used to be that it'd make you so drunk you might sleep on the road or drown; now it caused blindness. Nairobi's population surge meant that habitation had ballooned right on the shores of the river, the nervous system of Nairobi's giant informal and mostly illegal economy. What we now accept as hustle. Changaa brewing. Car washes. Trucks filling up to use the water for the vast construction going on in the city. Human waste. The city spewing itself into the river away from the eyes of the authorities.

A few years later I became an editor of *Kwani?*, a Nairobi-based literary magazine, and we started working across the city to document the 2008 postelection violence. When I asked a fearless photographer friend of mine who went everywhere in the city during the violence to take photos, he told me the one place he truly feared was Kiambiu. Even the police did not go in there, he said. That field behind my baby life in Buru Buru Phase 1 had become a nightmare more violent than the ogres of my dreams. The older slums were more manageable because they had come up in a kinder time and had old networks as their foundations. I thought about the chuki of those Jericho boys who had terrorized us in childhood because we were from Buru and I wondered whether Kiambiu is one of the places they had ended up and turned against those who were closest, those who were not of their tribe. At least like us they had a wilderness to roam and be free. In the new Nairobi that had all disappeared and all of us were trapped in an urban confinement of our own making, and have lost heshima and become angry enough to pick up machetes.

And yet while many of Nairobi's problems can be traced back to the river, not all has been lost—there have been attempts to clean it up again and again over the years. In 2009, 3 million tons of waste were removed from the Nairobi River. In the heart of Nairobi's Central Business District, where the river had been canalized, hawkers and mechanics were forcibly removed from a large area to build a park. There were murmurs that all this was self-serving and the buildup to a major redevelopment to build a Riverfront and sell units for millions of shillings—Nairobi's entry into gentrification. These overtures stopped, but then began again in earnest in 2018. Nakumatt, once Kenya's largest supermarket chain, was forced to evacuate one of its most lucrative branches in Westlands because it had built over a tributary of the Nairobi River. Before Nakumatt was kicked out, every now and then the supermarket would flood after heavy rains and would close for a few days, then resume business. Government intervention might be the only thing to help the river in the future, especially if taken beyond the most visible places, the Central Business District and the slums. Elsewhere, industrial dumping and illegal channeling of the river for irrigation to grow the city's vegetables continue. A few months ago, with yet another cleanup, bodies of babies and children started showing up in the river. Sociologists point to the ever-increasing pressure of life in the city, such that many are unable to take care of their children. But with the river it is better than it was twenty years ago.

Now you always hear commonplace comments about how oppressively hot Nairobi has become or how infrequent are its long and short rains. I wish I could put this down to nostalgia. I am sure that the Nairobi of my primary school years was always breezy even at 2:00 P.M. and the sun was high in the sky. Was it this way? I do know that in 2018, during a heat wave, motorists were warned against filling their gas tanks to the maximum to avoid spontaneous combustion. That's something new. Kanaro is regularly filled with garbage from Kiambiu. The Mathare River that regularly flooded Kanaro is now a trickle. The long and short rains now skip a few years and come down all at once as a deluge. Every decade we are told El Niño is coming again. I think of that dead body I saw in Kanaro and realize it was the end of many things. Bird-watching beyond Buru Buru, where Dandora eventually spread out to take over the wild. No more fishing anywhere on the Nairobi River. And to see dik-dik you now have to go on safari or to the Nairobi Animal Orphanage.

Nairobi River, still the city's nervous system, has been strangled by concrete and hustle. Without the water, the green is fast disappearing and only left in upmarket Nairobi. Nairobi residents now spend a significant part of their lives in traffic. When I recently drove along that road of my childhood past Mathare to the city it took me nearly two hours. The car crawled slowly along a road filled with small business stalls that sold secondhand clothes, padlocks, plastic utensils, coffins, and cheap cell phones. There were makeshift garages. Metal parts were littered everywhere. Mathare lay beyond this extra layer of hustle, where it had always been, but now covered in dust and smog. Hawkers and mechanics tried to catch my eye. When one finally did, he shouted, "Jua leo imetoka na jamii." The sun has come out with his family today. I

laughed and shouted back, "It's like this every day." And he nodded and asked me whether I wanted a checkup for my car. When
I finally crossed over into the city I could barely make out any
water underneath the bridge at the Globe Cinema roundabout.
The city had finally eaten up the river and all that was now emerging from its bowels was a brown and dirty trickle.

SPRING IN WADI DELAB, THE VALLEY OF THE (ABSENT) PLANE TREE

Raja Shehadeh and Penny Johnson

PALESTINE

WE HAD BEEN RELUCTANT to walk again in Wadi Delab, a deep valley that runs from our town of Ramallah to the village of Ein Qinya. For many years, walking there had been our refuge from the shocks and strains of life under Israeli military occupation. But now, with Ramallah confined to the narrow band of Area A under the temporary arrangements of the 1993–1995 Oslo Accords (now seemingly permanent), high-rise construction had strewn rubble down the hills and Israeli settlement expansion had contributed streams of waste and garbage. The springs that nourish our limestone landscape had suffered both from drought and a local mania for carving new roads through the hills, for paving over precious water sources. We had avoided confronting a landscape of ruin.

But finally, recently, abundant rain over the winter promised a verdant spring and we resolved to walk once more in Wadi Delab. While the "official" regional drought from 2005 to 2011—one of the triggers of rebellion in Syria—was over, our land between the Mediterranean Sea and the Jordan River, now occupied Palestine and the state of Israel, had suffered a series of winters with diminished rainfall. Coupled with human interventions in our landscape, voices of doom rang in our heads as we prepared to set out. A friend publishing a guide to wildflowers in the Ramallah region mourned the loss of plant habitat: "The orchids are gone," she told us in the dark month of February.

Yet descending into the wadi in April, there they were: pyramid orchids along the side of the overgrown path, beacons, we thought, of a small but precious hope. Away from the urban sprawl, we found that these delicate flowers persist even though the springs farther down were mostly dry. All town-planning schemes for Ramallah never took into consideration the movement of water and wind. The city's building boom over the last several decades has blocked the wind that blew through the valley and into Ramallah from the sea. With the abundant wildflowers that day in the valley, though, we could deceive ourselves and believe we were in the world as it had been. Yet this was a momentary delusion. Once we looked up, we saw in the distance several of the twelve Israeli settlements sprawled on the hills overlooking the wadi, most established after the Oslo Accords, forming a ring around Ramallah. Where gentle paths through the hills once connected villages and towns in the central highlands, roads carve into those peaceful hills today. Dispatched to Palestine in 1918 after suffering shell shock in World War I, poet Siegfried Sassoon roamed the hills around Ramallah and described Palestine as his Arcadia. This land, with its quiet beauty, has now become an arena for a state-sponsored land grab, land for settlements belonging exclusively to one religious group.

We live in a beleaguered land and it is hard to escape our human dilemmas. Turning to the living world that we inhabit, we face many losses: a shrinking Dead Sea; the once mighty Jordan River diverted for water-thirsty agriculture; a catalog of animals vulnerable, endangered, or extinct; and native plants at risk, despite the beauty of pyramid orchids one spring morning. For all that we resolved to continue walking in Wadi Delab in the course of our all-too-short spring, grappling with both hope and fear.

The old path we used to take, marked on the ordnance maps of the British mandate but much older than that, meandered along the contours of the hills all the way down to the wadi to the village of Ein Qinya and its once abundant spring. It was an attractive old path through the hills, one of many connecting every village and town to another in Palestine's central highlands. When we descended, near the top of the hill, we were once able to see a line of sea fossils and corals. Because of the small size of the fossilized sea creatures it was possible to tell that this was where the seawater had reached many eons before. Along the way we used to sit by the springs that marked our descent. We would peer into the *qasers,* old stone towers used by farmers to store their produce and sleep on the roof in the summer to protect their harvests. Now many of the springs are dry and only a few *qasers* stand in lonely splendor on the terraced hills.

These terraced hills are the work of many generations of farmers over hundreds of years. They turned a wavy, sometimes precipitous terrain into small plots of arable land, preventing erosion by building stone terraces so well constructed that they have lasted for many centuries against the forces of nature—a fine example of landscape art, where it was possible to read the history of human habitation and agriculture as well as the geological transformations over the ages. Over the past three decades, human intervention had done away with many of these wonders, often without leaving a trace. Bulldozers scooped the earth, erasing the patient work of centuries. Both the sea fossils and our old path are now covered with construction rubble.

These days, when we go walking, we begin in the middle of the valley, where an unpaved agricultural road offers access to the wadi. On a late afternoon walk with friends recently, we peer into a puddle of tadpoles as we try to cross the stone-choked wadi, recalling the small waterfalls that used to cascade down the valley in earlier springs. Perhaps we have come too late—whether late in this spring or simply too late in our troubled century. A stand of small wild irises cheers us and then hope comes from the sky. "Look up," our friend and sometime walking companion Gerard says. High above, a snake eagle catches a thermal current while migrating swifts pattern the sky above our valley.

Our long wadi has three names. Near Ramallah it is Wadi Kalb (Valley of the Dog); near the village of Ein Qinya it is Wadi Delab (Valley of the Plane Tree). But perhaps the third name is the most resonant these days, Wadi U'qda (Valley of the Knot), as we try to understand its current state.

In late April, setting out on a day's walk, we decide to begin at the lower end of the wadi, where young architects, artists, and environmentalists have launched a project, called Sakiya, or Water Giver, to tie back together strands of our lives that have unraveled: art, science, and agriculture, connecting, as they put it, "local agrarian traditions of self-sufficiency with contemporary art and ecological practices." As we approach, we wonder how this lofty language can be grounded in our wounded landscape. True, the spring of Ein Qinya, one of four springs near the village, still exists and has provided respite for travelers and water for farmers for centuries—indeed the springs of Ein Qinya used to supply all the water for Ramallah in Ottoman times. But the spring greens we spy in the fields are grasses, rather than crops. As in many rural settings in Palestine, agriculture has languished as the young seek work outside the village and rural lands suffer not only drought, but confiscation—Israel appropriated a patch of village land for the settlement of Dolev (which means plane tree in Hebrew), established in 1981, perched on a nearby hill, then more land for a military road, and finally classified over 80 percent of village land as Area C, where Israel exercises sole control.

The village olive trees reached almost to the top of the hill and we wondered whether the owners were allowed by the Israeli settlers to tend their trees. We asked architect Sahar Qawasmi from the Sakiya project whether the villagers who own the olive trees are permitted to tend to their orchards. Sahar said that the settlers allow a small number of villagers to do so for a limited time, but force them to leave by noon and patrol their access. As she was telling us this we saw a flock of birds, probably swallows, fly up and land over the trees, and we told each other how we wished we were as free on our land as these birds.

As we walk up another old path with Sahar, we find a young man hard at work planting in a hillside field. He is working on land given over to Sakiya by the Palestinian family that owns the house and surrounding land, along with an old stone house above the field, served by a spring called Um El Ayun (Mother of Springs); the house is currently being restored as an artists' residency. They were in direct view of the settlement and knew that if they carried out any new construction in the course of the renovation, the settlers might come and stop them because in Area C no construction can take place without a license from the Israeli authorities, which is close to impossible to obtain. We had visited this abandoned house and a nearby Islamic shrine (*maqam*) called Abu El Ayun (Father of Springs) so many times, wondering about their fate, and our hearts lifted as we saw the stirrings of life: rooms cleared of rubble, stone walls repaired, other walls whitewashed, a courtyard full of spring poppies.

A magnificent oak tree, at least a century old, dominates a hill just above one of the two houses. In Wadi Delab, there are in fact no plane trees, although, as Sahar explains, a young researcher has located one solitary plane tree in a nearby wider wadi. Perhaps, she adds, villagers in other times cut down the trees to build furniture and shore up their small houses. Certainly, we know, the oriental plane tree (*Platanus orientalis*) is now rare in the wild in both Israel and Palestine, although riverbeds in deep Galilee wadis are still lined with this magnificent tree. Sakiya has planted other trees so perhaps the absent plane tree may one day return to Wadi Delab. Indeed, on a nearby hill, a tree-obsessed Ramallah couple, Saleh Totah and Morgan Cooper, have founded an ever-growing arboretum (called Mashjar Juthour) to preserve native Palestinian trees and encourage young people to learn about and cherish native flora. But when they tried to build a wall around their property to keep grazing goats from their young trees, they were stopped.

At the higher end of the wadi, near our city of Ramallah, there are plenty of stray dogs that wander in Wadi Kalb, the Valley of the Dogs, as well as on urban streets. (The Ramallah-based Palestinian Animal League works on adoption and care for these beleaguered animals.) High above Wadi Kalb, in the sprawling town of Beitunia that abuts Ramallah and was itself once a wetland, a Palestinian scientist was recently studying sinkholes. Sinkholes are a matter of urgent investigation in the area of the shrinking Dead Sea, where at least five thousand of them now dot its shores. A doctoral candidate in anthropology, Simone Popperl, spent several years with Israeli and American scientists who study these Dead Sea sinkholes. She contrasts their realm of research activity with that of a Palestinian hydrologist from Birzeit University, who could not access the majority of Dead Sea sinkholes, many of which lie within the occupied West Bank but beyond an Israeli checkpoint. Popperl coined the phrase "geologies of erasure" to describe the restrictions on the collection of knowledge imposed by colonial and occupying powers. It rings true: we continue to walk in our still beautiful nearby wadi but we must, on occasion, look beyond it to understand and to act.

We cannot however, find much relief, let alone answers, in the growing pile of documents on climate change in the constricted territory now called, at least by some, the state of Palestine. On April 22, 2016, coinciding with Earth Day, the state of Palestine signed the Paris Agreement on climate change, along with another 174 parties at the United Nations headquarters in New York. (A year later, President Trump withdrew the United States from the agreement.) A flurry of plans and policy documents, several drawn up with both international and local expertise, followed. But like the Palestinian scientist studying sinkholes in a suburb, Palestinian plans and commitments to "climate adaptation" are somehow out of place. The Palestinian Authority's 2010 climate adaptation strategy and program of action identifies three regions as "having particularly high levels of climate vulnerability"—Massafer Yatta on the eastern slopes of the West Bank, the easternmost areas of the Jordan Valley in the West Bank, and Gaza. The first two are in Area C, the 60 percent of the West Bank under sole Israeli control; the Palestinian Authority can neither conduct an investigation nor implement a plan, just as its Palestinian inhabitants cannot build a house, dig a well, or install electricity or water infrastructure. Few Palestinians from the West Bank can enter the besieged enclave of Gaza, let alone initiate cooperative environmental projects so desperately needed as Wadi Gaza, the only wetland ecosystem in the state of Palestine, becomes increasingly degraded by wastewater, solid waste, and other toxic materials. Plans for a desalination plant have been consistently blocked by Israel. The groundwater from springs that have nourished the central highlands (West Bank) for so long has largely been diverted to Israel, which controls 80 percent of this water.

Soon this lovely but fleeting spring will be over and the winds from the Sahara—the *khamsin*—will blow a yellow wind over the land, drying the verdant green to yellow and perhaps our human hearts as well. Predictions of renewed drought have been sounded and will certainly come, if not next spring then the next. The consequences of drought may affect Palestinians and Israelis unequally, but we will all suffer unless respect and care for the land replace a scramble for territory. Sinkholes, in the end, sink us all.

In this springtime, however, the Palestinian Museum, high on a hill and shaped like an open book, hosted a remarkable exhibit with a telling name: "Intimate Terrains: Representations of a Disappearing Landscape." Three large, dark digital prints of "No Man's Land" by Steve Sabella reminded us of how conflict erases landscapes for humans and animals: a scattering of small green shoots provided moments of respite for the eye and heart. A three-panel video installation by Joumana Aboud and Elias Freij, entitled "Maskouneh" (Inhabited), lingered on landscapes of olive trees, waving grasses, and delicately stepping gazelles as though trying to preserve them, while looming human settlements threaten from the hilltops.

At the entrance to the exhibit hung a striking work by the Palestinian artist Sliman Mansour: "Drought" is an exquisite wall hanging made of the most prosaic of materials: mud and wire. Mansour created this work in 2005, the year that drought began all through the region, including Palestine. Sliman had made beauty out of our coming disaster.

On another wall, the words of our much-missed friend, the Palestinian scholar and writer Edward Said:

"Constructed and deconstructed, ephemera are what we negotiate with, since we authorize no part of the world and can only influence increasingly small bits of it. In any case, we keep going."

Come what may, next spring we will walk again in Wadi Delab.

THAT HOUSE

Tayi Tibble

AOTEAROA/NEW ZEALAND

In that house I lived in a pink lavalava.
Watched *Lilo & Stitch* with my sister
at least three times a day.
Delivered kittens in the kitchen and gave them away
to neighbors knowing too well
that *Ohana means family*
and family means nobody gets left behind
even if you want to be forgotten.
Something or someone always finds its way back
scratching at the screen door.

And in that house with the screen door
I showered with my underwear still on.
Played piano wet and limply
with my eyes closed. Escaping.
Up the tree to read all seven of
The Chronicles of Narnia until I fell
asleep and every morning
the sun was as bright and as startling as birth.
I developed an early kind of kinship

with all the ways the earth hurt.
With a toy stethoscope and that lavalava
I nursed wounds that made me wobbly
and only half visible, like a mirage.

And in that house with the piano
my mother was a mirror.
Pretty for as long as she could
hold herself together.
We wanted to stare but were afraid
that the pressure might cause cracks.
Couldn't tell if she would harden
like a diamond or collapse like sand.
The moon was in Capricorn and the man

of the house was busy shucking anything
he could get at with his machete.
Sundays were punctuated
with the hack hack hack and the nervous
rustling of Bibles. Everybody knew
what was happening and prayed silently
like good disciples. No altars
no candles, no fireplace

in that house so the wood
was stacked for the sake of
creating something looming.
As if a butterfly kiss might send
the entire thing tumbling. So we spent
whole seasons waiting with our breath
dissipating on the inside of our mouths
while he was out there

huffing and puffing on whatever
he could puncture with his teeth.

And in that house with no heat
I believed in the cold.
Thought I would grow old
like the piano and have to watch
that video forever.
But even winter eventually
weathers itself and when
the number was finally called
it was Spring
and the sprockets of blue and purple
were blooming too brightly
to politely ignore.

HAWAIKI

Tayi Tibble

AOTEAROA/NEW ZEALAND

My mother, tired
from pregnancy and being
alive, named her last son
Hawaiki
like the paradise.

Some people say
it is where we go
when we die.

They say we dive
straight off the edge
of Cape Reinga and into
the point where the sky
hangs so heavy with spirits
that it touches the sea.

Other people say
that is where we were
before we came here
by waka, or whale, or perhaps

that was where we were
before there was anything at all

where we meant something
before we discovered

like Eve
God's forbidden fruit
in the shape of an I.

I think it must be a womb
where everything is born
and returns to.

Life and death
are the color red.

They are the color
of a cosmic heartbeat
rising on his fresh baby flesh

pinched between fingers
and kissed.

BRUNO

Aminatta Forna

SIERRA LEONE

WE STOOD WITH OUR BACKS pressed to the outside wall of a wooden shack. A few yards away rose the wire fences of the enclosure. We were three: my husband, the keeper, and me. The keeper turned and said, "Madam, when I say run, you run." He pointed to another shack about twenty yards distant. He had a lazy eye, which was all I really had time to notice before he said, "Run, madam! Run!" I set off. About ten yards in, a rock came hurtling over the fence and hit the ground a few feet behind me. I ran faster until I reached the other hut, where I stood and watched my husband dodge a second missile. After that came the keeper, hopping across the uneven ground in plastic sandals.

"What was that?" I said.

"That was Bruno," the keeper said. "He doesn't like people and so he throws rocks."

I looked around the corner of the hut. There was an ape, huge and upright, holding a small boulder above his head. In front of him stood a pile of more rocks, stacked like cannonballs.

"And you sent me *first*?"

"Madam," said the keeper, whose crooked gaze somehow lent him a look of candor. "His aim gets better."

My son, who is eight, laughs, a great belly laugh, uncommon

in a child, even though he has heard the story several times. The scene I'd just described had taken place ten years before he was born. At this age, our son likes to hear true stories, in particular those from my childhood, of adventures in overseas lands, of how I met his father, tales of my years in boarding school in England and of corporal punishment, the idea of which appalls and thrills him. I think perhaps he likes these stories for the same reason I remember liking those of my parents' stories from the time "before me," which was to my mind some other, unimaginable dimension. This is my third or fourth recounting of the story of Bruno the ape.

Bruno is a legend in Sierra Leone. In 2000, I had returned with my husband for the first time in nearly a decade, during which a civil war had raged, the last embers of which now burned across a cindered landscape. People needed help, money, solace, and we tried our best to give them those things, visiting and receiving visitors several times a day, listening to stories of loss, giving where we could, and helping plan for a future few people had even dared dream of. One day, in need of an afternoon to ourselves, we went to the ape sanctuary a few miles outside Freetown to relax by pretending to be tourists. The sanctuary had been started by a Sri Lankan expat some years before, and he was there when we arrived, sitting cross-legged inside one of the cages, holding a baby bottle to the lips of an infant chimp. Visitors were rare and we waited while he found and seconded a keeper to act as our escort. Soon after came our game of dodgeball with the alpha, Bruno.

In 1988, passing through a village in the provinces, Bala Amarasekaran and his wife, Sharmila, came across an orphaned baby chimpanzee whose mother had been killed in a hunt. For twenty dollars they took the chimp home and named him Bruno, after the British heavyweight boxer whose title fight against Mike

Tyson took place the same day. Within a few years the baby had grown into a juvenile, already as strong as a man; a full-grown male chimp has easily one and a half times the arm strength of a human adult male. Smart, affectionate, and inquisitive, Bruno was also destructive, possessive, and territorial. One day, Bruno attacked a workman who had come to the house. It wasn't the first problem the pair had had with him, but it was the one that made them decide they couldn't keep him at home any longer. By then they'd already adopted, as company to Bruno, a second chimp, a female called Julie who'd been abandoned by a departing expat. The idea for a chimp sanctuary followed, and there was no shortage of animals, adolescents typically, some given up reluctantly by owners who'd lost control of their former pets, other rescues who'd arrived injured or scarred.

I've only ever known one chimp. His name was Cuba. I met him at the house of a friend of a friend when I was in my twenties. He didn't like people much and he disliked men in particular, though he loved the steward who took care of him and, I was told, he had been known to take a shine to a woman visitor or two. One day, walking alongside me, Cuba reached up and offered me his hand. Pleased at this sign of friendship, I took it. I thought, Cuba likes me. Cuba's hand was huge, long-fingered, dry, and he held on to mine with a firm grip, one that grew in pressure until I felt my knuckles grind against each other. I told him to stop. He didn't. I stood still and turned toward him. Stop it, I said in the voice I use for disobedient dogs. Cuba stared at me unflinchingly and tightened his grip. I cried out. The silent-footed steward appeared and hissed Cuba's name. Instantly Cuba released me and bounded over to the man, who turned and walked away, the ape at his heel.

Chimps should never be pets. When I look back at Cuba, I see how disturbed his behavior was. He spent hours of his day chained to a pole frame, from which he swung, one hand on the bar, the other gripping the chain around his neck that otherwise threatened to strangle him. A lot of young Lebanese men were visitors to the house. Cuba's party trick was to smoke cigarettes. He would ask a visitor for one, pointing at the open packet, and then he would perform, placing the cigarette in his mouth to be lit and bounding off to swing on his frame, holding the cigarette between two fingers and puffing on it to the sound of laughter. I remember too that he masturbated a great deal. Excess self-stimulation, including frequent masturbation, is one of the behaviors demonstrated by captive chimps, who have also been found to display signs of trauma and depression similar to those of humans.

A friend, Rosa, spent a good deal of time living in the forests of Sierra Leone studying the wild apes. There is a photograph of her smiling at a baby chimp she is holding in her arms. Bruno. In the late 1980s, Rosa teamed up with Bala on a project to locate and count captive pet apes, and their findings underpinned the need for a sanctuary. There were fifty-five chimps living in people's houses in the capital, Freetown, alone, most of whom would have arrived as infants after their parents had been killed in the hunt. People in Sierra Leone didn't used to hunt chimps. Local folklore says that chimps were once human—men and women transformed into apes as punishment for breaking the laws of the gods by fishing out of season. In my family village of Rogbonko, hurting or hunting the monkeys that live in the trees whose branches bend over the river is forbidden. Many of the old beliefs had their roots in food conservation. In the dry season the waters are low and fish scarce, the breeding season yet to begin. Back in the day, the priestess would have issued warnings against those minded to break her injunction—that to anger the gods was to risk being turned into apes—and then hoped people believed her. Some say people began to hunt apes for meat during the rebel war out of hunger; others blame the Liberian rebels, who did not share our eating restrictions. I see something else: the rise of the evangelical preachers in the latter part of the twentieth century, the cold reach of Christianity and its teachings of man's dominion over all animals.

The abandoned and abused chimpanzees that Bala and Rosa accepted into the new sanctuary would remain there the rest of their lives. Returning a formerly captive ape into the wild almost never works, Rosa told me, for the reason that wild ape troops carve the forest into territories, the boundaries of which are rigidly and violently enforced. Think of the forest like farmland, which can produce enough to support a family of a certain size, then remember what humans have done in order to protect their land, or to seize it in the first place. To survive, a newly released ape—which would already have had to be taught how to feed itself—would need to be accepted into a troop of wild apes without upsetting the existing hierarchy.

Rosa and I have a standing joke about our shared tendency to a mild form of misanthropy, a frustration with the shortcomings of our own species. Once I gave her the gift of a vanity mirror I found in a gift shop in Covent Garden, *Do I look like a fucking people person?* written on the back. Now I remember something else Rosa said to me about chimps, her expression as she spoke, the slight shrug of the shoulders that seemed to suggest that what she was about to say was an unavoidable truth. "They are us," she said.

And being like us has been the curse of the chimpanzee. Scientific experimentation on chimpanzees began in the 1920s when scientists and researchers purchased animals brought back by hunters from West Africa. Around the same time, chimpanzees started to appear as the comic sidekick in Hollywood movies. Cheetah from *Tarzan* first appeared in a movie in 1932, although there were no chimpanzees in the original Edgar Rice Burroughs novels. Two years earlier, the first primate research center in the United States was founded by the psychologist Robert Yerkes. Over the decades that followed, our attitude to chimpanzee experiments has changed. Writing in 1989, Jane Goodall, calling for an end to ape experimentation, described the chimpanzee as a "*being* . . . whose emotional states are quite similar to our own and who is capable of feeling pain, sorrow, happiness; a being who can trust and whose trust is very easy to betray." Today, several countries have banned ape experimentation, beginning with New Zealand in 2000. In the United States (the largest user of apes for scientific research), the National Institutes of Health in 2013 began to retire the majority of its research chimps, and soon afterward the U.S. Fish and Wildlife Service announced that it had designated captive chimpanzees an endangered species. Cheetah had become Caesar.

Like us, chimps form close and enduring friendships, their families held together by bonds of affection. In addition to their intelligence and apparent humor, those qualities that make people want to turn them into pets, chimps are, like us, also warmongering and homicidal. There are more attacks on humans by captive chimps than by wild chimps, though the answer may rest in relative proximity and thereby opportunity, also the fact that wild chimps have learned to flee from hunters and so humans in general. Bruno remained deeply attached to Bala and later yearned for him. Who knows if throwing rocks at human visitors was just the behavior of a protective alpha or bound to some deeper distrust of humans?

In February 2013, I was invited to assist with a fundraiser in London for the Tacugama sanctuary. Jane Goodall was there and so was Bala, alongside Paul Glynn, the author of a children's novel about Bruno, the sale of which was going to raise funds. A few years earlier, the sanctuary had made the news in Sierra

Leone and beyond. Something dramatic had happened. Led by Bruno, the chimps had staged a breakout. Bruno had escaped.

■ ■ ■

Tacugama Chimpanzee Sanctuary is reached by a long, narrow road, bordered by dense vegetation, which climbs steadily toward the summit of a low hill. Today there is a visitors' center and a path through the trees that leads to the building where the newly rescued chimps are sheltered before they are introduced to the group. The roof of the building serves as a vantage point out over a compound where the long-term residents relax, eat, and play. Beyond that lie many acres of fenced forest where the chimps will eventually live out the rest of their lives. In 2000, when I made my first visit, and in 2006, which was the year the chimps escaped, the whole place was much more modest than it is now: some cages, the compound, and a smaller parcel of forest.

Somehow the chimps succeeded in opening the gates to the inner compound. Details of what happened next overlap, vary, and sometimes contradict, but the essence of the story is the same. The chimps raced down the access road toward the Regent Road, which serves traffic to and from the capital. At that moment on the Regent Road, a taxi was passing, carrying two Americans and a Canadian; the men were contractors working on the building of the new American embassy. The driver was a local man, Issa Kanu. The visitors later recounted the story of a huge ape that materialized out of the bush and began to chase and then pound on the car. Issa Kanu tried to reverse away but misjudged the road and crashed. He left the vehicle. Or he was hauled out through the window by the enraged chimp. Another version of the story has Issa Kanu waiting alone outside the main gates of the sanctuary for the foreigners, who had gone inside in hopes of an early-morning tour, inadvertently releasing the apes who had already escaped their compound.

What is not disputed is that Issa Kanu was killed, his face and throat torn away. At first, news of the death was withheld by the authorities. When it came to light, Bruno was blamed, but by then the story of Bruno, who had still not been recaptured, was taking on the cloak of fable. Bruno's defenders pointed to another of the larger males called Phillip, who had returned to the sanctuary and replaced Bruno as the new alpha. The identity of the killer remains a mystery, because there were no witnesses who would have been able to tell the apes apart.

Police and soldiers were brought in to search the surrounding forest. The government warned villagers to keep their children indoors. Within days, many of the thirty-one escapees had returned of their own volition and most of the remainder were rounded up. Four remained at large. And of the four, one was Bruno. Bounty hunters in 4x4s drove out of the city intent on bringing him down. There were rumors of sightings, reports Bruno had been heard at night hooting in the hills, whispers he had been killed. Nothing was confirmed. The longer Bruno evaded his hunters, the more intense the speculation grew. In 2006, I was home, and I remember all talk was of Bruno: at weddings, in the marketplace. The papers devoted daily coverage to the hunt. People wore *I ♥ Bruno* T-shirts. At a party, Rosa got into an argument with an expat who thought it fun to sport a T-shirt that read: *I Shot Bruno*. Bruno, simian Spartacus, had the country rooting for him. In the years that followed, reports grew fewer. There came the occasional report of a sighting, but Bruno was never captured.

In 2017, my husband and I took our son to Sierra Leone for the first time. The rains that year were relentless. The traffic into the city was at a standstill; the beaches were empty. One day we went to Tacugama, where we waited in the shelter of the visitors' center for our escort and then made our way under sighing trees that dripped with rainwater to the viewing place. Some of the younger apes turned their backs and bent over to show us their arses; one pitched shit from the mound of a distant rock. Directly below, in their pens, the newly arrived apes howled and keened. My son seemed to be looking at everything but the apes we had come to see.

A room behind us contained a small display, mainly posters telling of Tacugama's founding and the dreadful plight of apes in Sierra Leone, who, when they are not hunted as food, are losing their forest thousands of hectares at a time, sometimes to farmland for villagers but more often to industrial-scale farming by international companies. On one wall I found a picture of me taken at the London fundraiser. I showed my son, who turned to our guide: "There's my mum."

The man looked at me and at the image on the wall. "Ah," he said, and smiled for the first time.

I described our visit in 2000 and how Bruno had thrown rocks at us. In turn, he told me that he had been one of the first to join the sanctuary as a keeper. Face-to-face with him for the first time I noticed his lazy eye.

"It was you," I said. "You were the one who showed us around."

We shook hands, and he called to another keeper, who came over and examined the picture and then me and shook my hand also. He referred to the first man as Pa Moses and told us Pa Moses had trained him. I asked Pa Moses what he thought had happened the day the apes escaped.

"They would call to them, you see, madam," the wild apes whose territories in the surrounding forest bordered the sanctuary. Some days an older female, whom the keepers named Congo, even ventured to sit on the other side of the perimeter fence and touch fingers with the apes inside. Sometimes she brought a baby with her and held it out for them to touch. Whether she was an emissary of sorts nobody knew, but the calls of the free apes, which came mostly at night, made the keepers uneasy because the apes in their care became agitated when they heard the cries. Still, no one saw the breakout coming. The keepers who fed the chimps and cleaned the enclosure entered and left through a double security gate; you had to secure the latch on one gate before you opened the next. The chimpanzees escaped through those gates. Some reports claimed the gates had been left unlatched. Pa Moses wasn't there that day, but he has his own theory. "They watched us. Maybe they had been watching for months. They saw how it worked."

Freedom would be tough for Bruno, for no alpha would accept another alpha into their troop. Bruno would have to found a new colony, perhaps somewhere distant. "That would be hard, but not impossible," said Pa Moses. For chimps can travel long distances, and when they do, they don't swing through the trees but run on the ground, covering many miles in a day. "The three who escaped with Bruno were the strongest of the males. Bruno took with him his best lieutenants. If any of the Tacugama apes could survive," said Pa Moses, "it would be those four."

Later, when we mention to people in Freetown that we visited the ape sanctuary, everyone responds the same, down to the shake of the head and little tsk: "Bruno. He escaped them all." And then they chuckle. They mean the posses who went after him, the police, the soldiers, the hunters. I listen and wonder how one ape came to mean so much to us, because people here, while not unkindly, are rarely sentimental about animals.

Rosa says Bruno's legend had begun before the war: visitors to the sanctuary were fascinated by the chimps, and schoolchildren arrived each day by the busload. Bruno, with his might and size, instilled awe. War came and the sanctuary was overrun by rebel soldiers twice, though the chimps amazingly survived; Bala and Pa Moses risked death to bring food to them. With the end of the war, Bruno's escape was the culmination of all that had happened, the end of the story. We were desperate for heroes in that time, for the truth of war is that there is no glory there. "He became the embodiment of things coming right," Rosa wrote to me years later.

When I ask my son, who has never known war, what he likes so much about the story of Bruno, he says he doesn't know. What if it had a different ending? I press. What if Bruno had returned to the sanctuary where he would be looked after for the rest of his life? My son frowns and shakes his head.

How soon do we learn it—the desire for autonomy? Bruno remained deeply attached to Bala, loved him, you might even say. We crave freedom even from those who love us and whom we love in return, even when freedom might mean death; it is a never-ending conflict of the soul. My son wants to be free of me, yet knows he cannot live without me. The last time we talked about Bruno, I asked what else he liked about the story: "What about the part when Bruno threw the rock at me?"

My son laughed, not his belly laugh, but a low, quiet laugh, like the broadening of a smile. "Yes," he said. "I really like that bit too."

SICK WORLD

Diego Enrique Osorno

Translated by Christina MacSweeney

MEXICO

SIERRA TARAHUMARA, CHIHUAHUA. The late afternoon is bright. The roar of the train spills over like the sound of a strong river current as it ascends and descends the mountains of the sierra. Steel whistle skirting clumps of white fleecy cloud. The wagons wind around chasms and rocks that, from a certain angle, are shaped like giraffes, frogs, and other gigantic animals petrified for eternity in the landscape. Immense panoramas stretch out in every direction: to the north, the mountains; to the south, more mountains that seem to be suspended in the air. A high cliff dominates the whole horizon. Life goes on at a walking pace. The predominant smell of oil fades into the scent of live oak, mechanical motion into the movements of goats tended by an indigenous girl as the evening turns to dusk and she adjusts her orange headscarf, her dress billowing in the strong wind. In this silence, the Rarámuri sow maize and beans, they gather firewood. The path begins to descend. Undernourished children run behind the wind. How many stars are there in the sky? The solitude of many Tarahumara nights is as hard as this stone.

The City, a with capital letter, is far from here.

Frailty. A fragile equilibrium based on the relationship between the indigenous people and nature marks the passing of the days in Rarámuri communities. If there is insufficient rain or the sun's rays beat down too strongly, everyone knows that the maize won't grow well. And if the maize harvest isn't good, what maize will they use to make *pinole*? And if there is no *pinole*, what will the Rarámuri eat until the season for mushrooms and the many varieties of herbs comes around? What's more, when food is in short supply so is energy. People are thin and weary. And if people are thin and weary, who will sow the next crop of maize? And if no one sows the maize, what will the community eat? If the community doesn't eat, the community will disappear, because it will leave or die out.

A four-year-old girl has diarrhea in the morning, and the following day her parents gather up her few possessions to bury them with her, wrapped in a torn red blanket. Death from malnutrition is ubiquitous among the inhabitants of these remote villages, a daily occurrence. Dying of hunger isn't in itself a tragedy for the Rarámuri: reports say that it is a chronic condition.

The tragedy that the indigenous governors discuss in their assemblies, what they don't understand, what they can't quite explain to themselves, is why the climate has changed so much in the past thirty years, why there is more rain in October than in the summer, or why the summer rains come in July. Why is there much less rain now, why does the sun feel stronger, why the hail, why the high winds?

And here, such climatic changes are deadly. They mean the fields are tired, pierced by light. As it is, wherever you look, there are more rocks and trees in the Tarahumara sierra than there is soil. The Rarámuri arrived several decades ago, displaced from their lands down below in places like Ciudad Cuauhtémoc and Parral, where Mennonites and businessmen now hold the fertile, arable land in usufruct. "Welcome to the region of the best apples in the world," says an official sign at the entrance to land that "civilization" took from the Rarámuri, offering them the option of staying on to live there, but as peasant laborers, servants.

The mode of resistance of this indigenous group, presently estimated to be some sixty thousand people, was not to confront the invaders. Their resistance consisted of leaving, coming to the sierra, with its forests rather than fields, and where, therefore, there were no white men, mestizos, or Mexicans wanting to change their customs, to impose new ways of doing things. The Rarámuri call the whites mestizos, and Mexicans "Chabochis," which means men with spiders on their faces, bearded men, but can also mean abuser, exploiter, greedy person, people who want everything for themselves.

Outside the official program of discussions on global climate change, in the Sisoguichi community, the Rarámuri governors hold a general assembly and address the topic in their own way. They speak about their indigenous rights and cultural resistance, about the water that used to be free and now has to be paid for, about the trees killed for money, about the air that in the past wasn't merchandise but now is. The Indigenous Pastoral of the Diocese of Tarahumara produced a record of that meeting held in the mountains. The first question the indigenous representatives ask is: What is happening to our communities? Those from the western communities respond that the hotels have polluted the water; that the communal land commissioner doesn't consult them; that there has been looting of firewood and stone, threats; that participation in church affairs is low, particularly among the youth, who are losing their traditional culture and lack respect.

The people from the north reply: We no longer eat our traditional food, our fiestas are dying out, the governor doesn't show his face, and local saints' days are not being celebrated. And in the center of the sierra the greatest concern is that young Rarámuri who migrate change their ideas about traditional culture (they strike out at the authorities) and invite the Chabochis to fiestas, where they don't belong; the Chabochis take drugs. One of the indigenous participants, Pancho Palma, addresses the audience and says that the white people work to earn money, that money creates divisions, and because of it, the mestizos fight among themselves for jobs. "If we, as indigenous people, follow the same path, that will happen to us too, and all our customs will disappear."

Soon afterward, Rafael Sandoval, bishop of the Diocese of Tarahumara, said the following to the governors in the assembly: "You are the oldest people in this land and so also the wisest. Your ancestors sincerely sought God and his commandments. And I ask your forgiveness because we mestizos have often denied your religiosity, your culture, your customs, even though God has always been with you. The only thing that God wants is for you to be yourselves. Remember that God is happy when you work, when you hold the Yúmari, when you pray, dance, and play music. The heavens are joyful. Money corrupts people. You don't hoard possessions and you are happy."

The Rarámuri people know how to share. This is very different from the egoism prevalent among us, comments Javier Ávila, a Jesuit priest and regional human rights activist. The history of progress for this indigenous group, says Ávila, is based on three fallacies. The first was the mines. The companies came and said that the mineral riches would bring benefits to the Rarámuri, but they ended worse off, with the hillsides full of holes and general devastation. The second fallacy was "green gold." In the 1970s, industrial exploitation of the forests began and things were even worse. Fewer streams, fewer trees, less water. "And the government is now sounding off about teaching them to care for the forest, when they were the ones who destroyed it. For God's sake!" Now, Ávila continues, we have the third fallacy: tourism. Since scenery became a consumer product, there's been growing interest in the sierra, although not in the Rarámuri. "The truth is that I don't know what's going on in those gentlemen's heads . . . or rather what's going on in their hearts . . . If they have hearts."

"They [the Rarámuri] watch what is happening with ever deeper sadness. They see that the white man has to cheat and steal to live. The governors have held a number of meetings to try to understand what is happening. These meetings have dealt with the notion of autonomy and also climate change." A few months ago, several indigenous governors visited the Jesuit priest and asked for his help in making a formal petition to the government for the removal of a statue, erected by that same government, in El Divisadero, a beauty spot with a train station, a street market, and a luxury hotel overlooking the Copper Canyon, described as one of the thirteen wonders of Mexico by TV Azteca. The statue they erected there, in a place considered to be the spearhead of the sierra's new fallacy (as Ávila calls the mega-tourism projects), was two Chihuahua dogs dressed in the traditional sash and costume of the Rarámuri. "There's a big tourism project here in Tarahumara, and for the government, the social repercussions are the last things they consider in those sorts of initiatives. This new neoliberal project is on the road to disillusion. They say a lot of people are going to arrive, and for those people, 'indigenous' is synonymous with drunk and lazy. They've never tried to get first-hand knowledge of them; it's all just stereotypes," the priest and human rights defender says.

And how are the Rarámuri likely to respond? The response, answers Ávila, will probably be the usual one. Say nothing and retreat. The Rarámuri are not aggressive, they don't get out their submachine guns and say enough is enough. That's how it was in the past after the mining and then the lumber industry came. They trust people; they see themselves being cheated and they move away. The same may well happen now. Or maybe not.

Luis Octavio Híjar, a former seminarian who has lived in the sierra for thirty years, thinks that the Rarámuri are different from the indigenous people of the south, who tend to be more long-sighted. This man, who coordinates projects for the Fundación Tarahumara José A. Llagunao, recounts that since he came to live here, he's witnessed an enormous number of abuses of the indigenous people. "We saw the Hollywood productions arrive, the white people, and they messed the Rarámuri up because they filmed them and meddled with their communities, and instead of giving them some of all that money their movies earned, they just took advantage of them and exploited them, but that didn't bother the Rarámuri. For them, the more you have the worse off you are."

Is it possible to write an article about what is happening in this Tarahumara sierra without falling into that trap of adding a touch of drama, a note of comedy, and a little action, the Hollywood formula desired by consumers? I put that question to Híjar. How would he do it? And he tells me that the first thing he'd do would be to explain what poverty and hunger means to them because, for the Rarámuri, hunger means that there's no maize. It's different for us. For us, poverty is not having a sewerage system, water, or electricity, but no indigenous person has any of those things. For them, the poor person is someone who desires what he doesn't have. The Rarámuri want to eat. For them eating is having food and having food means having maize. Period. The Rarámuri don't feel poor. They are the children of God and they feel sorry for the Chabochis, who are children of the devil.

"This is how it is," he says in his hoarse voice. "Freedom for the Rarámuri means being allowed to be themselves."

I chatted about that with a Rarámuri couple who had lived for a while in the city of Chihuahua. He worked in construction; she was a domestic servant. The impression the city had left in their minds was of a place where people only ever spoke about money, and money was needed for everything, particularly for living. Without money you couldn't live, you couldn't buy food, you couldn't walk in some places, or sit down in others, or even drink water. With money you could do anything: the person with money could buy status and was courageous, even if he was a coward.

Anthropological studies show that before the region was occupied by the Mexicans, the Rarámuri had no knowledge of poverty. Various Christianized Rarámuri believe that Hell is so full of Mexicans that there's no space left for indigenous people, and that the Mexicans who can't find a place there have come back to bring them problems.

The researcher Rodolfo Stavenhagen has written about the visions of "aid" that have circulated in the "Western" world in reference to the Rarámuri. One is the culturist view, which says that if they are to progress, external agencies must help the Rarámuri to destroy their culture; another, the class version, says that the Rarámuri need to break with their culture, initiate class warfare, and so gain their freedom; in the third, given the presence of an internal colonizer, only a socialist transformation would be capable of eradicating the distinctive features of their precapitalist economy and change them.

Looking at things from a different angle, through the eyes of a poet, after a month spent traveling on horseback through the Tarahumara sierra, the French surrealist Antonin Artaud wrote that the Rarámuri "live as if they were already dead." I thought of that line when I met Sandoval Moreno Batista, an indigenous man of over eighty who descended from a pickup that was making the journey up the ill-defined, rutted track in one of the many parts of the sierra where the only roads are those the people make for themselves.

At first glance, all that could be seen in the surrounding landscape was bushes, live oaks, and one or two strawberry trees that added a touch of red to a sun-drenched morning. Moving slowly, Sandoval Moreno Batista took a rustic walking stick from the cab of the vehicle and said good-bye in a quiet voice to his niece, Catalina Batista, and to us, the rest of the crew.

And then he started to climb the mountain.

His back bent, Sandoval made his way through the undergrowth, heading for a community six hours on foot from where we'd stopped. Six hours for the indigenous people of the region, but a stranger might need up to a day to complete the same distance. "He's going to visit his sister to see if she has any maize," commented "Cata," who is a health promoter for the Diocese of Tarahumara.

The left eye of the elderly Sandoval is almost completely closed; he can hardly see. The journeys that he makes have at times left him close to death. "He once disappeared for two days and we searched this whole track until we found him lying on the ground. He'd been bitten by a viper," said Cata, while Mariel Ramírez, the biologist, started up the engine of the pickup carrying us to Rarámuchi, a community located on one of the highest peaks. "My uncle was saved by some natural remedies. And there he goes again." By that time Sandoval Moreno Batista had completely disappeared from view, walking into the vast sierra.

When we finally arrived in Raramuchi after a couple of hours on the road, I met another elderly indigenous man whose vaguely muscular body stood out among the dozens of undernourished children. His name was Ramiro Juan and he was wearing a doctor's white coat with the logo of the Instituto Mexicano del Seguro Social on the left shoulder. He was the *Owiruame*, the word for a traditional healer in the Rarámuri language.

"They aren't unwell. It's the world that's sick," he told me in his slow Spanish, after I'd pointed at the line of malnourished children accompanied by their equally underfed mothers, standing before the nutritionist, Adriana de la Peza, who was handing out powdered milk. "The world is sick. There's very little rain now and the maize doesn't sprout. We have no maize now."

Behind Ramiro Juan, a flock of goats, tended by a woman, seems to be walking among the clouds. The goats can't find a single blade of grass to tear from the earth. They are scrawny. They continue their search, walking the clouds. Hunger as a fact of life.

THE PSYCHOPATHS

Joy Williams

UNITED STATES

BIG GAME HUNTERS are psychopaths.

Mentally ill is far too easygoing a term for them and the "game" they delight in.

Psychopaths. There's no other word for them—they who kill large numbers of iconic animals for trophies, and the rings, pins, and other geegaws doled out by one of the world's premiere ecocidal organizations, Safari Club International. SCI keeps an extensive and highly detailed online record book accessible to all, with accompanying photographs of grinning hunters with slaughtered elephants, lions, leopards, rhinos, and buffalo. These animals constitute a Grand Slam, which is a highly desirable goal for trophy hunters and one that can be achieved over and over again. In other words, the "thrill of a lifetime" or a "once-in-a-lifetime experience" of killing a critically endangered species like the black rhino can happen repeatedly for the same individual. One need only be compulsive enough, obsessive enough, morally dead and ethically unconscious enough to just keep on killing.

In 2015, a bumbling dentist, Walter Palmer, gained a bit of infamy by killing a collared lion, lured from a sanctuary preserve by handsomely paid "guides" (fifty grand!). He botched the murder with a bow and arrow—the grievously wounded animal had to be found and shot the following day. Palmer didn't want to do it because the kill wouldn't qualify for the record book. (What an artifact that horror will be in the future when there's nothing left but us banging around. . . .) Palmer wanted to kill a large elephant next but when he was told one wasn't readily available, he went back to Minneapolis. He had a tight schedule! Had to get back to his lucrative dental practice, which we hope went immediately into the toilet. But Palmer is chump change in the truly evil world of trophy hunting. He had a North American 12 Award from SCI (probably a nice certificate), for which he had to kill a dozen animals of different species, but he was still quite a ways away from the African Big Five Grand Slam, having killed only one qualifying animal, a white rhinoceros with a heartbreakingly magnificent horn. (The white rhino is now extinct, the last male having died in a Kenyan nature preserve in 2018. The black rhino is "officially endangered," a designation that pretty much means *gone*, a designation that functions as a baleful, inevitable count-down. It certainly doesn't mean that new protective laws will come into effect with severe penalties for breaking them.)

Though ambitious and remarkably not illegal, Palmer's kills are dwarfed by those of his clubmates like Barbara and Allen Sackman of Sands Point, New York. Barbara is pictured, grinning of course, just so pleased with herself—behind a black rhino (critically endangered!) she killed with a rifle; Steven Chancellor of Evansville, Indiana (five hundred kills in twenty-eight years of hunting, including six elephants, two rhinos, eighteen lions, and thirteen leopards); Renee Snider of Elk Grove, California (who enjoys killing cheetahs and polar bears and maintains that hunting enriches her life); and Thomas Hammond of Oakland Township, Michigan (who, having killed one hundred and fifty different species of animals, including thirteen lions, eleven elephants, and more than three dozen Cape buffalo, self-published a book titled *Only in Africa*).

How wicked these people are, how enslaved to evil, how soulless, how morally diseased. How pornographic really. The photographs of their kills are pornographic; their sentiments regarding their excitement, their pride, their delight in killing are pornographic.

And with tweaked regulations, fewer animals, and more corrupt governments, trophy hunting is bigger than ever.

These people are always rich. They have scads of disposable income and know the huge loopholes in wildlife protection. They scam the conservation message, they twist and play the philanthropy game. There's an establishment just outside of Tucson, Arizona—the International Wildlife Museum. It was founded by a C. J. McElroy, who is also founder of Safari Club International. A majority of the animals are from McElroy's own personal collection, the largest of its kind in the world. Over three hundred species from six continents. A remarkable array of splendid creatures, all monumentally, disturbingly dead, most murdered by McElroy's small and busy hands.

Wealthy psychopaths easily acquire permits to kill rare animals. And enabling governments eagerly buy the lie that their cash finances preservation efforts. Zimbabwe claimed that a large elephant shot recently by a "foreign client" showed that protection is working because the male had survived to grow such long tusks. But conservation and protection policies are in shambles everywhere. Rhinoceros poaching in South Africa rose from 13 in 2007 to 1,215 in 2014, a 9,000 percent increase. Mass poisonings of elephant herds occur. Or the animals are shot, their faces chainsawed away for the tusks and their bodies doused with cyanide, which poisons the vultures that congregate and alert enforcement (whatever that is) to the slaughter site.

Poachers are a big, big problem, doing their part to make the world an emptier and more lifeless place. But the thing is . . .

they're not even sportsmen! They don't kill for pleasure (though who knows . . .), but for profit, selling horns and ivory on the flourishing black market. They prefer not to have their photographs taken with their kills. In fact, they might kill *you* should you come upon them and wish to do so.

Trophy hunters frown upon messy poaching. For one thing, poachers have no real appreciation for the animals they're wiping out. But mustn't be judgmental . . . poor fellows, they're just trying to make a dollar or two in an impoverished land. Very little opportunity for the young people in these places.

Such thoughtful humanist sentiments allow the well-heeled, adventurous, psychopathic trophy hunter to glide into the altruistic argument for keeping their murder holidays—their safaris—socially acceptable. Trophy hunting provides "much needed money for communities living near game parks." Or as Safari Club International says: "It's an industry that Africa couldn't do without."

In other words: Africa is nothing, save for the great living resource that must be exploited.

Which sounds somewhat familiar, doesn't it, though updated for our times.

The planet is reeling under our continuous and varied and unchecked assault. Our concept of criminal behavior and psychological deviancy must evolve and include crimes against the earth and other species. Trophy hunters are robbing us all for vanity, thrills (apparently there's nothing like watching the light go out in a large animal's eyes), and tatty jewelry. They are robbing the earth of its strange and irreplaceable wonders. I am sickened writing this brief piece, sickened by seeing some of the hundreds of photographs of these people with their kills—hugging the astounding *other* they have destroyed, posing them, stretching them out, draping them over their shoulders, slinging their arms proprietarily around their heads and horns. These people feel neither shame, nor guilt, nor sorrow. They seem to feel . . . a horrid happiness. For they are smiling, almost always smiling. With a psychopath's smile.

■ ■ ■

By the way, the dentist Walter Palmer is still hunting. Hunting and killing. Killing and smiling.

■ ■ ■

. . . Or, as in the case of our very own president's issue, Donald, Jr., dangling the severed tail of an elephant he'd shot on one of his numerous safaris, a psychopath's smirk.

CORAL WATCH

Ishion Hutchinson

JAMAICA

Bubbling keys segue miles into days
and beyond. Some of us grow metal blights.
Others just numbed saffron, sighing *help*, *help*
in the gradual decline of water.
The sun spurs hard frost. We can't do much.
Someone, collect our bloated irises, please.

ON THE ORGANIC DIVERSITY OF LITERATURE:
Notes from My Little Astrophysical Observatory

Sjón

Translated by Philip Roughton

ICELAND

IN THE SUMMER of 2017, I spent seven weeks as an artist in residence at the Potsdam Institute for Climate Impact Research. The PIK, as it is commonly designated, is located in the buildings of the old Astrophysical Observatory on the summit of the willow-grown Telegrafenberg hill, which is also the site of the famous Einstein Tower, a white structure with rounded walls, designed in an expressionist spirit and named after Albert Einstein, whose theories on relativity are tested there. I was provided with a studio in the Kleiner Fotorefraktor, or little observatory, a smaller version of the main building, and allotted the task of determining possible talking points between literature and science in this era of climate change.

Concerning the importance of the PIK scientists' work for the rest of the world, no one need have any doubt. The men and women who work at the institute, mapping and studying the reactions of different natural phenomena to global warming, do so in the hope that their work in the field—at sea, on glaciers, sands, mountain peaks, and valley floors, at both poles—and in the digital physics models that they have developed on their supercomputers, will make invisible threats tangible and sound the alarm for those threatened—the public and administrations of countries and big businesses. The PIK's natural scientists have, however, begun to raise doubts concerning people's defensive responses (and have even begun to question whether mankind possesses the intrinsic ability to respond to its imminent extinction). And so they have called for collaboration with poets and artists, that segment of society that has, through the centuries, also made it its task to bring the hidden into the light and make it visible to the human eye.

One of the first ideas that I had after accepting the invitation to Potsdam was to make the nineteenth-century poet and naturalist Jónas Hallgrímsson my traveling companion and adviser in spiritual as well as material concerns. Jónas is the national poet of Iceland and the person who, beyond all others, taught his countrymen to behold the beauty in the natural elements, which, in days of yore, shaped the land that the Icelanders had settled, and which still challenge their existence with harsh weather and the violent agitation and outbursts of the earth. In his poems, scientific perspicacity regarding the nature of the physical world is combined with poetic humility toward its power. These works convey man's smallness in the face of creation, which is ferocious and lofty at once, a veil over the face of the Creator and a mirror of the being that the Creator made in His own image:

> Eternal snow shines in my eyes
> out and south and west it lies,
> in and east the same I see.
> Individual! Robust be.
> —"Snowbound"

Next to the collected works of Jónas Hallgrímsson on my desk in the little observatory, I lined up other books that I thought might be of use: *The Conspiracy Against the Human Race* by Thomas Ligotti; *In the Dust of This Planet: Horror of Philosophy*, Vol. 1, by Eugene Thacker; and *Staying with the Trouble: Making Kin in the Chthulucene (Experimental Futures)* by Donna J. Haraway—all of which deal explicitly with mankind's threats to itself and its possible disappearance from the face of the Earth. Mankind alone recognizes its worth as a species, and it is up to it to fight for its existence—against itself—with the same tools of the human intellect that now endanger it. I also had *Le Rire de la Méduse* by Hélène Cixous, which is a classic reminder of our ability to recreate our language and ways of thinking by finding them new wellsprings inside ourselves, in places not found on the maps of those banes of our existence: patriarchy and capitalism.

I soon realized that my project involved two main tasks. On the one hand, I needed to face boldly the physical and natural-historical findings of the PIK scientists, together with their predictions of the consequences of climate change for life on Earth. On the other hand, I had to find a way to answer the PIK's call to me, as a writer, to contribute to saving the world. Both required some effort. It would perhaps be easy to throw up one's hands and surrender in the face of the fact that human behavior in the past three hundred years has done so much damage to the environment that we are entering a new period of mass extinctions of animals and plants (behavior that is rooted in Western mechanisms of exploitation, colonialism, and privilege, simply put). And along with that inclination toward surrender comes a feeling of powerlessness, skepticism that one writer's literary creation can bring about results—no matter how high an opinion one has of oneself and one's works. What is more, I felt a twinge of the healthy stubbornness that crops up in most writers whenever an attempt is made to dictate to them, or to point out to them worthwhile and even urgent issues in the world today, however gently they are approached, or however glaring the need is.

"The Latest News of the Tipping Points" was the name of a talk that I attended, given by one of the professors at Telegrafenberg. In it, he reviewed the status of various natural phenomena that have already been significantly affected by global warming, including weather systems, icebergs, lakes, and seas, with the term "tipping point" referring to the moment when the changes to which these phenomena are subjected become irrevocable. When the Greenland ice sheet has melted below a certain elevation, it will no longer be able to sustain itself and will continue to melt to nothing; it is already in the process of vanishing, and this is happening faster than the most pessimistic forecasts predicted. It is such information that disheartens an Icelandic poet, that causes him to lose "robustness," as Jónas Hallgrímsson might put it. Yes, the big question is what it will take for mankind's "tipping point" to be reached. What will finally bring mankind to see clearly that global warming caused by climate change is nearing a point of no return, compelling it to raise its defenses and do everything in its power to slow down the changes and respond compassionately to the plight of those already suffering the consequences of those changes? A large part of the problem is, of course, that the societies most responsible for the changes are still the ones least affected by them. People living in the peripheral areas of the Earth, the so-called indigenous peoples, or in places where survival is so dependent on the sea level, precipitation levels during the rainy season, or the life (and death) of such essential entities as coral reefs or forests, are already wrestling with the consequences as they are manifested in wars, hunger, and refugeeism.

At a meeting I had with the director of the PIK, Dr. John Schellnhuber, shortly after my arrival in Potsdam, we in fact discussed the challenge faced by every writer to take on the changes facing the world and deal with them independently under the premises of literature. It is one thing to write articles and essays or discuss issues at conferences and in the media, and another to create literature that is shaped by the subject matter in dialogue with the history of its manifestations (the imminent destruction of the world or something similar, for example) in poems great and small, novels, and stage plays, ever since the earliest days on Earth of that storytelling creature, *Homo narrans*. We agreed that the arts of language and the natural sciences were siblings, and that nature alone, man in nature, and the nature of man are today, like all days previously, the subject matter of both. A recent discovery in the world of science was a moth that feeds on the tears of small birds. These moths flutter up to the sleeping birds, extremely quietly, land on the birds' feathery heads, extremely lightly, unfurl their proboscises and slip the tip beneath the birds' eyelids, and drink their fill without waking them. I told Dr. Schellnhuber that I had no doubt that this new discovery had already found its way into one or a number of the thousands of poems that had been written after word of it spread. Perhaps one of those poems could bring about a revolution in thinking? He believed that it would take more than that.

So it was that I spent the summer of 2017 in a little observatory in Potsdam, pondering the role that a writer could play in times of climate change and global warming, and the devastating consequences that these are having on man's environment and survival.

Toward the end of my stay, I acquired a copy of the book *Religion in Environmental and Climate Change. Suffering. Values. Lifestyle*, edited by the Norwegian theologian Sigurd Bergmann and Dieter Gerten, one of the PIK scientists. As the title of the book implies, it deals with the attitudes of different religions toward this threat to the earth. Among the book's subjects are Pope

Francis's encyclical *Laudato Si'*, in which the pope exhorts Catholics to take responsibility for nature, which God entrusted to man's stewardship, and to display compassion and brotherly love to those bearing the brunt of the disastrous consequences of climate change; at the presentation of the pope's encyclical at the Vatican, he had at his right hand Dr. John Schellnhuber, making it clear to all that Mother Church was walking hand in hand with science on this path. The book also discusses the denial of American eschatological Pentecostals (those convinced that we live in the "end-times," and who are anxious for Jesus's second coming) of the conclusions of the same sciences, and describes how the mythological worldview of the Sakha people in northeastern Siberia is changing as global warming negatively affects seasonal weather patterns and the subsistence modes that these people have developed over the centuries for survival at the boundaries of the inhabited world.

The correlation of the contents of this book with everything else that I had been reading, viewing, hearing, and thinking about, helped me formulate the following conclusion.

■ ■ ■

Only by putting literature into an ecological template can we understand what role writers might have in saving the Earth and humankind. In the ecological template, literature appears as an organic whole, stretching back to the dawn of humanity. Sometimes, literary works are spoken or sung, sometimes acted out or written, often in a language spoken by many, more often in the languages that belong to only a few. It is an entity that changes constantly according to content and circumstances, in both its clearest and most obscure manifestations, but that plays a key role at all times in the survival of the people who cultivate it.

The task of those of us who create literature in one way or

another during the era of climate change is thus—to put it simply—to ensure that it has a secure place in human existence. Together, we are responsible for the ecosystem of literature as a whole, whether it is the freedom of speech of conservationists in Uruguay and poets in China, the access of Syrian writers fleeing war to literary communities in their new countries and Dalit children in Jaipur to reading lessons, the preservation of the Paiute language in Nevada and the library in Timbuktu. It is up to each of us to decide how much light, and what type of light, we wish to shed on the upheavals facing us.

No less than in the natural sciences, the ecological approach to literature refuses different aspects of its ecosystem to be evaluated on the basis of hierarchy. The Sakha people's dying story of the blue-spotted Bull of Winter with its huge frozen horns might reflect the mentality that we need in order to survive as a species—the death of the moth that drinks the tears of small birds can eventually lead to the loss of the forest.

THE IMPERILED

Krys Lee

SOUTH KOREA

THE MOUNTAINS WERE BARREN pinnacles and flattened cones, vividly real until they were not there at all. It took one night's sleep for them to disappear. Only one night for the rows of identical apartments facing the woman's bedroom window to also disappear.

If it was a dream, it was longer than dreams should be. A scandalous length, the woman thought. Inappropriate, really. The woman propped herself up on the mattress that gave in like jelly, and craned for a better look until the glass pane chilled her nose. But no, no reassuring outlines, the mountains had been swallowed whole. Was she asleep, awake? It made no difference to the gray presence. The mass, an all-muscle billow, seemed to pulse with life as it roved across the sky. She wondered about the mountains, the thing against the window, but not about what happened to the blue sky, for in their country, blue skies were too long ago for remembering.

Our mountains, she began as calmly as she could, then stopped. What did you say? her husband shouted above the whir of the air purifier. To do nothing required her to see nothing, and they needed to do nothing since he was finally employed in his saturated field after scraping by on her salary, and since the sum total of their inheritance equaled: an impressive zero savings, one language between them (Korean), and her elderly parents living three floors above them. She said, Never mind, and he pretended to understand, but his eyebrows crinkled into puzzle pieces. The woman couldn't see beyond the great dome of smog that trapped them, but stress was as bad for you as fine particulate matter, so instead she looked for the gray orb of sun, and declared, It'll be sunny today!

The man nodded agreeably, dried his hair with one hand and pulled his shirt on with the other. The same white dress shirt was what he saw, though the woman changed it for him daily and bleached the whole lot once a week just before they went gray. Of course her husband was always time traveling to a galaxy of ideas so vivid that he hadn't considered that it was not normal, even perhaps unhealthy, for his wife not to leave the house for nearly two years. But the woman loved this about him, as much as she loved the wild hair he forgot to cut if she didn't remind him, the way he trailed after her on weekends like a love-starved mutt. How over breakfast that morning, he suddenly gazed at her with intense clarity and confessed, I'd be lost without you.

The woman, typical of the woman, became wary yet hopeful. She said, Now what's that supposed to mean?

I mean, loving you is the greatest meaning in my life.

This moved her and shamed her because he was the kind of person who didn't know how to love any less, and she, the kind who didn't know how to love any more.

The woman tamed her bristly black hair and had a first cup of coffee, a second, as she prepared breakfast. Squinted into the thick fog. Be sensible, she told herself, though she was more the sensitive type than sensible. Read the paper until Taeho, their six-year-old son, told her gently that it was upside down. He had started treating the woman as if she were a songbird whose bones could be crushed by the pressure of words, which wasn't the way she was, not at all.

Neither husband nor son mentioned the changed circumstances. Not, where did the mountains go? Or, today is different than yesterday. In fact they acted—or pretended—as if today were the same as yesterday, and yesterday, the same as the day before, when it was clearly different.

It would be all right, the woman made it all right with smiling banana slice faces on buckwheat pancakes, a dollop of fig jam, and fresh papaya. Pomegranate juice. Eat more, drink more, she urged, trying to act like a mother and wife.

Outside was the apocalypse. Maybe she shouldn't have left the church, or at least gotten baptized to hedge her bets.

What was that prayer? It was so long ago, she recalled only dribbles. Our father who art in heaven.

Her easygoing husband started in his chair. What did you say?

Nothing, she said, shuddering at the escaped words.

Her son stopped chewing. Are you—okay?

Of course I am. When have I not been?

Eomma, why don't you ever leave the house?

The woman froze. The unspeakable rose like a helium balloon that their son batted about. Other moms go to the park and parents' meetings, he said between bites. Everyone thinks you're not real.

Her husband looked bewildered. Also protective. Your *eomma*—

She stood up. You'll be late for school.

Why don't grown-ups have school, too? her son asked.

The woman kissed him on the head, the innocent.

The boy solemnly pulled on his mask, which made her sweet six-year-old look like a future criminal. She adjusted the straps and tightened the nosepiece until he squirmed in silent pain. What did you say, a sales clerk had once shrieked at the woman's muffled voice, looking at her as if she were about to rip off her mask.

The boy said, You know, I'm very brave.

How are you brave? she asked.

I go outside every day and I face the monster.

The monster?

He pointed outside. There it is, he said.

Its face was now pressing against the window as if it were trying to break in.

The woman's heart fluttered with fear. Oh, she said. Then, oh, again.

She hugged him, her brave boy living in a world that required him to be brave.

Like all the other days before, the woman took a deep breath of purified air, put on her own mask, and attempted to see the family off. She made it down the elevator, through the lobby, and to the building's entry. Only then she was stopped. I will not be afraid, she muttered angrily, once the fearless one at work, at college, in protests, now shuddering backward from what she couldn't see. Bye, *Eomma!* Then her boy stepped out into the globe of gas, and her man followed after him. Again the woman abandoned her loved ones, again she returned to the safety of the apartment.

Time to work. The kitchen table grew marked-up manuscript pages as the woman became absorbed in the novel. An editor's first job wasn't the editing; it was to be the finest-tuned ear to the voice of the novel, to cultivate a loving attentiveness. So much depended on the listening.

She was back inside words again, mesmerized. For what was work but a savoring of solitude? She fled her turbulent mind, did a second edit of a chapter before reviewing her notes. But eleven o'clock came, it was time to help bathe her father, and it was again ashes to ashes, dust to dust.

The other work took over. One, clean the air purifiers, call to ensure that her son had been allowed to wear his mask in class. It scares the other children, you see, the principal had explained, though to see it, the woman had to visit her son's classroom. He elaborated, the woman interrupted with, Where are *your* children studying? He had gone silent then because she knew, he knew, that people like him sent their children safely overseas.

Make lunch and run two portions up to her parents, water the dozens of snake and rubber plants converting carbon dioxide into oxygen. Take a wet cloth to the chocolate leather sofa, the stereo, to the slow seepage of filmy accumulation on surfaces that she had just wiped down the evening before. All the air purifiers in the world couldn't keep the demon dust out, it seemed. The have-tos gnarled up in the woman's head, her feet became lead.

She should have continued praying, she should have continued going to church. Our father who art in heaven, hallowed—or was it hollowed?

Back to work, but work was no longer the same. Within an hour she noticed the dust settling again on the sofa like a chronic dandruff problem.

A tiny white flake moved. As the woman scrutinized it, another mote of matter boogie-danced beside it. She attacked it with her dictionary before it sprang at her. So what if her husband's colleagues who did vague, admirable science things with bacteria would laugh at her ignorance? The woman knew it was alive.

■ ■ ■

After it took up permanent residence in their sky two years ago, the woman had stopped leaving the house. Unusually heavy Gobi Desert sandstorms, some politicians suggested. The climatologists warned of thermal inversion and trapped gases, but as usual, no one listened to them. From the twentieth floor, the woman had watched air-filter masks evolve into fashion statements, from rainbow-colored LGBT statements and Hello Kitty whiskers to sleek black ribbing. A friend claimed, Wearing masks means I can skip the makeup. It's a real time-saver! Their neighbor took up camping indoors in the living room. While the woman slowly grew unhinged in the country of optimists, businesses celebrated the many blue-ocean markets. Fingers were pointed, so many that politicians seemed to possess twelve fingers on each hand. Most of the fingers pointed at China, who pointed back at their country and their coal plants, diesel cars, and unregulated factories dotting the peninsula. The woman wasn't particularly interested in technical details or who was to blame. What mattered was that the darkened rag of a sky stayed. It stayed longer than necessary for it to prove its point.

The day grew long, an even thicker smog unfurled, descended. The woman sensed its stealthy, persistent movements; she smelled it curling around the apartments, the parks and schools, then crawling in through the nostrils and lips and ears toward the brain, the heart, the lungs of her son.

She stopped working when the few pedestrians disappeared from view. Scrubbed the floors instead until her palms were raw red. Dread grew as she cleaned and cleaned. She called her husband. No answer. Not the first time nor the second. No one picked up at the publisher, none of her friends responded. Her breath quickened.

Finally she did what she was afraid to do. She called her son.

A sound reassured her at first, until she realized that if you wished hard enough, you heard what you wished for.

Taeho? Her voice rose. Taeho? It had happened. The woman knew it had finally gotten to him, as it would get to all of them.

She sank to the floor. Had he taken off his mask? Or played soccer outdoors despite the rules they agreed on, and been seized by the fumes? She called again though there was no use in it. She wondered, and then she was certain.

She should have protected them. She should have joined an environmental organization, protested. She should have home-schooled him. She should have insisted they emigrate, even if they ended up scraping other people's shit from toilet basins for years. She should have done something instead of this *nothing*. She stopped cleaning. Started. Stopped. Breathe, breathe, the woman told herself as her quiet heart thundered. She followed the restless feet of her thoughts.

Finally she sat down, her chin resting on the mop. No matter how much she cleaned, it would never be clean, she would never be clean.

She tidied the manuscript and folded the laundry. One last time, still no answer. Breathe. She changed into a black A-line dress. She did not like to think of herself leaving a mess.

The woman retrieved her husband's favorite tie with giraffes, wrapped it around her neck, and looked for somewhere to hang herself. The light fixtures were precarious, the vent was awkward. The only feasible alternative was asphyxiation. She tested her strength, tugging until she felt her throat burn. Killing yourself was harder than she had imagined.

The fine dust hurtled forward, rattled the windowpane. But no, she looked closer. It wasn't dust. Or not only dust. Snowflakes spun and stuck to the windowpane, and though they weren't exactly white, they weren't exactly black either. She relaxed her hold and took deep, cool breaths until the fever diminished. What if it wasn't merely biblical nonsense and Jesus had actually walked on water? Maybe her family would be returned to her. Maybe miracles did happen, foolish as it was to believe in them. She looked down at the limp tie, at the fading tracks across her palms, and thought long about all the love that she had almost let go.

CONTRIBUTORS

Sulaiman Addonia is an Eritrean-Ethiopian-British novelist. *The Consequences of Love*, short-listed for the Commonwealth Writers Prize, has been translated into more than twenty languages. He currently lives in Brussels, where he has launched a creative writing academy for refugees and asylum seekers and the Asmara Addis Literary Festival (In Exile). *Silence Is My Mother Tongue*, his second novel, has been long-listed for the 2019 Orwell Prize for Political Fiction.

Juan Miguel Álvarez was born in Bogotá, Colombia, in 1977. He is an independent journalist on issues of culture and human rights and a frequent contributor to *El Malpensante* magazine, which is based in Bogotá. His most recent book, *Verde Tierra Calcinada*, was published in 2018.

Tahmima Anam is a novelist and anthropologist and the author of *The Bengal Trilogy*. She is the recipient of an O. Henry Prize, a Fellow of the Royal Society of Literature, and a *Granta* Best Young British Novelist.

Sarah Ardizzone is an award-winning translator with a special interest in sharp dialogue, multiethnic slang, and what Alain Mabanckou calls "a world literature in French." Her translation of *Petit Pays* (*Small Country*), by Gaël Faye, was a 2019 finalist for the French-American Foundation Translation Prize and the

Albertine Prize. Recently, she has been developing live multilingual performances for the Edinburgh International Book Festival. Sarah was born in Brussels and lives in Brixton, London, where she is a Royal Literary Fund Fellow and cochair of English PEN's Writers in Translation Committee.

Margaret Atwood, whose work has been published in more than forty-five countries, is the author of more than fifty books of fiction, poetry, critical essays, and graphic novels. Her latest novel, *The Testaments*, is a co-winner of the 2019 Booker Prize. It is the long-awaited sequel to *The Handmaid's Tale*, now an award-winning TV series. Her other works of fiction include *Cat's Eye*, a finalist for the 1989 Booker Prize; *Alias Grace*, which won the Giller Prize in Canada and the Premio Mondello in Italy; *The Blind Assassin*, winner of the 2000 Booker Prize; *The MaddAddam Trilogy*; and *Hag-Seed*. She is the recipient of numerous awards, including the Peace Prize of the German Book Trade, the Franz Kafka International Literary Prize, the PEN Center USA Lifetime Achievement Award, and the *Los Angeles Times* Innovator's Award. She lives in Toronto.

Edwidge Danticat is the author of numerous books, including *The Art of Death*, a National Book Critics Circle Award finalist; *Claire of the Sea Light*; *Brother, I'm Dying*, a National Book Critics Circle Award winner and National Book Award finalist; *The Dew Breaker*; *The Farming of Bones*, an American Book Award winner; *Breath, Eyes, Memory*; and *Krik? Krak!*, also a National Book Award finalist. Her latest book is *Everything Inside*. The recipient of a MacArthur Fellowship, she has been published in *The New Yorker*, *The New York Times*, *Harper's Magazine*, and elsewhere. She lives in Miami, Florida.

Tishani Doshi is an award-winning poet, novelist, and dancer. Her most recent books are *Girls Are Coming Out of the Woods*, short-listed for the Ted Hughes Poetry Award, and a novel, *Small Days and Nights*. She lives on a beach in Tamil Nadu, India.

Mariana Enriquez was born in Buenos Aires, Argentina, in 1973. She published her first novel, *Bajar Es lo Peor*, in 1995. *Things We Lost in the Fire* is her first book translated into English. She works as an editor and a teacher.

Gaël Faye was born in 1982 in Burundi to a French father and Rwandan mother. In 1995, after the outbreak of the civil war and the Rwandan genocide, the family moved to France. An author, songwriter, and hip-hop artist, he released his first solo album, *Pili Pili sur un Croissant au Beurre*, in 2013. *Small Country* is his first novel. A bestseller in France, it has been awarded numerous literary prizes, among them the Prix Goncourt des Lycéens, and is being published in thirty countries worldwide. He lives in Paris.

Aminatta Forna is the author of the novels *Ancestor Stones*, *The Memory of Love*, *The Hired Man*, and *Happiness*, as well as the memoir *The Devil That Danced on the Water*. Forna's books have been translated into sixteen languages. Her essays have appeared in *Granta*, *The Guardian*, *The Observer*, and *Vogue*. She is currently the Lannan Foundation Chair of Poetics at Georgetown University.

Lauren Groff is a two-time National Book Award finalist, and *The New York Times* bestselling author of three novels, *The Monsters of Templeton*, *Arcadia*, and *Fates and Furies*, as well as the celebrated short-story collections *Florida* and *Delicate Edible Birds*.

She has won the PEN / O. Henry Award, and has been a finalist for the National Book Critics Circle Award. Her work has been featured in *The New Yorker* and in several *Best American Short Stories* anthologies; in 2017 she was named one of *Granta*'s Best Young American Novelists. She lives in Gainesville, Florida, with her husband and sons.

Eduardo Halfon was born in Guatemala in 1971. He is the author of fourteen books published in Spanish, of which his latest, *Mourning*, received the Edward Lewis Wallant Award in the United States, the Prix du Meilleur Livre Étranger in France, and the Premio de las Librerías de Navarra in Spain.

Mohammed Hanif was born in Okara, Pakistan. He graduated from the Pakistan Air Force Academy as pilot officer but subsequently left to pursue a career in journalism. His first novel, *A Case of Exploding Mangoes*, was long-listed for the Man Booker Prize, short-listed for *The Guardian* First Book Award, and won the Commonwealth Writers Prize for Best First Novel. His second novel, *Our Lady of Alice Bhatti*, was short-listed for the 2012 Wellcome Prize. His most recent novel is *Red Birds*. He has written the libretto for a new opera and writes regularly for *The New York Times*, BBC Urdu, and BBC Punjabi. He currently splits his time between Berlin and Karachi.

Ishion Hutchinson was born in Port Antonio, Jamaica. Author of the poetry collections *Far District* and *House of Lords and Commons*, he teaches in the graduate writing program at Cornell University.

Daisy Johnson's first novel, *Everything Under*, was short-listed for the 2018 Man Booker Prize, making her the youngest author ever to be on the short list. Her debut book of short stories, *Fen*, won the 2017 Edge Hill Short Story Prize. Her next novel, *Sisters*, will be published in the summer of 2020. She currently lives in Oxford, by the river.

Penny Johnson's recent book is *Companions in Conflict: Animals in Occupied Palestine*. She is one of the founders of the Institute of Women's Studies at Birzeit University and an associate editor of *Jerusalem Quarterly*.

Lawrence Joseph is the author of numerous books of poetry, most recently *A Certain Clarity: Selected Poems*. He is also the author of two books of prose, *Lawyerland*, a nonfiction novel, and *The Game Changed: Essays and Other Prose*, in the University of Michigan Press's Poets on Poetry Series. He is Tinnelly Professor of Law at St. John's University School of Law and lives in New York City.

Billy Kahora is a writer from Nairobi, Kenya. His short fiction and creative nonfiction have appeared in *Chimurenga*, *McSweeney's*, *Granta Online*, *Internazionale*, *Vanity Fair*, and *Kwani?* He has written a nonfiction novella titled *The True Story of David Munyakei*. A short-story collection, *The Cape Cod Bicycle War*, was released in 2019. He has also edited seven issues of the *Kwani?* journal and other *Kwani?* publications. He currently teaches creative writing at the University of Bristol.

Eka Kurniawan was born in Tasikmalaya, Indonesia, in 1975. He studied philosophy at Gadjah Mada University, in Yogyakarta. He has published several novels, including *Beauty Is a Wound* and *Man Tiger*, as well as collections of short stories, including *Kitchen Curse*.

Krys Lee is the author of *Drifting House* and *How I Became a North Korean*, and the translator of *I Hear Your Voice* and *Diary of a Murderer: And Other Stories* by Kim Young-ha. She teaches at Underwood International College, Yonsei University, in Seoul, Korea.

Christina MacSweeney's translations have received critical acclaim, and in 2016 she was awarded the Valle Inclán Translation Prize for Valeria Luiselli's *The Story of My Teeth*. She has also contributed to a number of anthologies of Latin American literature; published shorter translations, articles, and interviews on a wide variety of platforms; and in 2018 participated in the events surrounding the Hay Festival in Dallas, Texas. Her most recent translations are *Among Strange Victims* by Daniel Saldaña París; *A Working Woman* by Elvira Navarro; *Empty Set* by Verónica Gerber Bicecci; and *Tomb Song* and *The House of the Pain of Others* by Julián Herbert.

Andri Snær Magnason is an Icelandic writer born in Reykjavik. He has written fiction, nonfiction, sci-fi, and poetry. His work has been published or performed in forty languages. His latest book is *On Time and Water*, a nonfiction work about glaciers, grandmothers, and holy cows.

Khaled Mattawa is assistant professor of language and literature at the University of Michigan. Born in Benghazi, Libya, he emigrated to the United States as a teenager. He is the author of four books of poetry, most recently *Tocqueville*, and has translated five books of Arab poetry. Mattawa has received a PEN Award for Poetry in Translation, a Guggenheim fellowship, two Pushcart Prizes, and a fellowship from the MacArthur Foundation.

Megan McDowell is an award-winning Spanish-language literary translator from Kentucky. She has translated works by Alejandro Zambra, Samanta Schweblin, Mariana Enriquez, and Lina Meruane, among many others. She lives in Santiago, Chile.

Ligaya Mishan writes for *The New York Times* and is a contributing editor at *T* magazine. Her criticism has appeared in *The New York Review of Books*, *The New York Times Book Review*, and *The New Yorker*, and her work has been selected for *The Best American Food Writing*. In 2019 she was appointed to the Mary Higgins Clark Chair in Creative Writing at Fordham University.

Lina Mounzer is a writer and translator living in Beirut. Her work has appeared in *The Paris Review Daily*, *Literary Hub*, *Bidoun*, *Warscapes*, and *Berlin Quarterly*. She has contributed long-form features on Middle Eastern literature, TV, and music to *AramcoWorld* magazine, *Brownbook ME*, and *Middle East Eye*, and she has translated work by Lebanese authors Chaza Charafedine, Hassan Daoud, and Hazem Saghieh.

Sayaka Murata is the author of many books, including *Convenience Store Woman*, winner of Japan's most prestigious literary award, the Akutagawa Prize. She used to work part time in a convenience store, which inspired this novel. Murata has been named a *Freeman's* Future of New Writing author, and her work has appeared in *Granta* and elsewhere. In 2016, *Vogue Japan* selected her as a Woman of the Year.

Susanna Nied is an American writer. Her translations include the poetry and essays of Danish poet Inger Christensen; they have also appeared in journals such as *Poetry*, *APR*, and *Harper's*. She has received the Landon Translation Award of the Academy of American Poets and has twice been named a finalist for the PEN Award for Poetry in Translation.

Chinelo Okparanta is the author of *Happiness, Like Water* and, most recently, *Under the Udala Trees*. Her honors include an O. Henry Prize. She has been short-listed for the International Dublin Literary Award, and for the New York Public Library Young Lions Fiction Award. She has published work in *The New Yorker* and *Granta*, and was named one of *Granta*'s 2017 Best Young American Novelists.

Diego Enrique Osorno was born in Monterrey, Mexico, in 1980. In his career as an author, he has written five books on drug trafficking and social movements in Mexico. His latest in English is *Carlos Slim: The Power, Money, and Morality of One of the World's Richest Men*. As a journalist, he has received several awards, including the Latin American Prize for Journalism on Drugs 2011 and the International Prize for Journalism Process 2011.

Yasmine El Rashidi is an Egyptian writer. She is the author of *The Battle for Egypt: Dispatches from the Revolution*, and *Chronicle of a Last Summer: A Novel of Egypt*. She is a regular contributor to *The New York Review of Books*, and an editor of the Middle East arts and culture journal *Bidoun*. She lives in Cairo.

Philip Roughton is an award-winning translator of Icelandic literature. He has taught modern and world literature at the University of Colorado–Boulder and medieval literature at the University of Iceland. His translations include works by the Nobel laureate Halldór Laxness, Jón Kalman Stefánsson, Bergsveinn Birgisson, Steinunn Sigurðardóttir, and others. He was awarded the 2015 American-Scandinavian Foundation Translation Competition Prize for his translation of Halldór Laxness's novel *Gerpla* (*Wayward Heroes*); the 2016 Oxford-Weidenfeld Prize for his translation of Jón Kalman Stefánsson's *The Heart of Man*; and a National Endowment for the Arts Literature Translation Fellowship for 2017.

Anuradha Roy is the author of four novels, including *All the Lives We Never Lived* and *Sleeping on Jupiter*, which won the DSC Prize for Fiction 2016 and was long-listed for the Man Booker Prize in 2015. She lives in Ranikhet, India.

Raja Shehadeh is the author of, among other books, *Palestinian Walks: Forays into a Vanishing Landscape*, which won the Orwell Prize in 2008. His latest book is *Going Home: A Walk Through Fifty Years of Occupation*.

Sjón is a celebrated Icelandic author born in 1962 in Reykjavik. He won the Nordic Council's Literary Prize (the Nordic countries' equivalent of the Booker Prize) for his novel *The Blue Fox*, and the novel *From the Mouth of the Whale* was short-listed for the International IMPAC Dublin Literary Award. His latest work, *CoDex 1962*, a novel in three books, has been called an "extraordinary performance" by *The Guardian* and "a show of virtuosity" by *The New York Times*. In 2001 he was nominated for an Oscar for his lyrics in the film *Dancer in the Dark*. Sjón's novels have been published in thirty-five languages. He is the president of Icelandic PEN and lives in Reykjavik with his wife and two children.

Lars Skinnebach is an award-winning poet and environmental activist. Born in 1973 in Denmark, he was raised in Greenland and returned with his family to Denmark as a teenager. His most recent volume, *TEOTWAWKI* (acronym for "The end of the world as we know it"), was published to critical acclaim in 2018.

Burhan Sönmez is the author of four novels, which have been published in more than thirty languages. He was born in Turkey and grew up speaking Turkish and Kurdish. He worked as a lawyer in Istanbul before moving to Britain as a political exile. Sönmez's writing has appeared in various newspapers, such as *The Guardian*, *Der Spiegel*, *Die Zeit*, and *La Repubblica*. He now divides his time between Istanbul and Cambridge.

Pitchaya Sudbanthad is the author of the novel *Bangkok Wakes to Rain*. He has received fellowships in fiction writing from the New York Foundation for the Arts and the MacDowell Colony, and currently splits his time between Bangkok and Brooklyn.

Ginny Tapley Takemori lives in rural Japan and has translated fiction by more than a dozen early modern and contemporary Japanese writers, ranging from such early literary giants as Izumi Kyoka and Okamoto Kido to contemporary bestsellers Ryu Murakami and Miyabe Miyuki. Her translations have also appeared in *Granta*, *Freeman's*, *Words Without Borders*, and a number of anthologies. Her translation of Tomiko Inui's *The Secret of the Blue Glass* was short-listed for the Marsh Award, and her translation of Sayaka Murata's Akutagawa Prize–winning novel *Convenience Store Woman* was one of *The New Yorker*'s best books of 2018 and Foyle's Book of the Year 2018, and was short-listed for the Indies Choice Award and long-listed for the Best Translated Book Award. Her translation of Kyoko Nakajima's Naoki Prize–winning *The Little House* was published in 2019.

Ian Teh is an award-winning British photographer currently living in Kuala Lumpur. He has published three monographs, *Undercurrents* (2008), *Traces* (2011), and *Confluence* (2014). Teh's work is part of the permanent collection at the Los Angeles

County Museum of Art (LACMA) and the Museum of Fine Arts, Houston (MFAH); and he has been published internationally in magazines such as *National Geographic*, *The New Yorker*, and *Granta*.

Tayi Tibble is a writer and poet from Te Whanganui a Tara of Ngāti Porou and Te Whanau a Apanui descent. In 2017 she completed her master's degree in creative writing from the International Institute of Modern Letters, where she was the recipient of the Adam Foundation Prize. Her first book, *Poūkahangatus*, was published in 2018 and went on to win the Jessie McKay Prize at the 2019 Ockham New Zealand Book Awards. She works as a publishing assistant at Victoria University Press and as a staff writer at *The Pantograph Punch*.

Annie Tucker is a writer and translator who lives in Los Angeles.

Joy Williams is the author of four novels, five short-story collections, and the book of essays *Ill Nature*. She has been nominated for the National Book Award, the Pulitzer Prize, and the National Book Critics Circle Award. She lives in Tucson, Arizona, and Laramie, Wyoming.

ACKNOWLEDGMENTS

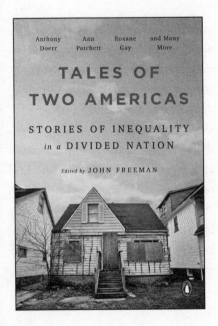